DETROIT PUBLIC LIBRARY

W9-ADQ-052

FRESH. CURRENT. AND TRUE TO YOU.

Dear Reader,

What you're holding is very special. Something fresh, new and true to your unique experience as a young African-American! We are proud to introduce a new fiction imprint—Kimani TRU. You'll find Kimani TRU speaks to the triumphs, problems and concerns of today's black teens with candor, wit and realism. The stories are told from your perspective and in your own voice. Kimani TRU is an exceptional line of books, written especially *for* African-American young adults, and will spotlight young, emerging literary talent.

Specifically developed with the tastes and interests of your generation in mind, Kimani TRU novels will tell coming-of-age stories that deal with the kinds of issues you face in today's fast-paced world, with compelling prose, realistic dialogue and the cultural references that are so much a part of your lives.

Kimani TRU will feature stories that are down-to-earth, yet empowering. Feel like an outsider? Afraid you'll never fit in, find your true love or have a boyfriend who accepts you for who you really are? Or do you feel that your life is a disaster and your future is going nowhere? In Kimani TRU novels, discover the emotional issues that young blacks face every day. In one story, a young man struggles to get out of a neighborhood that holds little promise by attending a historically black college. In another, a young woman's life drastically changes when she goes to live with the father she has never known and his middle-class family in the suburbs. In still another story, two sisters take different paths once troubling secrets are revealed.

With Kimani TRU, we are committed to providing a strong and unique voice that will appeal to *all* young readers! Our goal is to touch your heart, mind and soul, and give you a literary voice that reflects your creativity and your world.

Spread the word...Kimani TRU. True to you!

Linda Gill
General Manager
Kimani Press

 KIMANI PRESS™

Cassandra Carter

Fast Life

KIMANI
tru
™

If you purchased this book without a cover you should be aware that this book is stolen property. It was reported as "unsold and destroyed" to the publisher, and neither the author nor the publisher has received any payment for this "stripped book."

FAST LIFE

ISBN-13: 978-0-373-83076-3
ISBN-10:   0-373-83076-9

© 2007 by Cassandra Carter

All rights reserved. The reproduction, transmission or utilization of this work in whole or in part in any form by any electronic, mechanical or other means, now known or hereafter invented, including xerography, photocopying and recording, or in any information storage or retrieval system, is forbidden without written permission. For permission please contact Kimani Press, Editorial Office, 233 Broadway, New York, NY 10279 U.S.A.

This is a work of fiction. Names, characters, places and incidents are either the product of the author's imagination or are used fictitiously, and any resemblance to actual persons, living or dead, business establishments, events or locales is entirely coincidental.

® and TM are trademarks owned and used by the trademark owner and/or its licensee. Trademarks indicated with ® are registered in the United States Patent and Trademark Office, the Canadian Trade Marks Office and/or other countries.

www.KimaniTRU.com

Printed in U.S.A.

When I found out that I would have to come up with a dedication page, I immediately thought to myself, "Who in the world am I going to dedicate this to?" I didn't write this for a particular person, nor does it really relate to or uplift anyone I know. Then I came up with the brilliant idea to dedicate it to myself. Now, before you get carried away, let me explain. I'm not being conceited. When I say "myself," I mean more or less those out there who are *like* me. I am addressing any young Woman—or man for that matter—who has dreams as big as the world itself and is determined to somehow make them a reality. I want to show them that no matter how many people tell you—*you can't achieve it, you're not good enough, it's not possible*—and just however many "haters" you come across, they can't hold you down. (Shout-out and kisses to my haters! Without them, where would I be?)

I dedicate this book to all the kids who have ever felt out of place or stood alone and apart from the clique; those who have gone through it time and time again but still manage to keep it moving; to those who sometimes feel like it's them against the world; and to all those about their business at a young age, steadily on a mission to rise to the top. This is for you!

ACKNOWLEDGMENTS

I want to acknowledge my mother, Susan, who has worked her hardest to pull us through all the rough times faced by our two-person family. You have loved and been there for me from the day I was born. I truly couldn't ask for a better mother or friend. Love ya lots.

My "Mom-Mom" (grandmother), Sandra, who has always believed in me and supported me in any of my endeavors, and is always willing to lend a helping hand. You recognized my talent and are so genuinely passionate that I get out here to make my mark on the world. I also wish to thank you for turning me on to my artistic side. Ever since I can remember you have had a strong hand in introducing me to art and things of the spiritual sort.

To my "Pop-Pop" (grandfather): We seem to be growing closer with every year that passes. Thank you for all your wisdom and generosity, and I love you.

To my cousins Nicci, Amanda and BJ, whom I have practically grown up with and consider more like my siblings than my cousins. I love you all.

To my aunts, who are ever so loving and are such a trip (not to mention they spoil me rotten), Lori and Lena. I love you, as Aunt Lori would say, "whole bunchies."

To my uncle Stu, who has worked with me throughout this entire process and who took my work seriously, even at my age. To have your approval and you behind me on this meant a lot, because I know you don't sugarcoat anything for anyone! Thank you so much for keeping it real and seeing such promise in me.

To Ms. "Why," aka Ms. Wojtowicz: You are the best of the best, and anyone who has ever had the privilege of having you as a teacher knows this! I know I'll never have another teacher like you. Thank you for seeing my potential and being there for me as a friend as well as a wonderful teacher!

And finally to all of those whom I may have forgotten to mention who have inspired me, supported me, believed in me, guided me along throughout life and are reading this now! Thank you, and I am truly grateful!

CHAPTER 1

Five, four, three, two, one, brrring!

The bell sounded, signifying the end to another day at John Marshall Metropolitan High School. Kyra Jones snatched her black JanSport backpack off the floor and rushed out of the classroom into the crowded halls.

Finally, the day is over! Thank God! 'Cause I swear, if I had to walk to one more class in these shoes my feet would fall off. Damn Manolos! I knew I shouldn't have worn these to school, let alone bought 'em, period. But damn, they're settin' off this new pink shearling my baby Kai picked up for me on his run to Detroit last weekend. Plus, they're the real Manolos. None of that fake Steve Madden these broke-ass girls 'round here be rockin'—as if nobody don't know they ain't real. But you say that, they swear otherwise. They be havin' the nerve to try and stare me down, too, peepin' all extraclose tryin' to see if mines is real. But they already know the deal. They steady tryin' to lessen my rep as the hottest chick, even though this is only my second year here. But everyone knows that Makai and I are king and queen. We run this. I mean, Kai, for one, is geared and stays holdin' stacks. Not to mention he is sexy as hell! He got that whole sexy-thug thing goin' for him. I know any chick in here would love to get their hands on what's mine. Every chick want him, and everybody else wanna be like him. But I don't trip. He never cheated. Our love is real. And as far as everybody else goes, I don't worry, 'cause I know Kai can handle his. There are little whispers and whatnot, but no one ever dares to step. No use. They would be laid back down automatically.

But don't get me wrong—not everyone stay hatin'. I got my two best friends: Natasha, who is cool as hell and been down with me since kindergarten, and Mercedes, who probably done hooked up with the whole varsity basketball team and their daddies but is still cool. And well, Kai, he got his li'l crew, Reggie and them. They're high rollers, too. But none of them are anythin' like my baby Kai. As for all the haters, I just brush 'em off. A chick like me got more important stuff to worry about. They're just tryin' to catch me slippin', which even in these four-inch heels ain't happenin'.

Kyra made her way through the crowd, holding in the urge to grimace from the pain in her feet and from the thought of the D minus she had gotten on her biology test. She knew her mom would have plenty to say about that. She always did.

As she stood at her locker putting away her books, a pair of big, warm hands slipped around her slim waist. Accompanied by the scent of Curve for Men cologne, that meant only one thing: Makai.

"Damn, baby. That shearling is bangin'," he whispered into her ear from behind.

"Yeah, my man got it for me," Kyra boasted with a smile.

"Who's your man? Do I know 'im?"

"Well…" She began her reply as she turned around to stare

into his eyes. "Everyone knows him. He's about six feet, light-skinned, hazel eyes, keeps his hair in braids, got a killa smile with some luscious lips. He stay fly, too. He's sexy with his."

"Oh, I'm sexy wit' mines, huh?" Kai smirked.

"Hell yeah."

Makai leaned in and pushed Kyra up against her locker and kissed her. Engrossed in each other, they were unfazed by passersby. That was until Natasha came and interrupted them.

"Ahem! Ahem! Excuse me. *Excuse me!*" Natasha loudly announced her presence while tapping her friend's shoulder to get her attention. "Sorry to interrupt y'all's li'l make out session, but Kyra, are we still hittin' up the mall or what? We need to get those 'fits for the Black and White Party."

"Girl, we got plenty of time! That party is on Friday, and it's only Monday. Damn. This better be the biggest party of the year like everybody been sayin' for the past three months."

"I didn't ask for all that mouth. You wanna say everything but give me an answer. So what's it gon' be?"

"We can go after school on...hmmm...Wednesday, okay? Is that okay, baby? 'Cause you know I'm gonna need you to hook me up with some cash," Kyra said, her voice sounding innocent as she addressed her boyfriend.

"You know I gotchu, girl. Don't I always take care of you?" He angled her chin as he spoke and addressed her while looking deeply into her eyes. "You know I have to make sure my baby is rollin' fly through that party. You're gonna be the sexiest chick in there. No doubt," he added, and followed up with a peck on the lips.

"*Second* sexiest," Natasha piped up.

"Whateva!"

"*Anyways,* I'm gonna get going. But do me a favor?"

"*What,* Tasha?" Kyra's patience was wearing thin, and it

was clear that she was annoyed by her friend's interruption. She was more than eager to return to her previous activity.

"Get your grumpy ass some before we go, 'cause you're not rollin' with me acting like this." Her joke lingered as she hustled down the hall.

"Girl, shut your mouth!" Kyra half hollered, half laughed at her best friend. Natasha was known to be a trip sometimes.

"So are you ready to go, baby girl?" Makai had Kyra's undivided attention with those simple words before they headed down the hallway toward the exit.

The chilling Chicago wind whipped at Kyra's face and seeped through her clothes as she rushed to Makai's new red Cadillac Escalade sitting in the parking lot.

Makai was steadily coming up, and his role in the game was becoming more evident with each day that passed. He had a car so expensive that most people ten years his senior couldn't afford the monthly payments, let alone buy one outright. He didn't even have his license.

Kyra settled into the warm black leather interior and watched him navigate the Escalade. She studied him as he lit up a black cigar and leaned far back in his seat. His hat was so low she could hardly see his hazel eyes. Her gaze traveled down to his red T-shirt and his dark, baggy jeans all the way to his matching red Timbs. He was just so gangsta with his, and she loved it. She loved him.

As the car pressed on, Kyra was momentarily distracted when she saw a familiar-looking girl a little ways down the street. She was in the company of a tall, lanky boy. Kyra could see from a distance that he didn't have heavy pockets. Not at all.

When Makai pulled closer, she put a name with the face of the young woman. It was Mercedes, with a man by her side, as usual. It was rare to see her without one. Kyra rolled down her window and motioned for Makai to slow the car down.

"Mercedes! Call me later! I see you pimp!"

She rolled the window back up and sat back in her seat, laughing hysterically as they made their way down the street.

"Wasn't that that LaMonte walking witcha girl?" Makai asked, glancing over at his girlfriend, who continued to laugh.

"Yes! Ugh! What is she thinkin'? He is so *ugly!* And look, it's freezin' outside, and her ass is walkin' 'cause he's too broke to buy himself a ride. He look like he got beat with the ugly stick, like he *stole* somethin'." Kyra was almost in tears from laughing so hard.

"You crazy as hell, I swear," Kai said, now laughing a little himself.

"That girl always got a man. Just last week she was wit' Andre, and now she's with LaMonte already," Kyra said. "Chick just be runnin' through 'em."

"You know my nigga Reggie hit that, too. Sorry to say, but your girl is a ho, *H-O.* Why do you even hang wit her?" Kai asked. "I don't want you to get a bad rep 'cause of the nasty stuff she be doin'."

"I mean, I'ma let her do her thing. Who am I to judge what she do? That's my peoples." Kyra did her best to defend her friendship with Mercedes.

"I feel you, I guess," Makai said while turning up his stereo system. They continued to roll with the music blasting until they reached a red light. Makai calmly turned the black knob, decreasing the volume from his custom-made speakers. Then he fell back, relaxing deep in his seat as he stared over at Kyra.

"What?" She let out a giggle in response. She knew what that look meant, but playing dumb made it all that much more exciting. It was too tempting for her not to play hard to get.

"Girl, you know what's up. Don't play wit' me." Makai's tone was seductive as he licked his lips. That was one thing he knew never failed to turn her on.

"Let's go to my crib. My ma won't be home until seven or somethin'."

"A'ight, cool." He blew the gray smoke from his nostrils and extinguished the black in the ashtray as he pulled off from the light.

"Damn!" Kyra huffed in disappointment at the sight of her mother's blue Jeep Cherokee in the driveway of her home. Their plans were ruined nearly as quickly as they'd been made.

"It's cool, baby girl. Some other time."

"But Kai, it's been *so long*. I really want to," she whined.

"Shit is gonna be really busy this week. But I'll see what I can do, a'ight?"

"Yeah." Kyra couldn't hide her disappointment as he leaned in for another kiss.

"Love you."

"I love you, too."

After a few more quick pecks, Kyra grabbed her backpack and headed into the house. As soon as she set foot in the door, she slipped off her shoes and let her bag fall to the floor. She hadn't even had a chance to sit down when her mother burst into the room with a smile spread wide across her face.

"Hey, baby doll! I've been waiting for you to get home! I have some great news! You will never believe it!"

"What happened?" Kyra asked, never one for guessing games. She never had the time or the patience.

"I got the promotion!" Geneva Jones shrieked as she took a seat next to her daughter.

"That's cool, Mom. Congratulations," Kyra said, her voice uncaring.

"Wait. That's not all! Mr. Reynolds, the man that owns Allerton Crowne Plaza, wants me to be the *head* accountant at the new resort they opened on Providenciales! The company is going to cover nearly all of our travel and moving expenses!"

She waited for her daughter to respond, but Kyra just looked confused. Geneva could feel things taking a turn for the worse.

"Hold up. Where is Provincies?"

"It's *Providenciales,* and it's on a small Caribbean island! We're going to be living on an island! Can you believe it? We even have us a little house on Prince Paul Island just waiting for us, furnished and all!"

"But I thought you just said—"

"Oh, and Prince Paul! Let me tell you! It's just this cute little island where people who work on Providenciales live. I even have some pictures, if you want to see." She was rambling on as she shuffled the photographs in front of Kyra. "Isn't it gorgeous?"

Kyra didn't look at the pictures. She just sat completely still, unable to move. Her mother had to be joking. She couldn't be serious. Before Kyra had a chance to speak, a screaming tea-kettle interrupted their conversation.

"Oh, let me get that." Her mother disappeared into the kitchen. Within seconds, Kyra followed close on her heels, entering just in time to see her mother pour hot water into a mug and drop in a tea bag. Geneva began stirring the tea and gently blowing on it to cool it down, barely acknowledging her daughter's presence.

"So are you tellin' me that we're movin'?" Kyra asked. She was emotionless as she stood in the kitchen. Her feet refused to go any farther. As her mind began to turn, she found it difficult to function.

"Yup!" The excitement still hadn't left her mother's voice.

"You're jokin', right?" Kyra managed a weak laugh, hoping her mother would say yes, and burst into laughter. She just had to hear her say that they weren't *really* moving, that it was all a joke. But things like that never happened.

"No, I'm not joking, silly! We have to be packed by Thursday. Our flight is early Friday morning. It shouldn't be so bad with packing, because we aren't taking any furniture. This stuff is so old anyway." Her mother took a moment to sip her tea.

"Man, what? Friday? You mean *this* Friday, as in the day of the Black and White Party?"

"Oh, I'm sorry, sweetheart. I forgot all about that. But just think, by Friday night you will be in the Caribbean! You won't even be worried about that little party. I know I can't wait." Her mother seemed unaware of the change in her emotions. But Kyra could no longer contain her feelings. Even if her mother was blind, she could still hear.

"It's the biggest party of the year, Mom! I've been tellin' you all about it for the past, what, three months! I have to be there! And besides, what am I gonna do about my friends? Makai? School? What about Chi-town, period!" Kyra panicked as her anger slowly grew.

"Oh, it will be okay. You can keep in touch. With all the stuff you kids have access to these days, I'm sure it will work out fine. Plus, it's not like you won't make new friends or even meet a new boy you could really like. I mean, it's not like you and Kai are in love or anything."

"Yes, we are. I love Makai."

"Girl, you don't even know what love is. You're only sixteen. That's puppy love. You don't know the first thing about *real love*." Her mother laughed softly at Kyra's teenage foolishness, then lifted her mug for another sip of tea.

"Whateva, Mom, you don't know *what* we have," Kyra said, defending her relationship as she folded her arms across her chest and leaned against the laminate countertop.

"Like I was saying, it will be a good experience for you. This move will give you a chance to grow and mature. Give you a real opportunity to learn. I mean, think about it. It gives you a chance to see somewhere else in this world besides 'Chi-town,'" Geneva Jones concluded before walking back into the living room and flicking on the television. She assumed she had put an end to the conversation, but Kyra had much more to talk about and followed close behind.

"What are you talkin' about? I can do all that here! I learn at school. I like Chi-town. I love Chi-town. I grew up here, and I *don't* wanna leave. Especially not to go to some little-ass island in the damn Caribbean! I mean, St. Louis or Detroit or somethin' would maybe be a little more acceptable, but I mean, it's a whole other country!"

"Look, we are going whether you like it or not, Kyra La'nae Jones. End of discussion," her mother said adamantly.

"You have lost your fuckin' mind," Kyra mumbled. Her mother was in her face in a matter of seconds.

"No. The only person who has lost their fucking mind is you, talking to me like that! I'm not one of your little friends. I'll slap the taste out your mouth, girl. You are *not* grown!" she scolded.

"Now, you listen! Chicago is not safe. You be out there running around with those little hoochies and your little drug-dealing thug boyfriend like your little ass is really something around here. Well, guess what? I can't afford to pay the mortgage anymore. Bills are piling up, and I'm racking up debt like nobody's business. *So* we are going somewhere better. Shit around here has been hard since your father died. He loved

Chicago, too, Kyra. He loved the streets just like you do. Now look at him. He left me a widow and he's six feet under. All because he got caught up in that same shit Mickey—"

"Makai," Kyra said, correcting her mother as she rolled her eyes.

"—*Makai* is it now. You need to be as far away from him as possible, if you ask me."

"But I love him, Momma!"

"What do you want to do with yourself, Kyra? What? Become a hustler's wife, just like I did? You want to have a child to raise on your own and struggle to make it? That nigga doesn't love you. You'll see that. Someday it'll hit you. I promise you that. The sooner it does, the better—for your sake. He probably has hundreds of girls all over this city. I know the kind, Kyra. Hell, your father wasn't faithful to me, and we were married!" her mother declared, rubbing the wedding band on her finger to make her point. "I mean, Kyra, look, we can't stay here. It's not that I don't want to. I grew up here, too, you know. But I'm doing this for the both of us. I'm doing this in your best interest, and I know you probably don't see or understand that now, but..." She trailed off, her tone now soothing. But Kyra wasn't buying it.

"Yes, we could! We could stay here. We could get an apartment. Take a loan. I dunno, somethin'! But no! Some rich, fat-ass white man dangles a pretty little island and some extra dollars in front of your face and you're just ready to pick up and go! What would Daddy say?" she added in protest.

"He's not here! So what *I* say goes! It's been that way for ten damn years, so I would've hoped you were used to it by now. And don't try that 'What would daddy say?' shit on me. Not everyone has a little sugar daddy throwing money their way twenty-four-seven like you do. This is how I have to get mine, by working. I'm not going to let this opportunity slip away just because you're acting like a selfish brat. But you know what, never mind. I'm not saying anything else but deal with it. Deal with it." Geneva Jones's eyes were cold as she and Kyra exchanged glares. "Now go to your room. You done messed up my mood," she ordered as she upped the volume on the television and rummaged through her purse for a cigarette.

Kyra rushed upstairs to her room, slamming and locking her bedroom door before the tears forming in her eyes could fall. She wouldn't let anyone see her that weak, not even her own flesh and blood.

As she held herself against her door, trying her best to make sense of what had just happened, a muffled, catchy jingle played from her coat pocket. Her cell phone was ringing. She grabbed her flip phone and turned it off. She had no desire to speak to anyone after the news she had just heard. She didn't want to do anything.

Kyra crawled into her small, comfortable bed. She'd been lying there only minutes when the distant sound of gunshots distracted her. Unlike some people, who become frightened or nervous, Kyra was familiar with the sounds of the streets and so continued to lie still. She listened until, after five more gunshots in rapid succession, it was finally silent. She tried to gather her thoughts, but it seemed impossible. Her mind soon became overwhelmed with anger and confusion, and her body gave way as she fell into a deep sleep.

CHAPTER 2

"*It's six-thirty, Chi-town, and it's time to get up with your man Crazy Howard McGee! Stay tuned for the question of the day coming up next! 107.5 WGCI!*"

Kyra slammed the Off button on her alarm clock radio, silencing the host of the morning show. She dangled her feet over the edge of her bed while a yawn slipped from deep inside her. She glanced at the clock again and fought the urge to bury herself under the covers again. The soles of her French-pedicured feet made contact with the cold hardwood floor as she searched for her slippers and her robe to prepare for the day. It was sure to be a long one.

As the warm water of the shower flowed over her body, she mulled over her mother's announcement and the argument that followed. It all still left her body tense.

That was when it hit her. *How could she do this me? She didn't even ask me or nothin'. How could she act as though this is a good thing? This ain't nothin' good. If she was really doin' this for me like she's claimin', then we would be stayin' here, in Chi-town. We would be stayin' home.*

"You better hurry and get out of there before you're late for school! You haven't even eaten yet!" Geneva Jones cautioned from the other side of the bathroom door.

The unexpected knock on the door jarred Kyra from her thoughts.

She didn't bother to answer. Kyra sucked her teeth in response and turned off the water. She hurried to her room to avoid seeing her mother. She decided that it would be best to have as little contact and conversation with her mother as possible.

Kyra was sitting on the edge of her bed, lacing her black, fur-lined Timberland boots, when she heard loud, bass-filled music and the honk of a horn outside her house. Her ride to school had arrived.

She quickly snatched up her black Baby Phat jacket and her cell from the nightstand before running downstairs.

Kyra hurried into the kitchen, where her mother was already seated, enjoying her morning cup of coffee. She noticed the plate set for her but didn't touch it except to grab the two pieces of toast, leaving the eggs and bacon behind.

Makai, Kyra's daily ride to and from school, beeped his horn again, and she had just turned to leave when her mother spoke.

"You're not going to eat anything?" Her stare was attentive as she looked her daughter over.

"No," Kyra replied without turning to face her. Just looking at her was enough to piss her off.

"Well, I really think we should talk," her mother said.

Makai beeped his horn again, louder this time. He was getting impatient.

"I gotta go."

Lunch couldn't come quickly enough for Kyra. She found out in her African Studies class that her grade had dropped twenty percent because she hadn't done her report on the empire of Mali. In English class, she was reprimanded for paying more attention to a brand-new copy of *Vibe* magazine.

Mercedes and Natasha took their seats in the booth at McDonald's with their trays full of burgers, fries and shakes while Kyra opted for only a small Coke.

"Okay, see. I know something big must be up because you stay stuffing your face, especially with some Mickey D's. Spill it. Oh, *and* I want details," Mercedes said before taking a long sip of her strawberry milk shake.

"My mom got a promotion," Kyra mumbled, scanning the scenery on the other side of the window.

"Aww, girl! You had me worried fa real! Why are you so sad over that? You should be happy as hell. Last I knew, that meant more money. But I don't know, I guess that's just me," Natasha said, shoving a handful of fries in her mouth.

"Yeah, I know. The only problem is that it's in...well, it's *on* Prince Paul."

"Where the fuck is that?" Mercedes asked.

"It's in the Caribbean. We're movin' Friday."

The table instantly fell silent.

"Hold up, what the fuck? Wait a minute. Friday? As in this Friday, when we're supposed to be going to the Black and White Party?"

"Mmm, hmm."

Mercedes's voice was quiet. Natasha still hadn't said anything. No one spoke for a moment, and a cloud of awkward silence fell over the table.

"I got an idea!" Natasha piped up as she slid her tray away from her.

"What?" Kyra asked, only half interested in what her friend had worked up.

"We can all go and chill at my crib for a while. My mom ain't coming home till five. Fuck school."

"Okay," Kyra laughed. School was the last place she wanted to spend the few days she had left in Chicago.

After passing around a half-full bottle of Hypnotiq and watching TV, the girls quickly found themselves bored. The bottle was brought out to liven things up, but it failed to change their moods or to get them drunk.

"Damn, that's some bullshit. I don't even have a buzz," Kyra complained as she dropped the empty bottle onto the carpet.

"Yeah, I know...but oh! I got something that will get you way past a buzz. Hold on." Mercedes went digging in her purse before she even finished her sentence.

As she pulled out what she had been looking for, a wide, mischievous grin spread across her face. Natasha jumped up from her position on the bed, snatched the blunt from Mercedes's hand and quickly moved toward her nightstand drawer to get a lighter. She sat on the side of her bed and lit the joint, which was already between her lips.

"We're definitely gonna have to chill before you go. How about Thursday night we go out to get something to eat?" Mercedes suggested.

"As long as we go to—"

"—the Cheesecake Factory," Mercedes said, finishing Kyra's sentence for her. "We know, we know. Shit, everyone knows that's your favorite place to eat."

"Man, shut up and just pass that right here."

Mercedes threw her legs over the side of the chair and blew smoke up toward the ceiling. She passed off the thick blunt to Kyra, who took deep hits.

"Oh, and I don't know who you're telling to shut up,

because I *will* tell Makai you smoking, and he *will* get *all* in that ass. You know he got you on lock," Mercedes teased.

"Man, whateva. What Kai don't know won't hurt him," Kyra said, coughing a little.

She knew Makai didn't like it when she smoked; he had told her a few times in the past. It would really get him angry.

"And why the hell are you all worried about me and Kai? What will LaMonte think about you smokin'?" Kyra shot back.

"Oh! I think she's trying to blaze!" Natasha laughed.

"Whoa! Okay, let's get this straight. LaMonte is *not* my man and he *never* will be. I gave him some of this—" Mercedes stood up to model her golden body and flicked her straight, shoulder-length hair over her shoulder "—because I was getting those passes for us. Shit, I sure as hell didn't do it because he was fine *or* paid. That nigga was just saying how he got the passes from his cousin who's a bouncer at Pandemonium and that he could hook me up. *So,* I figured I would use what I got to my advantage, and I got what I wanted. You see? If y'all were smart you'd be doin' the same stuff I'm doin'. Sleep wit' 'em, get paid," Mercedes explained.

"Damn, I didn't mean it literally," Natasha joked.

"A'ight, so what did you get from Reggie, then?" Kyra said.

"Oh, you slept with Reggie's fine ass?" Natasha asked, all excited. Reggie was one of the biggest ballers in the neighborhood, and one of the finest.

"Yeah, I slept wit' him. How do you think I got this?" Mercedes bragged, holding up her brown Gucci G-print purse.

"Uh-oh! Turn this up!" Kyra said, turning her attention to the television. Her body was slowly beginning to wind like a caterpillar to the beat of Lil' Wayne's latest music video.

Natasha turned the television set up to its loudest and began to dance along. Before Kyra knew it, they were all up dancing to the music and enjoying the high. They continued to dance and sing together all afternoon until they got the munchies and raided the kitchen, finishing off a pitcher of cherry Kool-Aid, a bag of Famous Amos chocolate chip cookies and two party-size bags of Cool Ranch Doritos.

Kyra enjoyed herself that day. She and her girls hadn't had fun like that in a while. That was something she wouldn't have in Prince Paul.

Brown. That was all Kyra could see when she opened the door to her living room, which was full of folded cardboard boxes.

"Where were you?" her mother asked. Her hands were on her hips, her attitude reflecting her displeasure as Kyra entered the house.

"I was at Tasha's."

"Well, sit down, because I certainly have some words for you."

Kyra wished she could run up to her room and close her door, shutting out everything and everyone, including her mother.

"First off, I don't know who you think you are. You skipped school today! A few teachers called and said you had unexcused absences in their classes, which means you skipped. Then you come in late. It's five o'clock! Your ass should've been through that door two hours ago! You didn't even bother to call and let me know where you were." Geneva Jones drilled the words into her daughter. Kyra didn't even have a chance to defend herself before her mother continued, "Then I guess they figured while they were at it, they would bring up the subject of grades."

"Oh God…" began Kyra.

"Oh God is right! That's what you are going to need when you get out here because that's all you're going to have to your name, your faith in God, *if* you even have that! Your biology teacher said you are now getting a D for the class, because apparently some test y'all just took—which I haven't even seen, by the way—lowered your overall grade. Then, your African-American Studies teacher, Mr. Braxton, said your grade in his class fell twenty percent, and now you *are* failing! I mean, your grades aren't the best, and they really never have been. But dammit, Kyra! I don't know how much I have to stress to you how important it is for you to get good grades. You can't get into college with these kinds of grades, and don't think for a second you will be bringing grades like these home once we get to Prince Paul. You need to get yourself together, girl."

"I got myself together, Mom. College just ain't for me. I'm not some genius that knows biology and black studies. I'm passin' all of my other classes, though, right?"

"Just barely! I mean, what are you going to do for the rest of your life, Kyra? Have Makai give you everything on a silver platter? Before you know it, you will be out of high school. You only have two years left. You really need to think about your future."

"I'm not goin' to have Kai give me everythin'. I know that much."

"What are you going to do, then? Tell me," her mother impatiently demanded. To tell the truth, Kyra wasn't exactly sure what she had planned for her future.

"Look, all I know is that when you hit eighteen, your ass will be at some college somewhere learning something. You understand? Now take these and start packing your things." Geneva Jones shoved two brown boxes into her daughter's arms and walked off.

As expletive after expletive ran through her mind, Kyra tore open her closet doors, revealing row upon row of shoes and clothes. Louis Vuitton, Dolce & Gabbana, Gucci, Prada, Versace, Rocawear, Baby Phat, Chanel, Apple Bottoms, Azzuré—the list went on and on. Designers that most people only dream about, Kyra had in her closet.

She squatted down to the floor to fill the second box with her shoes. After clearing out most of them, all stored in their original boxes, she saw that there was only one box left, far back in the shadows of the closet.

The shoe box was red, old and covered in a thick layer of dust. It was plain and had no designer name on it, but it was more precious to Kyra than any pair of Prada boots. It was where she kept everything she treasured.

She removed the lid from the old red shoe box and began slowly, piece by piece, sifting through its contents. She came across an old bracelet Makai had given her for their first Valentine's Day together, some old arts-and-crafts friendship bracelets Natasha and Mercedes had woven for her out of colorful plastic string in seventh grade and pictures.

There were tons of pictures of her with Mercedes and Natasha: in middle school, at their eighth-grade graduation, at homecoming last year, at Six Flags, at the Navy Pier, all over the place. She even came across one of Natasha in elementary school. She smiled at her friend's missing teeth and big smile.

She continued to flip through the collection of photos she had gathered over the years and came across one of Makai. She had been with him since she was in the sixth grade. They had shared six years of love, and he always took care of her. He would do anything for her, and she would do anything for him. Makai was her everything. He was all she knew. He was her first love, her first kiss and the first person to explore her body and all of its forbidden places. He was her last love. Kyra wanted to be with him forever, and she was sure he was the man she would marry. She already had their wedding planned down to the smallest detail, and even had the names of their children picked out. But she couldn't shake the feeling that now with her moving so far away, everything between them would come to an abrupt end. An end she wasn't in any way prepared for.

She grew anxious and put the picture away, her gaze fixing on another one. Her father was a tall man, his skin a deep chocolate color. A neatly trimmed goatee brought out his well-defined jawline, with his hair crisply cut into a fade. He stood there smiling, his pearly whites shining. He had on nice clothes and a thick gold chain.

He was holding her in his arms. She was in a pink dress and pink shoes, with pigtails that curled all the way down to her chin. She couldn't even remember how it felt to be held by her father anymore.

Then there was her mother. Now, she was beautiful then. Still was. She had on a cream-colored dress, one of the skin-tight ones they wore in the eighties. Her dark brown, wavy hair was shining, as were her eyes. And that smile—so perfect. Kyra couldn't remember her mother being that happy in a while. When he was alive, they'd never wanted for anything, and good times had not been hard to come by. Kyra did remember when that all changed, though. The day her...*their* lives had fallen apart. That day *family* lost its meaning in her life. It was Sunday, June 1, 1997.

It was a beautiful day. The skies were clear, the sun was shinin', with a nice breeze. I remember it like it was yesterday. I was only five, and me, my mom and my dad went to this big-

ass barbeque at some park. It was live. So many people were there: some of Dad's friends, some of Momma's friends, some of our family and even some of my friends from school, Natasha bein' one of them. Me and Tasha had been playin' catch, and she threw the ball too high for me. I went runnin' after it, past Momma and her girls, talkin' loud with gossip, and Dad and his people, rowdy, playin' a game of dominoes. I had finally caught up to the ball when I stopped. There was this van comin' up the street. I dunno what did it, but I knew somethin' was wrong. It sent a chill through my body. Call it intuition.

That's when someone lowered the window real slow and stuck out what I knew to be a gun by the reflection of the sun off the metal. I couldn't move. I called out for Daddy, I guess out of instinct. When I was scared, I could always go to him. Next thing I knew—Pop! Pop! Pop! There were bullets flyin' every which way, from the van to Daddy's friends and back. My dad even pulled a gun from his waist. Everythin', the music, the laughter, yells, birds, the whole world seemed like it got quiet, and all you could hear was the gunfire. I saw people runnin'. I tried to move, but for some reason I couldn't. It was like I weighed five hundred pounds or somethin'. That's when one of the guys from the van aimed straight at me. He even pulled the trigger. But the bullet never hit me. Daddy pushed me out the way and knocked me to the ground. He took the bullet himself.

After he was hit, the van sped off. The gunfire was now replaced by cryin' and shoutin'. My mom was hunched over Daddy's body, screamin' out for help and tellin' him not to leave her and that she loved him. Some other people were around her, too, but there was another crowd around Uncle Anthony, 'cause he had been hit, too. I didn't waste any time runnin' over to where Dad was layin'. He was covered in blood, and so was my mom. It even got on me. I never saw so much blood in my life. I remember holdin' on to his hand so tight. I started tellin' him that I loved him, and I started to cry. That's when my mom started screamin' for someone to come and get me and that she didn't want me to see this. But if you ask me, it was too late. Besides, no one moved me anyway. I fought off the one person who tried. They didn't try again.

As I kneeled over him, he focused his eyes clearly on me. He opened his mouth just enough to talk when he started to choke and cough on his own blood. He wanted to tell me something. What, I'll never know. I imagine it was him telling me to be strong and that he loved me. I can only hope that is what he wanted to tell me, because before he got the chance, he struggled for his life for only a few more seconds until his eyes were still and he was gone. Just like that. If you have ever seen someone die, you'd know it's nothin' like in the movies.

After that, the realization set in on everyone that he was dead. The chaos suddenly ended and left this uncomfortable, almost suffocating presence that just surrounded all of us. My mom, who was still tryin' to calm and relax him, started to lose what little composure she had left until she broke down and began to sob even harder. So did I. I could barely even breathe. I remember screamin' for him to "Wake up!" and "Come back!" and that I loved him. I even kissed his cheek. But nothin' worked, and the only things that came were ambulances, a five-hour wait at a hospital and a funeral.

Things really fell apart then. The mothafuckas that did it were arrested but never convicted. Just because my father was a major playa in the game doesn't mean he didn't deserve justice. They should be under the jail. But I guess that's the system for you. It wasn't even two days before the DEA *crawled out from under a rock and, combined with his greedy-ass family, cleaned out everything. Money, jewels, cars—anythin' they thought would be worth somethin'. Since Momma's family had never really been there through the years, we basically lost all ties after that. I still dunno if Momma was more angry that everyone came and took everythin' from us or that Uncle Anthony, who is now known as Lucky, survived that day after being shot seven times when Daddy was hit only once. Whatever the case, we don't deal with them anymore. Our attitude toward the police never changed, though. Everyone knows how they get down. You just expect better of ya fam, even though you shouldn't.*

After it was all said and done, my mom was a widow and she had to raise a child on her own at the age of twenty-two. That was when the unhappiness began—June 1, 1997. A day I will remember forever. The day my father died. And to think that he sacrificed his own life to save mine. If only I had moved. If I had ducked or ran. If I had done somethin', Daddy would probably still be alive and we wouldn't be movin' anywhere. But I know I have to do what I believe he would have wanted me to, and that is to be strong. I have to be strong, if not for me, then for him.

Kyra was still staring at the picture when her mother's knock at the door jolted her from her reverie. She didn't have a chance to answer before her mother barged in, phone in hand.

"Here, it's Natasha…" Her voice trailed off when she saw the picture.

Kyra noticed her mother staring and quickly placed the photo in the box and resealed the top, hiding it as though she'd never had it in the first place.

CHAPTER 3

A winter white Dolce & Gabbana pantsuit with matching boots, a black and gray striped chinchilla fur jacket, and every diamond Makai had ever bought her was what Kyra wore. She decided that since she was going to go out, she might as well go out with impeccable style. She would roam the halls of John Marshall High one last time, allowing girls to envy something they wish they had and guys to lust for something they could never obtain.

She was looking so sharp that even after she was gone they would still talk about her. Kyra Jones: the flyest, sexiest, most stylish female ever to grace the halls of John Marshall. She just knew it. She couldn't wait to see Makai, either. She knew he would be all over her. Plus, she planned to tell him about the big move today. But after waiting for twenty minutes that morning, it was obvious he wasn't showing up.

As she stood in front of the living room window, peeking out at the driveway from behind the blinds, she was full of hope that Makai would pull up in his Escalade at any minute. By the time her mother came down the stairs, all hope was gone.

"What are you still doing here?"

"Kai's not here yet," Kyra responded, turning back to the window.

"Don't worry, I'm sure he probably just overslept or something. Now fix your face and let's go. You're already late, and I don't need to be late on my last day," Geneva said, taking her keys from the battered leather bag draped over her shoulder and walking out of the house. Kyra followed reluctantly.

It was an uneasy ride. The only noise in the car was the radio, but even that was silenced with the push of a button when the DJ mentioned the upcoming Black and White Party on Friday.

"Still mad about that party, huh?" Her mother was trying to begin a conversation.

"You look really pretty today. I see you really outdid yourself." Even with the compliment, Kyra still focused her dark brown eyes ahead as her mother pulled up to the school entrance. Her mother was grasping at straws. Geneva Jones knew her daughter well. She had been just like her when she was Kyra's age.

"Bye. I love you," she called, as Kyra stepped out of the Jeep, slamming the car door in her mother's face.

Kyra rounded the corner to the hallway where her locker was located. And there he was. Makai was leaning against her locker waiting for her. His worried look went unnoticed as she approached.

Before she could begin to say anything, without warning he slammed her into her locker with such force it made her hold her breath.

"Got something to tell me?"

"What the hell is your problem?" She studied his deep,

steady gaze. He was staring at her with a seriousness she had never seen before.

"Why the fuck am I hearing shit about you having some little adventure to the fuckin' Caribbean coming up?" Makai raged as he pinned her harder against her locker. "Do you know what this shit makes me look like? A fool. And I ain't nobody's fool, Kyra. Not even yours. Everybody's buzzing around here talking about shit going on witchu while my ass is fuckin' clueless. I mean, shit, I thought you loved me. Did you think you were just gonna up and leave or something?"

"I do love you," she murmured as she shrank under his intense glare. Her mind was racing with faces of those who could have been the snitch. She'd only told her girls.

"No you don't, 'cause if you did you would've told me ASAP."

"I was gonna do it today, I swear I was. I just didn't know how to say it. I dunno…"

"You know I don't trust nobody, and now this got me thinking. You could be up to all kinds of shit and not be telling me a damn thing. Wit' what I do, I can't risk dealing wit' people like that."

"So what are you sayin', Kai? I didn't tell you somethin' about me movin', and now I can't be trusted or somethin'? What, you think I turned into a cop overnight or some dumb shit?"

"I'm sayin' that I gotta do what I gotta do. I can't have no shady bitch on my team."

And with those words, Kyra slapped Makai across his face so hard the hall echoed with the sound of her palm's impact. She didn't know what had gotten into her, but in six years of dating he had never called her a bitch. She made sure he would never do it again.

Kyra watched as the man she loved stared at her as if she were worthless to him. It was as if she were looking into the eyes of a stranger. He looked as though he would strike her down for anything she did within the next second. And with a sudden move he seemed like he was about to do so, but instead he punched the locker, missing her face by inches. Her eyes were tightly shut, until she realized he hadn't hit her.

After an exhausting day, Kyra lay twisted around her bed-sheets, wide awake and fighting her manic thoughts for sleep. The glowing red numbers read 1:30 a.m. when she fixed her heavy eyelids on her ringing cell phone. *Who's callin' me this damn late?* She snatched the phone and quickly answered it to silence the ringer.

"Hello?" Her voice was thick with irritation as she lay back and closed her eyes.

"I'm outside. Don't keep me waiting."

Click!

What the hell is he doin' here? Kyra shot up, now wide awake. She didn't debate even for a minute whether or not to go. Makai had overreacted earlier, but she was quick to forgive him. Within seconds, she had crept down the stairs and out the front door undetected as her mother slept heavily upstairs in her bedroom.

When Kyra reached the car, she didn't say a word. She didn't even think of asking a question. Neither did Makai. She didn't ask a question not because she didn't want to or didn't have one, but because she didn't care. She trusted him and she loved him. She would go anywhere with him, no questions asked. She wanted to show him that. She not only wanted but needed him to know that.

Makai drove the car through the quiet streets while

grooving silently to a local jazz station and its slow jams. It didn't take long until his intended destination was revealed: the Navy Pier. It was the place they had had their first kiss; the place it had all started.

He parked the car and got out, all without speaking. Kyra followed as if she were his shadow. They walked along the dock for a while, staring at the water, the Ferris wheel and the huge white tour boats, until he suddenly stopped and took her hand in his.

Kyra grew nervous over the thought of pier security and kept shifting and looking around.

"Security ain't coming tonight. Calm down." Makai stared into Kyra's deep brown eyes with his dazzling hazels as he took a deep breath and readied himself to speak. Her body relaxed and she stood at attention, quiet and ready to listen.

"Kyra, I apologize for earlier. I was trippin' and, as much as I hate to admit it, I deserved that slap. I mean, shit, something had to knock some sense into me. It's just that you gotta understand that I love you and I felt like I was losing you. This shit got me fucked up. But at the same time, I know you must be going through it. So I want to let you know, in case you have any doubts, that I'm here for you. And I'll be here for you when you need me. Even when you move I'll be here for you." He took another deep breath and continued, "I promise you I'm gonna come down there and get you, shawty." His promise was as tender as his voice.

"What about all them other hoes you had on your dick today?" Kyra said as they stood beside the giant Ferris wheel.

"Yeah, they were sweatin' me, but you know I don't love them hoes. Fuck 'em. I only got love for you. Always have. Always will. You're my baby girl no matter what."

They then embraced for what felt like a lifetime, reveling in their moment in the cold winter air. They didn't move. They didn't speak. They just felt. Their love for each other was strong.

The whole scene was short-lived, interrupted when Makai scooped Kyra up without warning and carried her to the car. She laughed and squealed all the way. Even upon reaching the car, her laughs seemed endless; then she unexpectedly grew shy. She noticed he had been watching her every move, and now she found herself only tittering under his gaze as his eyes traveled over and analyzed what felt like every inch of her body. He could always make her melt.

"What are you lookin' at?"

"I'm looking at my sexy-ass wifey, that's what I'm looking at." Makai's statement was paired with a lick of his lips as he went on, "Come here." His words were more a command than a request, but of course, she obeyed.

She situated herself on his lap and was met with a deep, tongue-laced kiss and his wandering hands. It wasn't long before he discovered the zipper to her shearling. A devious smile came to his face when only a bra was revealed underneath. He slipped off her jacket and bra and began to massage and suck on her breasts as moans fell from her mouth and her breathing began to quicken.

Between kissing and nibbling on each other's necks, he reached down on the side of the seat, pulling the lever and re-clining the seat all the way back. They didn't waste any time removing the only things standing in their way: their clothes.

Kyra could feel him as the heat in her body rose. She wanted him inside her. He could feel her wetness, and warmth radiating from her body, and he knew he had her excited. He began to tease her with his tip by grinding it on her clit and sucking her neck just right. He knew he hit the spot that drove her wild—time and time again.

In no time, she began to jerk and bounce up and down with him, as he gripped her hips tightly, helping guide her movement as well as pushing himself deeper inside of her. He took her breasts in his hands as he watched her moan and scream in ecstasy.

He could tell she was getting closer to her climax because she grew louder with every bounce and he could feel her thighs tightening around him. He grew louder and felt himself becoming more excited, as well. When she finally screamed out his name as she came, her body instantly weakening and her cries diminishing into mere whimpers, he came with her—inside her.

They were both out of breath as they stared into each other's eyes. All was quiet except for their gradually slowing breaths. Kyra placed her lips softly to his, laying her head on his chest and listening to his heartbeat. Makai played with her hair, twirling it between his fingers as she held him tight and closed her eyes. She never wanted to let him go.

It was a place that was dark even on the brightest of days. It was a place of mourning and sorrow—a painful reminder of the missing pieces in her life. It was a place that never met a smile and never heard a laugh. Even with hundreds or thousands of people, it always seemed to be deserted. People passed through on occasion. Some yelled to God, asking why he had to take their loved ones, expressing the pain of their suffering heart and the fear of being alone. But for Kyra, today it was a place where a daughter went to say goodbye.

Kyra stood in front of the gray marble gravestone. She leaned down slowly and read the letters engraved across it: "Marcus Jones. Beloved husband and loving father. December 15, 1968–June 1, 1997."

As she gently ran her hands over the letters, laying the fresh flowers on top of the stone, she felt a soft breeze that reminded her that she didn't have on a jacket. But as the wind blew again, she felt him. Kyra felt her father. He was there, and he knew she was scared. He knew she was upset, and he knew how she missed him. He knew that they were leaving. He knew it all. She shut her eyes and listened to the wind. She listened to what she believed he'd wanted to tell her before he passed but had been unable to. She made her imagination bend until she heard those words in his voice.

"I love you, too. Daddy." She whispered the simple words before standing up.

She realized there was nothing more she needed to say. He knew everything going on, and he would be with her all the way, as always. He would even be in Prince Paul with her. Then suddenly a stronger, more forceful gust of air blew, riddling her skin with goose bumps.

She glanced down at her diamond-faced watch. It read three forty-five. She had left home at about three o'clock, and she knew her mom was waiting for her to get back so she could give her an earful. She planted a sweet kiss on top of the gravestone and turned away, leaving the cemetery and another part of her life in Chicago behind.

CHAPTER 4

The Cheesecake Factory, with its yellowish-pinkish curved walls and ceilings and its casual, relaxed atmosphere was the perfect place for their farewell.

They were seated in a round booth, Natasha and Mercedes on either side, and Kyra in the middle. They had been gabbing away all night, laughing and joking, reminiscing about old times. Their chatter stopped when their meals arrived—hot, delicious and scrumptious-looking.

"I'm about to tear it up!" Mercedes rubbed her hands together as she eyed the shrimp New Orleans dish being set in front of her by the waiter.

"I know that's right," Natasha agreed.

"Enjoy your meal, ladies," said the blue-eyed waiter whose name tag read ANDREW in bold black letters.

"Oh, believe me, we will." Mercedes shot the waiter the eye before he walked off—blushing—to attend to other tables.

"Cedes, you know you need to leave that li'l white boy alone. Flirting with him like that," Natasha giggled.

"Don't sleep on them white boys. They be havin' money! I mean, look, he got a job and it's legal. Plus he's a cutie. Maybe he'll give me a discount or something if I keep it up. Who knows? But hey, a number is good, too, 'cause to be honest, I'd do him," Mercedes shamelessly admitted as she stuffed a forkful of food into her mouth.

"Oh yeah, before I forget, Kyra, I got something for yo' spoiled ass," Natasha said, changing the conversation. She reached down into her purse and pulled out a thin box in shiny purple wrapping paper.

"Me, too," Mercedes chimed in, pulling up a long royal blue box. Kyra knew by instinct it was jewelry.

"Aww, you guys didn't need to do that for me!" Even though she acted surprised, deep down she had expected something.

She started with Natasha's gift. She tore the wrapping paper and revealed a CD.

"Aww, cute, really cute." She smiled at the memory of the day they'd played hooky at her friend's house.

"Okay, open mines now." Mercedes' anxiety was a sure sign that Kyra was bound to like her gift.

Kyra picked up the thin box and slowly removed the lid. There were three white gold bracelets, each holding part of a shimmering pink-rhinestone-encrusted letter.

"It's a three-way friendship bracelet. I had it specially made. It's rare, just like our friendship, and when you put it together, it makes a C for Chicago. I just had to make sure you never forget where you came from," explained Mercedes. Kyra passed each of her friends a bracelet, and they put them on, connecting the pieces that linked them as friends.

At the top of the John Hancock building was where Natasha and Kyra stood side by side, looking at the Chicago skyline—the lights, the buildings, the water and everywhere across the city. Kyra took it all in. She was so comfortable and took the city's vitality for granted. She never wanted to forget it.

"I'm gonna miss you, you know that?" Natasha broke the silence.

"I'm gonna miss you, too. I don't wanna go. I just...wish things were different." Kyra sighed as she looked out over the city.

"I don't want you to go, either, but I mean, look at the bright side. It's really nice there. It has all those white-sand beaches and crystal-clear water. It might not be so bad. I mean, you'll be basking in the sun while we're all up here freezing our asses off." Natasha never failed to try to put a positive spin on things.

"But it's not Chi-town. I don't care how much sand and water it has, it will never be here. It'll never be home. I mean, if this was a vacation, I would be geeked as hell. But to live? No! *Hell* no!"

"Well, you'll only have two years there, right? Then you'll be eighteen and old enough to do what you wanna do, including come back to Chicago and live with me and Cedes." Natasha grinned at her friend. She was still trying to lift Kyra's mood, even though she knew it was useless.

"But while I'm there, I won't have nobody, Tash. Not you, not Kai, Cedes, nobody. I leave and at least you still got Cedes."

"Yeah, you're right, I guess. But you can meet new people while you're down there. Ain't nothing wrong with that. I mean, don't get it twisted. All three of us are tight, but me and you, man, we been down since kindergarten! Cedes came in the picture in junior high. You got years on her! I mean, she's a good friend, don't get me wrong, but she ain't my sis like you are."

"I'm your sis? Fa real?"

"You know I never lie! And you know I'm gonna be down there for summer vacation, right?"

"Yeah..."

"Aww, girl, come here! I'm going to miss you something crucial!" Natasha tried hard to smile and laugh and hold back the tears as she hugged her longtime friend. It hurt her to be so helpless when someone she cared about was down and out.

Kyra wished she could confide in Natasha as she rested her chin on her shoulder. All she needed was a moment to tell her how, deep down, she was really scared. She was afraid of this huge change in her life, afraid she wasn't ready for it. But telling someone she was afraid was something she could never do. "You can't show your weakness" was advice Makai had passed on to her, and she followed his advice as if it were scripture.

The two of them broke free of their hug and fell silent again. Since neither of them really knew what to say, silence seemed best. Eventually, a security guard in the building came to tell them it was time to go, and the building was closing.

They exited the elevator and spotted Mercedes as Andrew was leaving.

"I see someone's awfully happy," Natasha commented.

"Yup, another success. But I got a problem." Mercedes held a small piece of paper on which seven digits and his name were scribbled in blue ink. "I don't know whether to get his ass to buy me a pair of Gucci boots to match my purse or if I should get him to pay for my hair and nails every week."

"Oh Lord. She got herself another victim," Kyra chuckled.

"It's not like we're getting married or anything. By the time he realizes what's happening to him, he'll be too damn broke to do shit about it."

The conversation on the way home had been buzzing over the radio, but as soon as they pulled in front of Kyra's, things fell quiet.

"Well, y'all, I'm gonna go. I'll talk to y'all later," was all Kyra could manage to say on her last night. The three had one last tight group hug.

Kyra had to avoid goodbyes, to avoid any kind of emotional moment. She wanted to keep the situation under control, and that meant not seeing anyone cry and holding back her own tears. She stepped out of the car and walked toward her house.

She stood on the porch in the chill of the winter's night and watched the Altima drive down her street and vanish.

FLIGHT 2353 TO NASSAU FROM CHICAGO, 1:00 A.M. scrolled across the large electronic screen in bright orange letters as they sat and waited. Kyra looked at her watch. In just half an hour, she would be on a plane headed to what many people considered paradise. She, however, considered it hell, and it was hot, too.

While waiting to board, she tried to call Makai. She just wanted to hear his voice one more time. She wasn't sure she would make it through the flight if she didn't. When he didn't answer after a barrage of calls, she rolled her eyes and sucked her teeth in frustration. Aside from his disappointing call that morning, she hadn't heard from him all day. He hadn't even sent her a text message. Nothing.

"What's wrong?" her mother said, sensing her daughter's frustration.

"Nothing. I'll be back," Kyra snapped as she snatched her carry-on bag and marched to a nearby kiosk.

Her eyes were blurry as she fumbled through the racks of magazines and rows of snacks and candies, but she ignored the impulse to break down. Instead, she quickly settled on *Ebony*, *XXL* and *Jet*, along with a king-sized Snickers bar, a snack-sized bag of Cheetos and a Pepsi. To her, they were not just the perfect snacks—they were now essentials for the trip.

"Flight two-three-five-three to Nassau from Chicago will now begin boarding. If you are an unaccompanied minor or a first-class passenger you are welcome to board."

The announcement echoed through the terminal as Kyra made her way back to the boarding area with a plastic bag of goodies and her small carry-on bag. She began heading toward the gate but stopped when her mother didn't follow.

"Mom, come on. We gotta board." She motioned for her mother to come along.

"They didn't call us yet. Sit down."

"We're not in first class?" Kyra said, as though she couldn't believe it.

"Since when do I have first-class money?" Her mother chuckled, but Kyra didn't find anything funny.

Seat 26A, a window seat, was Kyra's. She and her mother were among the last group of passengers to board and were now seated near the very back of the plane. As the plane took off, Kyra sat in the stuffy cabin and listened to her headphones. When the flight attendant came around, she didn't eat anything or drink anything. She didn't even speak. She just sat there going through her iPod selections, finally choosing several menu tracks. In between burying her head in a romance novel, her mother took a nap and ate the snacks the flight attendant doled out. Kyra scowled at her in disgust, barely able to control the urge to choke her mother in her sleep.

As tired as she was, Kyra couldn't sleep. Insomnia left her cranky. Kyra flipped through magazines, and even though they didn't hold her attention for long, she forced herself to read every article in each issue twice. She sometimes felt herself drifting off, but with the sudden jerks of the plane and a crying baby, a nap was impossible.

Man, this is some bullshit! Here I am on this big-ass plane that's stuffy as hell and smells like shit. That bitch back there needs to change that little rug rat's diaper and shut him the fuck up! He sounds just as happy about leavin' as I am, though, so I guess I can't really knock him for it. And Mom. Look at her ass. Over there all asleep. Lookin' all comfortable, too. Like this was nothin'! Like this was no big deal! Man, if I could parachute off this plane and go back to Chicago, I would in a heartbeat. But no, here I am goin' to a whole other country with nobody. I mean, Mom can be cool sometimes, I guess. But more times than not, she's too uptight. Why are we movin' here? This still don't make no sense to me! I mean, we could've found a solution. There had to be some way to fix the problem. But naw, she just wanna up and ruin my life. I feel robbed, robbed of my life or somethin'. I feel incomplete. It's like somethin' is missin'. And now here I am, on this plane that keeps rockin' and shakin'. Yup. This is it. I'm goin' from bein' one of Chi-town's finest to bein' some island girl.

Kyra looked down at her watch for about the millionth time. It was about seven in the morning. They would be landing soon.

Thank the Lord this flight is just about over. I've been on this plane long enough. Got me sittin' next to a woman I despise with every fiber of my goddamn being right now. I could just choke the shit out of her for doin' this! For makin' me go through this shit! For makin' me miserable! For makin' everythin' change! This is by far the worst day of my life!

CHAPTER 5

Kyra and her mother spilled out of the plane in the middle of the crowd of passengers. They had reached Nassau, Bahamas. The island was captivating. The sun was shining bright, the air was warm, and there were rows upon rows of palm trees. Yeah, Florida had these things, too, but Nassau had a much more exotic appeal.

They made their way outside with their baggage, trying to catch a ride to the ferry that would take them to the island of Prince Paul. Kyra stepped outside into the heat, which forced her to take off her leather jacket. It didn't take long to hail a cab.

Their cabdriver was kind, maybe a little too kind. He got lost driving to the dock, all the while engaging in friendly conversation with her mother as though nothing were wrong or out of the ordinary. He had that thick West Indian accent Kyra had imagined, and the looks to match. *This is goin' to be a long two years*, she thought. She sighed and leaned her head against the window.

Vomit floated in the water as Kyra hung over the side of the boat. She had gotten seasick on the ferry. Her face was pale and her stomach did more flips than a gymnast. She had ridden in small tour boats in Chicago before for fun, but that was a long time ago. Her body wasn't used to the swaying of a boat anymore.

She sat down on a bench on the top deck. She was tired and nauseated but refused to close her eyes. Her body was tense and aching. She stared out at the light blue water and the islands in the distance. She even thought she spotted a dolphin fin at one point. Her head tipped back and she looked up at the sky as birds glided through the air. She didn't like the new place, but she couldn't deny its beauty. She kept her comments to herself, while her mother was the complete opposite. "It's so beautiful!" she said to Kyra nearly a thousand times, and that was no exaggeration.

At around one o'clock in the afternoon, they pulled into a dock with a sign that read WELCOME TO PRINCE PAUL, POPU-LATION: 5,078. Kyra couldn't believe it. There were probably more people in her old high school than on the entire island.

"Okay now, we're up the road a mile or two," said Geneva Jones as she read aloud from the directions to their new address. "I can't wait to see the house up close. I bet it's gorgeous!"

"You want me to go find a cab?" Kyra asked, sipping her now warm Pepsi to ease her stomach as she stood on the dock.

"No. There aren't any. The island is only a few miles long. No need for one, really. We're just going to have to walk."

"Walk! In this heat? For a few *miles?* I don't think so."

"Don't start acting up already. You don't have a choice, so let's go." By the tone of her voice, it was clear that she wouldn't tolerate her daughter's attitude. Kyra huffed in exasperation but didn't say another word.

They strolled side by side down the dusty dirt road, passing what seemed like hundreds of palm trees and other plants whose names were unfamiliar. They passed by dozens of one-story homes and little shacks that served as tiny shops.

The homes were well kept and painted bright and lively colors. They were not run-down like Kyra had thought they'd be, and their colors blew the dull grays and browns of Chicago away. They had porches and green, grassy yards where, in some, children played as they were watched over by their elders.

As Kyra and her mother passed, heads turned. It was as if everyone knew they were foreigners. With a population of only 5,078, it wasn't difficult to tell.

Kyra and her mother had been walking for what seemed like infinity and a day when they finally stopped in front of a baby blue house. It was one story, like all the rest, and had a white wraparound porch with a chair swing in the front. There were white shutters flanking the windows, and a white door with a circular glass window in it. The stained-glass window had a design of flowers and small birds. There was a large front yard with the same thick green grass as the other houses on the block, and a dirt driveway, where a Jeep Cherokee just like their old one was parked. This was to be their new home.

"Oh, it's even more beautiful than I imagined!" Geneva Jones was giddy as she ran up to her new house, keys in hand. It was more than Kyra had expected, too, but her expression remained cold.

The inside was even lovelier than the outside. There was lots of white wicker furniture, some deep, dark mahogany tables, and in the living room, an entertainment center that held their TV and stereo system. There were a few colorful African paintings on the walls, as well. And there were small lamps and wide, leaf-shaped ceiling fans.

The dining room and kitchen were joined. There was a window over the sink looking onto the backyard, which had a small garden with colorful tropical plants and a patio set. There were also wide floor-to-ceiling sliding doors to get there from the kitchen.

Kyra's room had all white wicker furniture and soft pink walls. There was a queen-sized bed with a fluffy white comforter and lots of pillows, all in different shades of pink. There were a few chairs, a small glass table and a vanity. A nightstand on each side of the bed held a small lamp and pink flowers. The house left them both speechless, but Kyra refused to admit it. She made sure to find fault.

"My favorite color is blue."

It was around seven that evening when Kyra opened her eyes again. She got up and changed into a short jeans skirt and a light green tank top. She put on her white and light green Air Force Ones that Makai had had specially made for her the previous summer. She smoothed her hands over her braids and took a deep breath. She was here. This was it. There was no going back—not for two years, anyway. She remembered the promise Makai had made to her before she left. She was missing him like crazy, and a full day hadn't even gone by.

Kyra walked out into the hall to hear her mother's voice coming from the living room. She assumed her mom must be watching TV, since she was in the habit of talking to the characters as though they could actually hear her advice. But she was on the telephone.

"Yes, we just got in not too long ago. The place is wonderful...amazing. Oh, tomorrow at noon? Sure, sure.... Yes, she'll love it. That'll be great. Okay, see you then. Bye." Geneva Jones placed the phone in its cradle before turning to address

Kyra, who was now staring blankly at the television. "Are you ready to go to the market? I found out that they have one a mile or so down."

"Who was that on the phone?" Kyra didn't bother to so much as look at her mother. The television had her in a daze.

"Oh, that was my boss. He wants us to go up to Providenciales for the day tomorrow to have a tour, grab some lunch and show me around work."

"I don't wanna go. Can I stay home?" Kyra's complaints came between her glances at the commercials flashing across the television screen.

"No. Don't be rude. You were invited, and there is no reason for you not to go. You don't have anything else to do. Now come on. Let's get to the market before it gets too dark."

"Man, I do have a reason. It's called emotional distress."

"You're so damn dramatic. You act like this is the end of the world," her mother said, laughing off her statement.

Kyra redirected her focus and looked directly at her mother and said, "It is."

Kyra hung back while her mom walked ahead along the dirt road. She was in no rush to do anything. She made painstaking efforts not to dirty or crease her shoes. She kept her head down, watching for every hole and puddle while contemplating the fact that she had gone from a city to an island in a matter of hours. Oh, what time could do.

The market was busy with chatter that was audible from around the corner and aromas that filled the air. There were stands overflowing with an array of fruits and vegetables in every shape and color one could imagine. Kyra had never seen anything like it in her life. It was almost fascinating. Almost.

Kyra wandered around glancing at things, stopping to pick

up carvings and beaded jewelry to admire their craftsmanship. Her mother headed off in search of food items. But Kyra didn't mind making her way through the market alone. She was exhausted from thinking and was still in no mood to entertain her mother in conversation. The reality of her move weighed on her, and she was helpless to do anything about it. She was on the island now. But she was miserable in paradise.

After discovering a tobacco stand, Kyra bought two Cuban cigars, wondering if they would live up to their reputation. Then she slowly drifted to another stall that caught her attention. Her eyes roamed over all the candles. No two seemed to be the same. She picked up several, smelled them and set them down only to pick up yet another. As she sniffed each candle, she couldn't help but feel uneasy. Someone was watching.

Kyra lifted her eyes and spotted a group of boys standing in the shade of a neighboring tree. They appeared to be her age, maybe a little older. One had butterscotch-colored skin and a freshly cut head of hair. From his posture alone, she could tell he was muscular underneath his white T-shirt. Another one, tall and lean, had long cornrows and a light brown skin tone that was reminiscent of walnut.

Of the three guys, only one had dreadlocks, and he was the culprit. His skin was the shade of milk chocolate. He had a mustache, and a thin beard ran along the edge of his face and chin. Their eyes locked. And no matter how hard Kyra tried to turn away, she couldn't break his stare.

"How are you doing today, miss?" He spoke with a slight accent and was very polite. He blew all of Kyra's prejudices out of the water.

"I'm fine."

"So are you new to the island? I've never seen you before. What is your name?"

"None of your business." For the first time in their conversation, Kyra looked the stranger in the eye. She clutched the things she had bought as she gave him the once-over from head to toe.

"Well, None of Your Business, I'm Justin. And over there is my brother, Quentin, and my best friend, Michael." Justin smiled at her feistiness and pointed in the direction of his friends. "The one with braids is my brother and the one in the white shirt is Michael." Kyra could instantly see the resemblance between Justin and the boy he said was his brother.

"Look, that's nice and all, but if you came over here to get my number or somethin', then you're wastin' your time. You might as well walk over to your friends and make up a lie to tell them to keep you from bein' embarrassed."

Without another word, Justin smiled and rejoined his boys. They exchanged words for only seconds before heading in the opposite direction. As they walked down the dirt road laughing, talking and kicking up dust, Kyra stared at them curiously.

"Hey, are you ready to go?" Her mother's gentle tap on her arm made her jump.

"Yeah."

"What are you looking at? Uh-oh, I see. You like one of those boys, don't you? Which one?" She poked fun at her daughter.

"None of 'em. You know I'm with Kai."

"Yeah, yeah. Anyway, what did you buy?" her mother asked looking at the bag resting in Kyra's hands.

"Some candles. I got some pink and white ones to match my room," she said, leaving out the exact inventory.

"That sounds cute. We should get going, though. We have to walk all the way home, and I still have to fix dinner." She shifted the full basket of goods in her arms. It was obvious that her energy was dissipating.

"Okay," Kyra said, still preoccupied, making sure to glance down the road one last time before starting on their trek back home.

Something inside Kyra had clicked when she saw Justin. She didn't understand it. Something she didn't understand made him linger in her mind all evening. She didn't like his dreads, but he was very, very, very attractive. Occasionally, she would snap out of her infatuation when thoughts of Makai resurfaced. Kai was her heart, even if her mind played with the memory of her encounter with Justin for the rest of the night.

CHAPTER 6

At noon the following day, Kyra and her mother were crossing the water that separated the islands of Prince Paul and Providenciales. The sun was shining, but there was no breeze to offer relief from the heat. The sky was clear, and the water was the crystal blue the Caribbean was famous for.

As the ferry parted the waters, Kyra sat on a bench in the small closed cabin and stared out the porthole. In the distance, she could see the hotel resorts that dotted the coastline. Kyra admired the long stretches of sandy white beaches. Providenciales appeared to be a lively place with lots of people, and she liked that. Prince Paul was as nice as it was quiet. Being from Chicago, she wasn't used to that. She loved the hustle.

Once the ferry pulled into port, Kyra's mother navigated their Jeep onto the dock amid a slew of other cars and people. The island of Providenciales was larger than Prince Paul, and home to more businesses. Downtown, Kyra made a mental note of the shops and boutiques. She also noticed other places—nightspots, a spa and an old-style movie theater.

The Jeep came to a halt in front of the Sands at Grace Bay Resort, putting an end to Kyra's sightseeing. The short ride to the oceanside hotel was not long enough to prepare them for the beauty of the six three-story buildings that comprised the hotel and the lush tropical landscaping that surrounded them.

Kyra could still hear the roar of the waves as she entered the lobby. She appreciated its laid-back décor as her mother headed over to the reservation desk, where a tall, dark, thin, muscular man was waiting. He had glistening dark brown eyes, and his dark brown hair was in little dreadlocks. His fitted tan suit hung well on his handsome frame.

"Hi, I take it you are Mrs. Jones." The man took her mother's hand in his and shook it firmly, smiling to reveal his straight white teeth. She smiled back at the gentleman.

"Yes. And you are…?"

"My name is Matthew Daniels. I'm your new boss. We spoke on the phone."

"Oh! Hello. I'm sorry!" Geneva let out a small chuckle, re-alizing her mistake.

"And I take it this pretty young lady is Kyra?" Matthew said, turning his attention to Kyra and shaking her hand.

"Yes, this is my daughter." Her mother beamed with pride.

"Nice to meet you. I see where you get your beautiful looks from."

"Yeah." Kyra plastered a fake smile on her face and offered a limp handshake.

"Well! Should we get this tour moving? I don't know about you two, but I haven't eaten all day, and I cannot wait for lunch." Matthew let out a nervous laugh in an attempt to enliven the mood.

"Me, neither," Geneva said, even though she had eaten breakfast before they left the house that morning. Kyra couldn't help rolling her eyes at the useless lie and her mother's rusty method of flirting.

* * *

By the time they made it home, Kyra was thankful to be there. She slipped her shoes off at the door and was in midstride when her mother called out to her.

"Hey, put your shoes back on. We have to head to the grocery store if you plan to eat tonight. Matthew told me about a place at lunch, and I would like to pick up a few more things."

"I don't wanna go."

"And I don't want to hear it. Let's go. We can even take the car if you want."

"Dang! Okay, I'll go." Kyra let out a sigh as she gave up the fight and headed out the door beside her mother.

The old-fashioned grocery store was located on the east side of the island and was outfitted with a 1960s-style gas station in front. There were absolutely no credit card machines or security cameras.

Kyra tiptoed behind her mother as she watched her weave through the aisles, pick an item up, inspect it, and then place it in her basket. She was feeling anxious and her palms were sweating. She bit her lip in a feeble effort to exercise self-control, but she couldn't help herself.

"So what do you think of Matthew?"

Her mother paused for a moment, clearly caught off guard by the nature of her daughter's question.

"Well, he seems like a really nice guy, very intelligent, handsome. Oh, I don't know. But that reminds me, earlier I got the impression that you didn't care for him. Why were you acting like that toward him? He hasn't done anything to you."

"He talks too much. Blah, blah, blah. He needs to have a Mute button. Plus, he seems a little *too* nice. He was probably just actin' like that because he's feelin' you—at least, I hope so, for his sake. Anybody that soft is a disgrace. He has no manliness to him."

"Oh, stop it! He is not *feelin'* me or whatever you want to call it." She clutched the small plastic basket, and for the first time in the conversation turned her eyes toward her daughter. "What made you think he likes me?"

"Mmm, hmm, see, you asked me why I think he likes you. That must mean you like him, too, don't you?"

"No. I barely even know the man. And yes, I realize that he does talk a lot, but he holds good conversation."

"Yeah, I bet." Kyra rolled her eyes.

"Well, maybe if you said more than two words to the man you would know."

"I'm just sayin' you don't want to rush into things."

"You know you need to stop. I know what you're doing. But don't you even start in about your father, because I can tell that's what you're beating around the bush about. And I just want you to notice how I didn't bring up anything else about you drooling over some dreadlock wearing skinny li'l boy. How you've been staring off into space today is more than enough to make me think you *like* him. Now shut up and just let me shop if all you want to talk about is me and Matthew, because in all honesty, it's really none of your business."

Kyra would have usually snapped back with a smart remark, but she couldn't say a word. Her mother had her there, and by the tone of her voice, Kyra knew not to push her any further or she'd run the risk of raising her mother's fiery temper.

Once they were back at home and settled, her mother started to prepare dinner. Kyra shut her door to block out the clanging of pots her mother was using in the kitchen. She listened to the lock click in place and began making a call on her cell phone. She was surprised she could even get a signal, being where she was.

The light shone against her cheek and was blinding in the darkness as she perched on her bed, swinging her feet until, after five rings, someone picked up.

"Hello?"

"It's me! Don't tell me you forgot me already!" Kyra felt instantly relieved when she heard Natasha's familiar voice.

"Hey! I didn't even look at the caller ID. My bad."

"It's cool. So whaddup?" She was now at ease, able to release the tension in her muscles. The thought that her friend might have forgotten about her had raised fear.

"Uh-uh. I need to be asking you that! How is it? Is it beautiful like what I be seeing on TV?"

"Yeah, it's all right."

"So what you been doing since you been there? Hit a beach or something yet?"

"When we got here we had to take a ferry, which had me all throwin' up. Then we had to walk to the house in the hot-ass sun. It's crazy hot down here. Then me and my ma hit up this little market yesterday, and I met this boy named Justin...."

"Uh-oh! Tell me 'bout him!"

"He cute and everythin', and he was cool, I guess. Even with his dreads."

"Hmm, sounds like we might have a little crush on our hands?"

"Hell naw! Ain't nobody like my baby Kai. Man, I miss him," she cooed.

"Yeah, yeah. I know ain't no nigga hitting those draws but him."

"Heffa, shut up! Ain't nothin' poppin' off down here."

"Well, let me fill you in on what's been happening up here in ya hometown! Now, as you know, the Black and White Party went down last night. It was fiyah! It was just too crazy, girl! Tons of celebs rolled through, too. And yes, Cedes did get an autograph from Chingy." Natasha chuckled as she continued to fill Kyra in.

"Damn, it sounds like it was so fun," Kyra said, doing her best to hide her sadness.

"Yeah it was. I wish you had been there, though."

"Me, too. But uh, speakin' of Cedes, how's she doin'?"

"She's umm...okay, I guess. Same ol' Mercedes doin' what she always do. Just out running the streets being a ho."

"Damn, you harsh for that."

After the conversation with Natasha, Kyra hung up and dialed Makai's home and cell numbers. She even sent a text message to his two-way. She called more than once on each line and soon grew frustrated and upset. The sound of his voicemail was beginning to disturb her, and she threw her phone on the floor. Makai had never been so hard to reach in all of their years of dating. The new mystery of what he was doing and the possibility of who he could be doing it with left Kyra feeling insecure, with too many doubts. Nightmarish scenarios ran through her mind as she snuggled under the covers and flicked on the TV. She didn't bother to pay it any attention before she drifted off into a light sleep.

Sunday afternoon Kyra's mother burst through Kyra's white double doors into her bedroom with a package. "Wake up, sleepyhead! It's almost one o'clock, and you got something in the mail!"

Kyra sat up, aggravated by her mother's unwelcome entrance. She took a seat on the edge of her bed as her mother handed over the package. Kyra tore at the package and even began to think it was a gift from Makai but realized no one had her new address yet. If that wasn't enough, once she opened the package it revealed a short red plaid skirt, a white button-down shirt, knee-high black socks and shiny black shoes. Topping it off was a small gray cotton sweater.

"What in the world is this?" Kyra asked as she looked over the clothes. She held the items as if they were disgusting rags.

"It's your school uniform. I want you to try it on to make sure it fits."

"I'm not wearin' a uniform. Especially somethin' this... this...hideous, 'cause *ugly* sure ain't the word."

"Shush and go try it on."

Kyra sucked her teeth and dragged herself into the bathroom with the uniform clutched in her hands. All the while, she hoped that maybe the uniform would be too small or too big and that she could wear her own clothes until she got another one. Maybe with luck she could buy some time. But luck was not on her side. It was a perfect fit.

"Okay, now turn around. You look so adorable!" Geneva Jones squealed as she watched Kyra do a slow turn. She was beaming while her child frowned.

"Adorable? I'm sixteen, Mom, and you're usin' li'l kid

words like I'm four. This is so ugly! Do I have to wear this?" She whined and fidgeted in what felt like a Halloween costume.

"Sorry, it's the rules. Besides, I personally think it's for your own good. I see how you girls dress these days, and if you ask me, they need to have uniforms everywhere. If one thing isn't hanging out it's another. You would think you girls would be ashamed to be so exposed. Whatever happened to leaving something to the imagination?"

Monday morning Kyra was up and ready to go. She had her backpack over her shoulder and had applied her own style to her uniform. Her braided ponytails finished off the look. She proudly pranced into the kitchen, where her mother sat sipping her cup of coffee.

"Mom, I'm ready to go," she announced.

Her mother turned around in her peach-colored pantsuit. She almost choked on her coffee when she saw her daughter's outfit. She eyed her from head to toe, from the skirt pulled up higher than it should have been to the shirt knotted to showcase her pierced navel. Kyra's sweater was fastened with only two buttons, so as to flaunt her cleavage, while gum danced between her teeth.

"Uh-uh! You can't go to school looking like that! You're going to wrinkle your blouse like that!" Geneva Jones quickly set her mug down and rushed over to straighten out her daughter's uniform.

"Mom! Quit! I needed to do somethin' with it! Ain't nothin' wrong with showin' some stomach and legs. It's hotter than a mug out there. And it's only what—seven a.m.?"

"Honey, I really don't know what to tell you. This place isn't like your old school. You are just going to have to grin and bear it," her mother said, turning to the sink to pour the remaining coffee from her mug.

"No shit," Kyra mumbled under her breath. "Anyways, can you drop me off now?"

"No. I have to be at work by eight, and I still have to take the ferry. I don't have time to drop you off. You have to get to school by yourself from now on."

"Man," Kyra sighed. "Okay, where's the bus stop?"

"Kyra, there are no buses. God forbid, but you have to walk."

"Walk? I ain't walkin' to school every day. It seems like we walk everywhere around here!"

"It's not that far. Walking never hurt anybody. Now, here's a map for you to find your way if you need it. It came in the mail with the uniform. I'm pretty sure you'll see someone walking along and can ask them where it is if you need any help." She handed over a small laminated map before snatching her leather bag from the countertop. "I gotta go, sweetie. Have a good day." She kissed Kyra on the cheek as she bolted out the door.

As she walked along the roads, Kyra could see people in the distance, groups of students or men and women on their way to work. Kyra was unsure of her direction, but she was too proud to ask anyone for help. Instead, she walked on, passing a small swamp, low-cut pinewoods and a small lake before approaching a path that stretched for what appeared to be several hundred feet. As she wandered down the shaded lane, she was very grateful for the cool shadows provided by the large green trees on either side. Rays of sunlight pierced between the leaves, and a constant gentle gust of wind calmed her. The light combined with the breeze enabled Kyra to keep her composure when she caught a glimpse of her intended destination.

The one-story brick building at the end of the road would be her new school.

Prince Paul Academy was in large black letters on the front wall. The building had only one floor but was spread out. There was a dirt basketball court outfitted with chain nets, a large green recreational field, and a few picnic tables outside. Things didn't look too bad after all.

Kyra had imagined that her new school would be some one-room shack made of wood, similar to those used during segregated times in the rural South. She'd was sure there would be no running water, heat or enough books for the students.

Kyra slipped through the thick wooden doors of the school, past the crowds and cliques and the eyes outside that examined her curiously, and inside to a surprisingly bustling school.

"Excuse me? Hi, I'm Kyra Jones. I'm a new student." Kyra politely announced her presence to an older woman sitting behind a desk outside the principal's office, only to receive a stern look. The woman simply looked down at her typewriter as if Kyra weren't there.

"Umm...I was wonderin' if you had a schedule for me. I dunno where any of my classes are. I'm new."

"Yah, yah. I hear ya, chile. Yah said yah new. Yah have Ms. Kingsley." The secretary didn't even look up as she pecked on the keys.

"Okay, what after that?"

"I say yah had Ms. Kingsley, now step!" the old woman snapped. She glared at the stranger before her, and Kyra was by no means slow in making her exit.

She exited the office feeling confused and angry. It was seven fifty-six a.m. She had four minutes to get to class, and she didn't have any idea where she was going. Any chance of getting help seemed impossible. She definitely didn't want to ask for help from a teacher. She assumed they would be just as impolite as the secretary, or worse.

That was when she saw her coming down the hallway. A tall, slender girl with slightly curled, shoulder-length hair, light brown skin and piercing, glowing blue eyes strolled in with grace as others rushed around her. Kyra could tell she was a goody-goody just by looking at her perfectly pressed uniform, the way she had her books clutched to her chest, and the straight, white smile on her face that seemed permanent. Kyra knew the girl would help her out. She seemed too nice not to.

"Umm...excuse me? I need some help," she called out to the girl just as she began to pass by.

"Sure, what's up?" The girl responded with such familiarity, it was as though she already knew Kyra.

"I'm new and I dunno my schedule. That mean-ass secretary said I have Ms. Kingsley, but..."

"Follow me. I have her, too. We better hurry, though, or we'll be late."

The classroom was spacious. A big wooden desk was in the front of the room. The blackboard served as its background. Many smaller desks were arranged in rows, and windows lined an entire side of the room, offering a view of a small, tranquil pond. The room was rather plain. There were no colorful posters or pictures to give life to the it, only the wall clock and a speaker.

The bell sounded as soon as the pair stepped into the classroom. Everyone quieted down and stared in Kyra's direction. All eyes were on her. There were a few open seats, and the girl who had helped her to class occupied one in the rear. The teacher was taking attendance from a small brown book, and Kyra was intently watching her, awaiting instructions. From what Kyra could tell, the teacher looked to be about her height, young and with a thick figure. Her hair was a red, dusty color and was pulled into a bun with loose strands dangling at her temples. Her face was overrun with freckles, and her eyes were a vivid green. She wore a pair of thin-framed glasses and a white floral-print dress with flat-heeled crimson shoes.

The teacher removed the glasses propped on her nose and let them hang on the chain around her neck. She seemed to be completely engrossed in notes she had written in one of the margins. She glanced up from her notebook for a moment to scan the room and then rose from her position propped against the desk. Seeing her new student brought a smile to her face.

"Hello. You must be Kyra. Kyra Jones, right?" The woman and walked over to shake Kyra's hand.

"Yeah, that's me," Kyra managed to answer, despite being preoccupied with returning the stares of the class, which was silently evaluating her.

"I apologize for keeping you waiting. I was just reading my notes on you. I was expecting you tomorrow, but I am glad you are here." Her voice was probably velvety and smooth in private conversation Kyra thought, but was powerful when projected. "Class, this is our new student, Kyra Jones! Kyra, I know its clichéd and all, but would you mind telling us a little about yourself?"

"Yes, I would."

"Oh, come on, don't be shy."

Kyra hesitated for a moment before giving in to her teacher's request.

"Okay...umm....well, my name is Kyra. I'm sixteen. I'm from Chicago, umm..."

She was trying to think of something else to say when her breathing stopped. She spotted Justin in a far corner of the room. She didn't know how she hadn't noticed him before, but there he was, and he was staring dead at her.

"...and I moved here about three days ago," she added hurriedly finishing her sentence.

"See, that wasn't so hard now, was it? It's nice to get to know you a little better. How do you like the island so far?"

"It's okay." Kyra knew she had to have offended some in the room, but if she rubbed them the wrong way, then so be it.

"Class, get out your homework from the weekend while I fill Kyra in on a few things." The teacher motioned to her new pupil and took her aside. "I'm sure you know that I'm Ms. Kingsley and I'm your teacher for this year. Here at the academy we have the same class all day and cover different subjects. It's kind of like the elementary school system in the U.S. We cover mathematics, science, history, English and some Spanish. We will cover each subject for an hour every day, with an hour lunch break at noon. Your parents should have gotten all other information regarding school hours, breaks, et cetera, in the mail with your uniform. Oh, and about the uniform, you have to wear it every day. Don't be fooled, Friday is *not* dress-down day. If you need another one, you can order it from a catalog.

"But enough of me talking your ear off. Let me give you a seat so we can get going." Ms. Kingsley peered up from the paper and surveyed the class several times before finally giving instructions.

"Okay, Kyra, you will sit in the back row next to Angel Cartier and Justin Hartwell." She pointed out what was to be Kyra's assigned seat.

"Hey, cutie." Justin showed off his heart-melting smile as Kyra took her place in the back of the room.

"Hi," she managed to mumble as she dropped her bag on the floor. She kept her eyes straight ahead as she readied herself for the day's lessons.

While Ms. Kingsley delivered her lectures, first discussing science and then math, Kyra found herself daydreaming. Her mind wouldn't settle down. She didn't pay attention to the first two lectures of the day, leaving her lost when Ms. Kingsley handed out a stack of math worksheets. Kyra stared at the first paper as if it were written in Japanese. She didn't comprehend a single problem on the sheet. She had been sure she would be more advanced than the others in the class, but instead, their studies were far more advanced than anything she had ever done. She was only a sophomore, and they were doing senior-level work.

After about ten minutes, the teacher called for the papers to be passed forward. Kyra held on to hers and then slowly raised her hand to for assistance. Mrs. Kingsley walked to the back of the room where Kyra was sitting.

"Ms. Kingsley...um, I never learned this stuff back in Chicago." Her admission came in a whisper that no one else could hear.

"Well, we can get you a tutor to help you catch up. Who in here is good at math?" Ms. Kingsley's question to the class immediately blew Kyra's cover. Most of the students who raised their hands were boys. One curly-haired boy in the front of the class with laughing dark brown eyes shielded by long eyelashes caught Kyra's attention. It didn't take long to figure out just from his looks that he was the class clown.

"Richard, put your hand down. We all know you are not the brightest student when it comes to math. All you do is act a fool."

"Aww, come on, Ms. Kingsley, you know I'm smart. Well, at least that's what you said last night."

"Boy, you couldn't hang with me for five minutes. Who are you fooling?"

Ms. Kingsley was still quite young and had some sass to her. She was genuinely kindhearted and wasn't cold like most teachers. Kyra had already taken a liking to her.

"Now, enough fooling around. Justin, you will be her tutor. You're good at math and you sit close enough to her that you'll be able to help out during class." She nodded at Justin and walked back to her desk.

Justin smiled at Kyra, who slid lower in her seat and folded her arms on her chest.

After the history and English classes, the bell rang for lunch. Everyone in the class stood, stretching their legs before hurrying to the cafeteria or outside with friends.

Kyra was left behind. She was picking up her bag from the floor when someone approached her.

"Would you like to eat lunch with me?"

Kyra looked up to see Angel, the girl who had helped her get to class. She wasn't at all keen on accepting what she considered charity, but she didn't like the idea of eating lunch alone. She was alone enough already.

The girls ate in silence at a small round table under the shade of an umbrella. A basketball game between some boys served as their source of entertainment until Angel finally took the initiative.

"So, you're from Chicago, right?" Angel asked while wiping her hands with a napkin.

"Yup, lived there my whole life."

"I just wanted to let you know that with you being new and all, if you need anyone to help you out or anything—"

"Thanks." Kyra cut her off before sipping her Coke. Even after being assigned a tutor and accepting Angel's lunch invitation, she wanted to hold on to what little pride she felt she had left.

"Rahh!" A boy with intricately designed braids ran up behind Angel, scaring her and making her jump. She turned around and playfully hit him in the arm and laughed. Kyra sensed their familiarity, which was confirmed when Angel give him a soft peck on the lips. He was one of the boys from the market the day she'd met Justin. He was Justin's brother, Quentin.

"Baby, you scared me half to death! Now stop playing around. I want you to meet my friend Kyra. She's new. Kyra, this is my boyfriend, Quentin," Angel said, introducing them.

"Whaddup?" Quentin acknowledged her with a nod of his head.

"Yeah, I saw you before. You're Justin's brother, right?"

"Yeah, you're that girl he was talking about," Quentin said with a slight chuckle, which stopped when his girlfriend elbowed him in the side.

Kyra was curious to know what Justin had said about her, but before the opportunity presented itself, the other boy from the market took a seat at their table. He was light skinned with thick lips. She had no doubt that it was Michael.

"Ooowee! Who is this fine thing right here?" Michael licked his lips.

"She's that girl J was talkin' about from the market," Quentin informed him.

"Oh," Michael said, before his mind drifted off to other matters. "So what's up, Q? You down for a game of ball?"

"Nah, I'm not really in the mood. Where's Justin at?"

"Probably breakin' Veronica off by the pond," Michael joked. His comment made Kyra's ears to perk up right away.

So Justin has a girlfriend? Veronica. That name just sounds stuck-up. I wonder if she's pretty. Hell, I know her ass ain't prettier than me. She kept her thoughts to herself as she half listened to the conversation going on.

"You know he dumped her *sanfi* ass a long time ago," Quentin said with a laugh.

"What the hell is a *sanfi?*" Kyra asked. She had never heard the term before in her life.

"*Sanfi* is when you are dishonest, manipulative and will sweet-talk anybody. A gold digger, you know." Angel was first to offer an explanation.

"Oh."

"Yeah, she's a newbie. She's not up on that slang yet."

The voice originated from behind her. Kyra spun around and set eyes on Justin, who was without a smile. He greeted everyone except Kyra and took a seat next to Michael. His arrival changed the whole mood of the table.

"I'm going to play some ball," Michael announced. He stood up from the table and began to dribble the orange ball.

"Baby, do you want to go back by the pond and relax?" Quentin asked. Angel nodded and said a quiet goodbye to Kyra as she walked off with her boyfriend, giving in to his loving tone. Everyone had practically run off to give Justin and Kyra some privacy.

"So who's Veronica?" Kyra blurted out as she ran her finger around the rim of her soda can.

"She's my ex. Why?"

"Oh, I was just wonderin'."

"Yeah, okay, but now it's my turn to ask you a question. Would I be wrong to assume that little Ms. Chicago didn't think us island folk knew any slang or talked without an accent?" She was silent as he went on. "It's all right. It's a common misconception. It's just that I could read your type from the day at the market."

"Please, you don't know about my type."

"Oh, is that right?" He smiled at her spunk.

"That's what I said, ain't it?"

"Well, even though I would *beg* to differ, that's not what's important right now. I just want to know when you want me to tutor you?"

"*Psh,* you're not *really* tutorin' me. I'll ask Angel or somethin'. There's no way you're about to be up in my house...in my room. No, no and no."

"But Ms. Kingsley said so. Anyway, there are such things as libraries, you know? I mean, who said we had to do it at your house? I think you want me to do it at your house, don't you?"

"Say what? No! Ugh, yeah, right!" She was trying to hold back her smile. "I didn't even know if you guys *had* a library around here. Remember, I'm new? And besides, where else would we go? Your little shack by the swamp?"

"So I see you got jokes. Do you got a man, too?"

"Oh, so now what? You wanna try and holla!" She let a laugh slip through.

"No. I just want to ask him how he puts up with all that attitude of yours."

"Whateva."

"But naw, on the real, I'm just tryin' to get to know you." He took a seat closer to her.

"Mmm, hmm, sure you are."

"You want to know what I think, Kyra?"

"Not really, but I feel like you're goin' to say it anyway, so go ahead, *Justin.*"

"I think that you want me to come to your house and that you want me to holla at you. You want me to come over to your house and tutor you on all kinds of stuff." Justin moved in so close to Kyra's face she could feel his breath on her lips as he spoke. The way he looked in her eyes, it was if he was trying to seduce her. It was working.

"Ugh! Bye!"

She threw away her garbage and headed for the school building. As she neared the school doors, her path was blocked. Kyra sized up each of the three girls in front of her.

Kyra assumed the girl who stood front and center was the leader of the clique by her in-your-face stance. She was tall and thin but had a large bust. Her silky jet-black hair was long and curled at the tips. Her lips were thick and full, and her cheekbones, as well as the rest of her facial features, were well defined. She had long, curly eyelashes, and her jealous eyes were a pure shade of brown. The girl was beautiful, but Kyra would never admit that to anyone.

"Who do you think you are?" the leader said in a voice loaded with attitude.

"Excuse me? I dunno who you think you are, but you need to move up out my way and you need to do it now." Kyra was quick to shoot back a similar attitude almost instinctively. She was never one to run from a confrontation.

"Obviously you don't know who we are. This is my friend Nicole," she said, pointing to the mixed-looking girl, "and this is Bridgette." She pointed to the girl with too much makeup. "And me, I'm Veronica," she introduced herself, placing her hand on her chest.

"Okay...so what's your point?"

"My point is that me and my girls run this school. So don't think that you're about to come down here regulating shit, because you're not. You're nothing but a newbie, and you need to keep in line, because if you step out you *will* get dealt with and it *won't* be pretty." Veronica bravely stepped into Kyra's face as she made her threat. In truth, she was all talk and no action, but to protect her status and image she made sure to pretend otherwise. It worked on her other peers, but Kyra wasn't having it.

"Hold up. First off, I dunno who the fuck you're threatenin'. Second off, this school you runnin' ain't nothing' to be proud of, and if I wanted to, I could run this in a day. Yeah I'm a newbie, but don't you ever come over here with some bullshit like this, 'cause others up in here may be scared of y'all, but I'm not. Don't even jump stupid with me. You don't know me. So now if you will excuse me…" Kyra growled back, attempting to pass the girls when Veronica stopped her with a shove to the shoulder.

"Bitch, who do you think you're talking to?"

"You and your punk-ass crew. And don't touch me again if you want to have that hand still attached to your skinny little body."

"We should whoop your ass right now for everyone to see."

"Trick, I wish you would even *flinch* at me." She moved so close to Veronica they could've kissed. She meant every word.

"Ha! Please. It's three against one. You don't want none. Face it, you don't want drama. Just keep your place and keep your distance from my man." Veronica backed up and placed her hand on her hip. Kyra's being so close to her made her uncomfortable.

"And who the fuck is desperate enough to go out with you?" Kyra scoffed.

"Justin Hartwell. Don't act like you don't know who he is. You were just over there with him. I saw you." Just then it clicked for Kyra. This was the same Veronica mentioned at lunch.

"What the...? I should slap you just for sayin' some dumb shit like that. Let me lay it out for you: I don't like him. You can have him."

"Oh, don't worry, I've already got him. And keep your ass away from Michael, too. My girl Nicole is with him." Veronica snottily nodded back to her friend.

"Watch your mouth. I hate to do it, but I will beat all y'all on my first day of school."

Kyra was about to swing on Veronica when Quentin and Angel showed up and stepped between the girls to avoid the conflict.

"Don't start any stuff with her. You know she's new, Veronica. You're not even with Justin anymore, so you need to let it go," Angel said.

"Little girl, don't come over here trying to speak to me on some shit you don't even know about. Just let your little friend know she needs to watch her back as well as her mouth," Veronica threatened as she and her crew continued to walk toward the building. The bell rang, and the rowdy crowd began to file back into school.

"I'm glad we have an understanding!" Bridgette yelled from the doors. She wanted to make sure Kyra heard her.

"Ooo, I'm gonna beat her ass!" Kyra raged through clenched teeth. Bridgette giggled before she disappeared inside. She had elicited just the reaction she had been seeking.

"Don't pay them any mind. Just don't play into their games. They do it to everyone on their first day, and Veronica definitely does it to anyone she even *sees* within a few feet of Justin," Angel said.

"Yeah, she still claims him, even though they've been over. Don't even worry about it," Quentin said.

"But she's disrespectin' me, bottom line. I ain't no ho, and

I sure ain't quick to back down. If she wants some, she can come get some."

"Don't fight her, Kyra. She's not even worth the trouble. She thinks that just because her family has money that makes her better than everyone else, and it doesn't."

"Did I miss something?" Michael walked up slowly, zipping his pants.

"Mike, man, where were you?" Quentin asked, noticing his friend's unzipped khakis. Quentin quickly excused himself from the company of the females to hear another one of his friend's scandalous tales of sexual conquest.

"Are you all right?" Angel turned her concerned look back to her new friend.

"Yeah, I'm fine. They're nothin', like you said."

"Okay, good. Let's get back in before we're late." Angel sighed and flashed a reassuring smile before they rushed back inside.

For the rest of the day, Kyra half listened to the lessons. She could see Justin frequently looking over at her, but she would only glare back, and he would look away.

CHAPTER 7

The final bell of the day hadn't even finished ringing before Kyra was out the door. She brushed by the crowd into the sun and its suffocating heat to start her brisk walk home up the tree-lined lane. She had reached the middle of the path when she felt someone clutching her elbow. She spun around with her eyes narrowed, expecting a fight.

"Are you okay?"

"Do I seem okay? Go on somewhere. You're causin' more trouble than you're worth," Kyra snapped at Justin.

"Veronica is nothing to trip off of, trust me. She's just too red eye of you. That's all."

"Red eye?" Kyra asked.

"Oh, my bad. Red eye means she's jealous of you."

Just then, Richard, Veronica and her girls sped by in her car. Kyra heard the music blare, and the car stirred up dust in the air as they rolled past. She bent down quickly and picked up a large rock to pitch, but Justin's hand grabbed hers. He slowly brought her hand toward the ground and let the rock fall. His hand replaced the hard mass as he locked eyes with her.

"Let me go." Kyra snatched her hand away and continued to walk. Justin kept up with her.

"So...wasn't that that one boy from our class in the car with her?" Kyra asked after walking a few steps. Once her anger subsided, she slowed her pace to listen to Justin.

"Yeah, he's her brother. Richard Pierce. Their father owns some resorts on a few islands. So that pretty much makes them uptown rich—you know, in other words, stuck-up as hell."

"That would explain the car, then, too."

"Basically."

"So now what I'm wonderin' is why on earth did you two ever break up? You guys seem meant for each other. She's stuck-up and you're just...you. So, hey, I don't see why y'all didn't click."

"Hey, sometimes things just don't work out. She just still tries to claim me because she knows she messed up and she doesn't want to see me with someone else. And her brother, Richard—if you're even thinking about dealing with him, be careful."

"Yo, chill, motor mouth, I was just wonderin' if they were related or not. I never said I wanted to holla at the boy."

"Did you just call me a motor mouth?"

"Sure did."

"So you're saying I talk shit?"

"No, chill. I'm just saying that it sounds like you like to gossip."

"Okay, new girl, let me set you straight on something. I'm just trying to look out for you."

"Don't get no attitude, I was just sayin'."

They walked to the end of the lane in silence.

"Thanks, then...I guess," Kyra said.

"You're welcome. So...where do you stay?"

"What does it matter to you?"

"Damn, you're so feisty! I like that. It's cute."

"Ugh, Justin, stop!" She laughed.

"Nah, I'm just messing with you. I *was* going to walk you home, but..."

"A'ight that's cool but don't try no funny stuff. No, you can't come in to get a drink or use my bathroom, understand?"

"Okay." He held his hands up in surrender.

"Your house is really nice."

"Thank you, and thanks for walkin' me home. That was fun."

"You're welcome. But I'm going to get going, so I'll see you at school tomorrow. And don't forget about me tutoring you. When should we start?"

"How about I just let you know. I'll call you or somethin'."

"But you don't have my number."

"Then give it to me."

"Okay..." Justin reached into his backpack and retrieved a pen and paper, then scribbled down his number. He had been caught off guard by Kyra's forwardness but was pleased by it, as well.

"Here. Let me give you mine, too." She neatly jotted down her digits before passing the scrap of paper to him.

"Okay, I'll see you tomorrow. First light. Bye, baby girl." He gently tipped her chin and headed up the street on his way home. Kyra could feel the goose bumps on her skin from when he had called her baby girl. Makai always called her that.

Kyra unlocked the door and walked into the air-conditioned house. The cool air flowed over her body as she took a seat in the living room and picked up the phone. She was going to call Makai.

She called all his numbers but got no answer. She called over and over, until the sound of the ringing was stuck in her head and gave her a headache. Whatever he was doing, she couldn't shake the feeling that it wasn't right.

Kyra leaned back into the cushions of the couch. She missed her boyfriend and her friends, and she seemed to worry more now than she ever had before. She felt stressed and overwhelmed from having to adjust to so much "new." Everything was new. Everything had changed in the blink of an eye.

I just wish that I was back where I was last Monday, where the only thing I had to worry about was how much my feet hurt. That was the last thought to cross Kyra's mind before she had no worries and was gone to the world, and to her problems in it.

CHAPTER 8

In a multimillion-dollar mansion on the other side of Prince Paul Island, Quentin, Michael and Justin were all seated around Quentin's large bedroom engaged in a lively conversation while playing a video game.

"Where did you go earlier?" Quentin demanded. "We were looking for you, but we couldn't find you anywhere. Some people said they saw you walking with the new girl, and the only new girl I know of is Kyra."

"Yeah, I walked her home."

"And...did you hit that or what?" Michael nosily added.

"I just walked her home. I hate to be the one to tell you this, but not everyone sticks their dick in everything that moves."

"Oh, you got jokes." Just then, Michael's cell phone ring tone sounded. He took it out and examined the caller ID. "It's Nicole."

"See, he got one of his hoes calling now," Quentin laughed.

"That's not funny. She be straight stalking," Michael said, putting the phone back in his pocket. The look on Michael's face when he had first told his friends about his night of sex gone wrong had been memorable.

"Forget both of y'all. Just take a look at you two. Quentin, Angel is too much of a goody-goody, dawg. And J, man, you were strung out on Veronica for the longest. Now here you go trippin' off that new girl. Before we know it, you're going to be taking her out, buying her things, straight tricking your dough and you *still* won't get some!"

"A'ight." Justin stood up and began to speak. "As much as I *hate* to say it, yes, I loved Veronica, and yes, she had me messed up. But you can't say I didn't get her ass good. Yeah, I have money, and yeah, I got status, and she thought she could get some to add to her own. But did I ever buy her shit? No. Did I take her places? Hell no. Why? Because I found out what she was doing around the way a while back. I was just using her after that, until I got tired of her. Then I dipped. And as far as Kyra goes, I'm not even going to tell her about my cash flow. I want to see if she'll like me for me. I'm sick of all the gold diggers. From now on, the fact that my family owns the island is on lock, you got me?"

"Okay, okay. Yes, you were kind of pimpin' when it came to Veronica. I'll admit that," Michael said.

"I don't know what it is, but Kyra does something to me," said Justin. "She's just…different. I don't know how to explain it. We all know I've been with my share of girls. We all have. But I'm for real on this one."

"Oh, I think I'm going to be sick." Michael gagged, faking as though he were going to vomit.

"Mr. Hartwell, the barber is here." One of the maids who tended to the estate made the announcement from the doorway of the bedroom. Her hands were folded on her apron and her face was stern.

"I'm not cutting my braids, Harriet, no matter what my father says," Quentin protested. His father had been pestering him for months to cut his hair.

"No, it's cool, it's for me," Justin clarified. He hopped up from his seat and handed off his controller.

"See, there that shit goes right there! I told you!" Michael pointed and snickered at his friend's decision to change his appearance.

"Shut up. It's not even like that. It's just...time for a change."

The next day, Kyra awoke with a plan in mind. She decided to take what she creatively dubbed a "chill day." Things had been moving too fast lately, and she desperately needed to slow things down. It was time to take it nice and slow, nice and easy.

She woke up at her usual time and got dressed in her uniform, creating the illusion that she actually intended to go to school that day. She walked outside in the rain and saw her mom off. She made sure her mother was out of sight before she back-tracked home to take off her uniform. She was in no rush to do anything.

She watched HBO movies and ate almost an entire half gallon of chocolate chip cookie dough ice cream. It was mid-afternoon when she went out onto the front porch and sat in the swing. She watched the rain fall as she inhaled the smoke of the rich tobacco from one of her hand-rolled Cuban cigars.

She was intently watching the wet scenery when she spotted a dark figure approaching her house from the road. She sat up and leaned forward, hoping to see who it was. The rain fell so hard it was almost blinding.

"Who are you?" she called out with a hint of fear in her voice as the unknown figure crept across her lawn.

"Girl, chill, it's me."

It was Justin. He walked onto the porch and dropped the

hood of his black sweatshirt. Kyra's eyes grew wide and she threw the cigar butt into the rain.

"Oh my God, what did you do?" she shrieked as she stood up and walked over to him for a better view.

"What? You don't like it? I cut off my dreadlocks. It was time for a change."

"Change isn't always good. But in this case it is."

"So you like it, then?" Justin asked curiously, secretly scared she would say no.

"Yeah, it looks a'ight." She smiled as she ran her hand over his freshly cut hair.

That was an understatement, because to her it looked really good. *He* looked really good. She could clearly see all his facial features, and the rain glistening on his face was adding to his appeal. He was looking too tempting.

"So why didn't you come to school today?" he asked as he leaned on the railing of the porch.

"'Cause," she sighed, "I just needed a day to myself."

"I thought you might've been sick or something. I came by to check on you," Justin lied.

"Thank you. You didn't have to do that."

Silence fell between them.

"Look, I know you said you needed a day to yourself, but do you mind if I join you? Being by yourself can get lonely, don't you think?"

"Sure. I don't care."

"I can start tutoring you if you want. I brought my stuff," Justin said, swinging his backpack down to the porch.

"Okay, that's cool. Come on in."

"Nice room," he commented as his eyes explored her furnishings.

"Thank you."

"You have an awfully big bed...."

"Don't even try it. We're studyin'. Now let's get started." Kyra laughed.

Justin removed his math book from his bag. "Do you want to do this over there?" he asked, motioning toward the chairs and the small glass table.

"No, we can do it right here," she said, hopping onto her mattress. "It's more comfortable."

"Now, what we're studying is trigonometric graphs, identities, and equations...."

As Justin began to explain what they were and how to solve them, Kyra zoned out. She stared at his face, his hair and the large diamond earring that hung from his ear. Either it hadn't been there before or she hadn't noticed it. She stared at his well-defined biceps, making their presence known through his wife beater. She stared at the tattoo on his arm and the smoothness of his skin. She stared at his lips. They were moving, but she heard no sound. She made note of how soft they looked and thought about what it would be like to kiss them. She looked at the thin beard along the edge of his jawline and at his thin mustache, tracing his face until she stumbled across his big brown eyes. She couldn't tear her gaze from them.

Justin felt her stare and looked over at her and stopped talking. His gaze met hers, and she didn't look away. He then leaned in and kissed her, freeing his tongue to caress her mouth. Her tongue pushed back, and he slowly laid her on the bed. He continued to kiss her and began to work his way to her neck, then spread her legs and laid his body between them. Kyra couldn't believe she was doing this. The only person she had ever been with was Makai, and here she was about to have sex with a boy she had only known for two days. Still, her body wouldn't let her buckle under the guilt when his hands glided over her body and began to work her shirt up over her head. She shook under him.

"Don't be scared. It's okay," he whispered reassuringly in her ear as he eased his shirt over his shoulders.

He began to kiss her chest and his hands unbuttoned her shorts to ease them down. He skillfully managed to take her panties along with them.

"Are you sure you want to do this?" He looked into her eyes as he lay ready to penetrate. With a nod, he pushed himself slowly into her body.

Kyra gasped for air as he began to slowly push himself deeper into her. She dug her nails into his back. She felt her body heat rise and she couldn't contain her pleasure-induced moans. She felt her body become tense with excitement as he placed his lips to her ear. She couldn't wait to hear what he had to say.

"Kyra! Kyra! Wake up, Kyra!"

The thrill ended when she snapped out of her daydream to see that she was still sitting on her bed, fully clothed and staring at Justin as he shook her.

"Oh, my bad, sorry." She looked away from him, extremely embarrassed and so ashamed. She couldn't believe what she had just fantasized. She had never even considered being with another man besides Makai, and her erotic dreams had always been reserved especially for him.

"Did you even hear anything I just said?"

"Maybe we should do this later. My mom is goin' to be home soon, and she'll trip if she sees you in here. Thanks for comin', though." Kyra began to rush Justin out of the house.

"Girl, what's wrong with you? Are you okay?" Justin barely managed to get the words out as Kyra was practically shoving him toward the door.

"Yup, I'm fine. See you tomorrow. Bye!" Kyra threw his things at him and shut the door. She leaned back against the door and took a deep breath. She was in dire need of a cold shower.

The schedule for the remainder of the week was unchanging for Kyra: wake up, go to school, exchange glares with Veronica, come home, call her friends in Chicago and get no answer and then be bored to death until she went to sleep.

After the day Justin came to her house, she felt different around him, almost uncomfortable, and avoided him. She wouldn't speak to him, and when he spoke to her, she replied with one-word answers. It wasn't that he did anything wrong, but she felt as though she had made a mistake by thinking the way she had. She couldn't deny that she was attracted to him, but she didn't want to make any moves she would later regret.

It was Friday, and Kyra was stuck at home. Angel invited her to a movie, but she declined. Instead, she opted for sitting in her living room in her red Scooby-Doo pajamas and watching "106 and Park."

Ring, ring!

The shrill ringing of the phone interrupted the daily count-down of the top hip-hop and R & B videos.

"Hello? Mom, where are you?"

"I'm at work. I have a lot to do, so I'll be home late." Her mother sighed into the phone, the stress evident in her voice.

"Oh, okay."

"I just wanted to call you to tell you not to wait up and to make dinner, because we all know that if I'm not there to make it for you, you might starve to death. Are you going anywhere tonight?"

"Nope. Just stayin' home."

"Say what? It's a Friday night and Kyra Jones is at home. I must have the wrong number," she joked.

"Ha, ha! Real funny, Mom." She chuckled a little bit. She knew her mom was right. In Chicago, Kyra was nowhere to be found on a weekend.

"All right, well, I'm going to go and try to get all this work done. I'll talk to you later. Love you. Bye."

"You, too. Bye."

Kyra hung up the phone and then picked it back up when the show was over. She decided to call Mercedes. She hadn't talked to her once since she'd moved. She dialed the number and waited for an answer. It rang about four times, and just when she went to hang up, someone answered.

"Who dis be?"

As soon as she heard her boyfriend's voice, Kyra hung up the phone. She moved her fingers shakily and called Natasha. She couldn't believe what she had just heard.

"Whaddup?" Natasha sounded as though she had been awakened from a light nap.

"Tasha…" Kyra choked as her throat began to tighten. It was a clear sign of her oncoming tears. "You asleep?"

"Yeah, girl, I got this job down at Burger King for me to be able to come down there this summer. It's been whuppin' my ass. BK ain't no joke. But you sound like something's wrong? You okay?" Natasha said. She was becoming more aware of her friend's tone of voice.

"I just called Mercedes, right, and tell me why somebody picked up and it sounded like…it sounded just like…Kai. I swear it was him, and you know I know his voice. It was him. I swear it was. It *was* him! What the fuck?"

"Oh shit," Natasha mumbled under her breath.

"What, Tasha? Tell me. Please just tell me they not really messin' around, Tash. Please."

"Okay. Damn! Chill! Shit, I didn't want to tell you this," she sighed.

"Tasha, you better tell me," Kyra demanded.

"Basically Mercedes and Makai been having their little thing on the low-low, I guess. The night you left, he showed up at the Black and White Party. The guy she left with…it was him. I tried to talk to her. I asked her what the hell she was doing. I even reminded her that you and him are still together even though you moved, but she said she didn't give a fuck. She told me that they been fuckin' for the past few months. We got in a big argument and everything, and we almost started boxing right there in the club. We would've, too, if security hadn't been on some bullshit. After that night at the party, she started talking shit on you and she was showing up to school looking like she was big ballin' or something. I stopped talking to her as soon as I found out, 'cause I wasn't about to be associated with her, especially with how she was doing you," she continued. "I'm sorry. I didn't know how to tell you. I mean, I tried to make everything seem normal until I got the chance…. I'm so sorry, girl,"

"I gotta go." Kyra hung up. A powerful rage filled her. She knocked over the vase of flowers on the end table in her bedroom, which shattered against the wall. She found her small box of keepsakes and shredded all pictures of Makai and of Mercedes, leaving a trail of scraps all over her room. She threw away all the gifts from Makai. The last thing to go was the friendship bracelet Mercedes had given her. It was dropped in the trash can.

The phone rang what seemed like a million times the next morning, but Kyra never moved to answer it. Her mother would come in and tell her that the phone was for her, but she still would not respond. Her mother intruded to clean up the mess, asked tons of questions that went unanswered and opened the curtains, but Kyra rolled over with a groan and slid deeper under the covers. She didn't move and she refused to eat when breakfast was prepared. She didn't do anything but lie there and sulk.

Around three in the afternoon, Justin showed up. Kyra could hear her mother talking to him out in the living room. She managed to move a little, but she still couldn't get up. Not even for him.

"Nice to meet you. You can see if she'll talk to you, but I doubt it. I just don't know what's wrong. The girl won't eat and she won't come out of her room. She hasn't been out once all day," Geneva Jones said, briefing Justin on her daughter's state, sounding mildly vexed.

"Okay. Thank you, Mrs. Jones."

"Call me Geneva."

Justin gently pushed the door open and entered Kyra's bedroom. From what her mother had told him and from what he could see, something was seriously wrong. He surveyed the trash can. It was filled with dried roses, scraps of paper and shards of glass.

"Kyra…" There was no movement. She made no noise at all. "Everybody's going out to get something to eat, and we wanted to know if you wanted to come. I've been calling you all day…."

Still there was nothing. Justin moved to Kyra's bed and sat next to the outline of her body. He set his hand on what he estimated to be her shoulder.

"I'm here, Kyra. Whatever it is… I'm here."

Suddenly, Kyra moved. She slowly peeled the covers from her face to reveal her bloodshot eyes. She sat on her knees and pulled him to her, hugging him so tight it seemed that she didn't want to let him go.

"It's okay. It's okay." Justin comforted her with a squeeze back.

She still hadn't said anything, but when she pulled away she looked into his eyes with longing.

"Do you want me to stay with you?" He was visibly concerned as his hands traced over her braids.

"No, I want to come with you. I...need you right now...." Those difficult words slipped out of Kyra's mouth. It was the first time she'd made this confession, not only to him but to herself, as well.

Kyra and Justin strolled into the restaurant to see their friends seated around a large round table—loud, smiling, laughing, joking and talking. Mama Caribbean's Café was tiny, but it was packed wall to wall. There was rhythmic reggae music blasting from a few speakers set around the room, and most of the patrons were teenagers. It was obvious that this was one of the teenage hangouts.

"Hey, Kyra!" Angel called, and waved. She was snug under Quentin's arm.

Kyra took a seat next to her while Justin sat on the other side of the table by Michael, who had brought a date. His date wore fake blue contacts, bright red lipstick and a tacky blond wig. She was outfitted in a pair of Daisy Dukes and a bright pink halter top with matching flip-flops.

"Hey, aren't you that one girl who was about to beat up Veronica the other day?" Michael's date blurted out.

"Yeah, somethin' like that. Justin, pass me a menu," Kyra said as she reached out her hand, grabbed a menu and began looking it over.

"Everybody's talking about it! Anyways, my name is Lynette."

"Hi." Kyra was nonchalant and made a conscious effort not to look Lynette in the eyes for fear that she might burst out laughing.

"Mike baby, where's the potty?" Lynette turned to Michael with a whine.

"Straight down the back hall, baby."

"Excuse me." Lynette shimmied her way past Justin and followed Michael's directions. As soon as she was out of sight, the whole table burst into laughter.

"I must say, you've really outdone yourself this time." Justin put his head down while laughing.

"Now, you know I don't talk about anyone, but I have to agree with J on that one," Angel chimed in.

"All y'all can go to hell. I didn't even want her to come, but when I tried to sneak out her house this morning she caught me, and I had to bring her," said Michael.

"Are you guys ready to order?" asked a tall girl with a short ponytail and glistening light brown eyes. She had a pen and pad in hand.

"Yeah, we're ready," Michael said, rubbing his stomach. "I'll have the rack of ribs with some fries, some banana fritters and a large Sprite."

"Damn, Mike. I'll just have a burger and fries with a chocolate shake," Quentin said.

"I'll have the same," Angel said, passing her menu to the side.

"I'll have the jerk chicken with shrimp on the side, and a Coke," Justin said.

"And you, miss?" the waitress asked Kyra.

"Um…I dunno…" Kyra was staring blankly at the menu.

"She'll have the same as me," Justin interjected.

"Okay, I'll be right back with your drinks," the waitress said, and walked away from the table, with Michael's eyes glued to her backside.

"Damn, shorty got an ass on her!"

"Why'd you do that?" Kyra leaned over the table and whispered to Justin.

"You looked like you were about to panic or something, so I thought I was helping you out. Plus now you can try some Caribbean food, *real* food."

"Well, it better be good, that's all I know."

"I'm going to pull her number," Michael schemed aloud.

"Didn't you come here with a girl?" Kyra commented.

"Yeah.... So?" He sounded as if it didn't matter, because to him it didn't. Kyra just shook her head at him in disapproval.

The waitress returned with a tray of drinks and handed them around. She was in the middle of tending to her other tables when Michael stopped her.

"Hey, uh...Wendy..." Michael called out to her, reading the name tag on her uniform.

"Yes?" In no time, she was again near their table and awaiting his request.

"You know, you're looking real good today in that uniform," he told her.

"Thank you. Is there something else you want to order? I have tables waiting."

"I want dessert."

"Okay. What would you like?" she asked, taking out her pen and pad to scribble down his order.

"You." He threw a wink at the waitress, which made her grin. "So can I get your number? We can go somewhere and chill tonight. I'll take you anywhere you want to go."

"Um...sure...but I get off at six." Wendy shyly smiled and walked away. She seemed flattered by his game.

"Hey, guys, I'm back. Sorry about that," Lynette said, returning after a ten-minute absence. "Did the waitress take orders yet?"

"Yeah," Michael said with an attitude.

"You can probably catch her when she comes back around," Angel added.

"No she can't. I'm not paying for anything. Look, Lynette, it's been fun, but you have to go," Michael said coldly.

"What?" She looked puzzled.

"I said you gotta go. I got people waiting on me, so you need to vacate."

"Oh, so you're going to try and play me? Even after you were all up in this last night! But you know what? It's all good. *It's all good.* I'll see you guys later. Bye!" Lynette exploded before storming out of the restaurant.

"Is everything okay over here?" Wendy asked upon her return with a their food.

"Yeah, it's cool, baby," Michael answered casually.

"Here goes your food. Enjoy. I'll bring the check around later."

"Mmm. This smells good," Kyra said, sniffing her plate with delight.

"Taste it," Justin suggested. He watched her to take in her reaction.

She took a piece of chicken into her mouth and slowly began to chew it. In seconds, her eyes lit up.

"Mmm...this is really good! It's kinda spicy, though."

"Oh, Ms. Feisty herself can't handle some spice?"

"Boy, please!" Kyra dug in.

"Hey, Justin baby!" Veronica squealed, entering in her

short, tight yellow dress and white cat's-eye sunglasses. She hugged him and planted a kiss on his cheek.

"What are you doing here, Veronica?" He was clearly irritated as he pushed her off and wiped his cheek.

"I just stopped by with the girls to grab a bite to eat, and poof! Here you are! What a coincidence!"

The phony smile on her face faded when she noticed Kyra. "What is *she* doing here?" Veronica said as she looked her enemy up and down.

"She's here because *I* invited her," Justin shot back.

Veronica started mumbling something in French. Kyra didn't understand a word, but Veronica shut her mouth when she noticed Kyra running her fingers over the knife next to her plate. "Hey, come on. The table is ready," Bridgette announced.

"I don't want to eat here anymore! Let's go!" Veronica snapped as she shoved past her friends and out the door. Nicole was so busy waving and smiling at Michael that Bridgette had to pull her out the door. Before everyone knew it, they'd left as quickly as they had come.

Between jamming to the loud music, finishing their food and small conversation, six o'clock rolled around quickly.

Kyra and Justin sat in the backseat of the convertible as Michael drove with Wendy in the passenger seat. The car zoomed along the empty roads as the sun began to set on the horizon. It was a beautiful sight. No one spoke, except for few flirtatious expressions tossed between Michael and Wendy.

"I think I'm gonna be sick," Kyra leaned over and whispered to Justin, smiling.

"I know, right," he answered, intoxicated by the smell of her perfume.

For the duration of the ride, Justin kept finding himself

looking over at Kyra. He took in her presence—her smell, her face, her smile, her body, her laugh, how she talked, her voice, how she dressed—everything about her. He thought she was truly beautiful, and in his eyes, she was the very definition of sexy. He just had to have her. They had a friendship on the surface, but deep down it was more.

"Hey, J, this is your stop, too." Michael let the car come to a halt in the driveway of Kyra's house.

"Stop playing and drive me home."

"I can't even do that playa. Wendy and I have plans," he said, turning to Wendy and sliding his hand between her thighs. She let out a giggle.

"Man…" Justin sighed heavily as he surrendered his own vehicle for his friend's benefit.

"You understand, right? I mean, you know how it is." Michael was enjoying toying with him. Justin stepped out of the car and scowled at his friend. He leaned down to be face-to-face with him as he spoke in a low and serious tone. "If you mess up my car I'll fuck you up, Mike."

Michael flashed him a mischievous smile.

"I mean it!"

Justin's threat hung in the air as Michael sped down the street. Justin mumbled under his breath. He turned around when he felt a soft hand on his shoulder.

"What was all that about?"

"Nothing. It's just that he knows he could've taken me home."

"I can ask my mom if you want, or I could—"

"No! I mean, no, thank you. You shouldn't go out of your way." His response was fast. He couldn't risk her seeing where he lived.

"Okay, if you say so," Kyra replied.

"Here. Let me walk you to your door."

The butterflies were fluttering in both their stomachs as they stood facing each other at the front door.

"Justin?" Kyra broke the silence. She had somehow overcome the difficulty of talking with the nervous lump in her throat. She had been used to dealing with Makai, but boys in general were still a mystery to her. She didn't want to make the wrong move.

"Yeah?"

"Thanks for everything."

"You're welcome."

"I also wanted to...apologize for how I acted after that day you came to my house. I just didn't know how to handle it."

"Handle what?"

"I had this kind of fantasy, I guess...well, not a fantasy, but I guess like a dream or somethin'...."

"About?" Justin prodded her out of excitement and curiosity.

"We...did it."

"Did what?"

"*It.*"

"*Oh!*" He was shocked but happy.

"I dunno why, though. I mean, you're my friend. Don't get me wrong, you look good to me, but to do that is kind of..."

"Weird. Yeah, I couldn't picture that, either." Both of them were fronting, obvious to themselves but not to each other.

"Do you wanna come in for a drink before you go?" she asked.

"No, I'm cool. I better get going. It's getting dark."

"Oh...okay."

"Bye."

"Bye." She planted a soft kiss on his cheek and turned to go inside, leaving him frozen for a minute and badly wanting to stay.

She watched from the other side of the door as he walked away, and she felt good inside. She had just found out about Makai, and as much as it hurt her, Justin helped to ease that pain. With him, there was something there. She could feel it. He was a friend, but there was something about him that made her want him to be more than that. And that was what scared her.

CHAPTER 9

The months flew by, and by late May, Justin and Kyra's relationship had grown. They flirted constantly, and it was obvious to everyone around them that they cared for each other. But no one, not even Justin or Kyra, opened up and shared their feelings.

The days carried on as usual. Everyone would go to school and chill, go to eat or go to Provo and catch a flick. Justin and Kyra went to the library for her tutoring sessions; Kyra felt that would be a "safer" move. The temptation for what she believed would be too-soon a sexual encounter at her home was too great.

Kyra made remarkable progress in her classes and was bringing home good grades, which made her mother happy. Angel and Quentin were as in love as they wanted to be, and Michael continued to pull girl after girl, being the bachelor that he was.

Things were going pretty well for Kyra. Her life, which had once felt like it was spinning out of control, now seemed to move at a steady pace. Of course, as Justin and Kyra grew closer, Veronica became more and more envious. Everything seemed to be going Kyra's way until she missed her period.

A Saturday-morning trip to the grocery store, ten dollars, a cheap pregnancy test and the most nerve-racking three minutes of her life proved to be a disaster. The results came in the form of two pink lines. She quadruple-checked the instruction packet and the stick to make sure she wasn't hallucinating, but it was true: Kyra Jones was with child.

Kyra heard five rings, five times, but she received no answer as she tried to reach Makai. Her patience was waning and she was ready to give up when her perseverance finally paid off the sixth time she called. On the second ring, he answered.

"Who's dis?" He yawned into the phone. It was only eight-thirty a.m.

The sound of his voice sent chills down her spine, a reflex she couldn't help.

"Kai..." Kyra whispered into the phone, trying to calm her racing mind.

"Kyra? How you been down there, baby girl? Sorry I haven't had the chance to call. I've been so busy. I miss you like crazy, girl. You just don't know...." Makai poured out excuse after excuse, trying to sound as devoted as possible.

"Baby, who is it?" Mercedes groaned in the background. Makai ignored her, but Kyra heard. She could see right through his fake affections.

"Look, Kai, I know you've been fuckin' Cedes, so cut the bullshit," she said.

"What? Baby, I don't know who you heard that from, but..." He acted as if he were genuinely shocked by the accusation.

"Don't worry about where I hear shit from."

"Oh shit..." Makai mumbled under his breath. "Come on, girl, you know I love you. I wouldn't even do you like that."

He put the phone closer to his mouth as he whispered into the mouthpiece.

"Yeah, right, whateva. Me and you ain't shit. I got someone else now anyways, besides your sorry ass," Kyra lied. She liked Justin, sure, but he couldn't be officially claimed.

"What? Okay, okay I got you, shawty. I see you out here. You wanna up and move and act all brand-new and shit. So tell me, if we ain't shit, then what the fuck are you calling me for?"

"Because...I'm...pregnant." The words dropped from her mouth.

"And?" He sighed as though the news was petty and irrelevant.

"And? It's yours! What do you mean *'and'*!"

"You just said you have someone else down there. It could be his. All I know is it ain't mine."

"Don't even try to fuckin' play me like that, Kai! You know it's yours! The only man I've ever fucked in my whole damn life is you!"

"This ain't even my problem. Don't call me at some eight-thirty in the fucking morning talking about this bullshit. I got too much shit on my hands right now, and I don't need a kid, too."

"And what, you think I do?"

"Fuck this and fuck you, Kyra. You were right, I'm with Cedes now, so stop calling me. This shit ain't my problem. Get rid of it." He coldly cut her off.

"What the fuck you mean, Makai? *'Get rid of it?'*"

"It's simple. Get an abortion," Makai heartlessly advised. Click!

When she reached the island of Providenciales, she didn't have a clue where she was going as she walked along the busy streets. Provo and Prince Paul might as well have been on two separate planets when comparing how peaceful things were. The bombardment of noise almost reminded her of Chicago, a place she'd never thought she would despise but now did.

She continued to walk along as the sun brought forth sweat from her pores, then stopped abruptly. HEALTH CLINIC was in big red letters on a small building a little farther down the way. She had questions she could not answer, but they could.

"I just got the results from the lab." The doctor shut the door to the small examination room behind her.

Kyra had been pacing the length of the room for the past twenty-five minutes, but now she stood motionless and at attention. "And?"

"No need to worry. It was a false alarm. You are not pregnant."

Kyra exhaled a deep sigh of relief.

"Sometimes at-home tests don't give the most accurate results. You missing your periods could be a result of stress or birth-control-pills. I actually want to talk to you about some methods of contraception…"

Kyra sat in the room and acted as though she were listening. The truth was that she hadn't listened to anything the doctor said since she'd gotten her results. She had her answer, and that was all she needed.

School was nearing its end, but an anniversary was nearing, as well. It was death: the death of Marcus Jones, Kyra's father. It seemed like every month since the move, something traumatic happened: the move itself, discovering the betrayal of Makai and Mercedes, the pregnancy scare and now the painful memory of June 1, 1997.

Kyra's schoolwork became less important and she wasn't her usual self. It was apparent to everyone that something was wrong, but when asked to elaborate she would only respond with a meek smile and an "I'm fine." Her response never varied. She wouldn't open up to tell anyone about her father. Not even Justin. It was just too personal and far too painful for her. Besides, how exactly do you go about telling someone you saw your father murdered when you were only five years old?

Kyra sat in a trance in her wicker chair. She was in a dream-like state, lost in her own world, staring helplessly into space, when the doorbell rang. Its unexpected echo throughout the house caused her to shuffle to the door in hopes the visitor wouldn't ring the bell again.

"Hey," she greeted Justin as she opened the front door to him.

"What's good?"

"Nothin', just, uh...workin' on some homework. You know how it is. What are you doin' around here?"

"I was just rolling by with Q and Mike, so I figured I would stop by and see you." She looked past him to see Quentin and Michael waiting in the convertible outside. She waved and they returned the gesture.

"But anyways, do you need any help with that homework?"

"No, I got it."

"Good. See, that tutoring paid off."

"I dunno how."

"It's 'cause ya boy is so smart!" Justin popped his collar in the form of a boast. Kyra couldn't hold in her laughter. She hadn't really laughed for days.

"So...are you ready for Friday?" He asked his question

from the kitchen, where he was busy helping himself to a grape soda.

"Friday?"

"Yeah, Friday. Don't tell me you forgot *again*." He sipped the ice-cold beverage. "My birthday party at Club Xscape. Ring any bells?"

"Oh yeah…" Her memory was slow to click in, but now she remembered.

She fell silent and stared off. Justin had been born on the day her father had died, and every time he talked about his birthday, it only reminded her just how quickly that day was approaching.

"Are you sure you're okay?"

"Yeah, I'm fine, why?"

"Because every time I talk about the party, you get this look in your eyes. And lately, I don't know…you just seem down. You seem kind of out of it. I mean, if you don't want to go, that's okay. Just let me know."

"I'm sorry. It's nothin'. I'll be there. You know I wouldn't miss it." She painted her face with a false smile to reassure him.

"Good. You know it wouldn't be the same without you." Justin kissed Kyra on the cheek and looked her in the eyes for a minute before leaving. He and his boys disappeared down the road, stirring up dust just as they had the first day she saw them.

Friday, June the first. The day fell upon Kyra faster than she had thought, but no one could control the hands of time. It was the end of the day, and she sat in class waiting for the bell to dismiss her.

Brrring!

The bell rang, and all the students headed for the hallway,

Kyra included. But right before she reached the door, Ms. Kingsley stopped her.

"Kyra, do you have a second? I would like to speak with you." Ms. Kingsley had perfect timing. She caught Kyra right as she reached the door. The teacher stood up from her desk, taking her glasses from their place on her nose. Kyra felt the anticipation of freedom leaving her. Kyra stopped without saying a word. She already had an idea what this was about. She had been through it more than enough times at her previous high school.

"Kyra, what is going on with you lately?" Ms. Kingsley asked. Her face was concerned as she shut the door to her now-empty classroom.

"What are you talkin' about?"

"In class you aren't paying attention like you used to. You zone out. Is something the matter?" Ms. Kingsley asked as she leaned her weight on the edge of her desk.

"No..."

"Well, if there is, you can talk to me, okay?"

"Okay, thanks." Kyra quickly turned to leave the room. The idea of confiding in any authority figure was bizarre to her.

"No. Not so fast. I also wanted to talk to you about your work. Your grades are steadily declining, and I'm missing several homework assignments from you. When you first came here you were shaky, but then you were doing so well. Now I'm not so sure. Whatever it is you have going on, your academics are suffering because of it."

"Look, it's nothin'. Next week I'll make up all my work. I swear I will. I just had some stuff on my mind lately, that's all," she said, putting her hand on her forehead and running it over her hair.

"I'll give you the benefit of the doubt only because I like you.

But don't you try to put one over on me. I know you know how that goes. I saw you and Veronica on your first day. It looked like you were going to claw her eyes out."

"I was," she chuckled.

"Well, that's all. You need to get on home. I'll see you on Monday."

"Okay, bye." Kyra shut the door behind her and took a deep breath. That was close, she thought.

"Oh yes.... That sounds great.... I am too old for that...! Where is it...? Oh really...? How long...? God, I haven't been out that late in ages! Well, sure, alright, I'll be there at nine on the dot. Bye-bye." Kyra reached her house to find her mother in the middle of a lively telephone discussion. She was very excited about something and was smiling uncontrollably, with giggles here and there.

"Who was that?" Kyra asked curiously.

"A friend from work. They invited me to go dancing tonight. A lot of people from work are going."

"Oh. You know what day it is, right?"

"Yes. It's the first. I don't think I can forget it." Her mood turned bitter.

"Are you doing anythin' for Dad before you go out?"

"No. I didn't plan on it. There's not too much I can do."

"Well, could we pour out some liquor or somethin', light a candle, I dunno. I just want to do *somethin'* for him. I can't leave flowers like I usually do, so..."

"You already do, sweetie...." Her mother paused for a moment before speaking again. "I have some Hennessy up in the top cabinet above the refrigerator." She pointed to the storage place and gave her daughter a crooked look.

"Why are you lookin' at me like that?"

"Because usually you would be losing it right now with me going out tonight. Are you okay?"

"I'm fine. I'm goin' to Justin's birthday party tonight, anyways."

"I didn't know you had plans tonight. What time will you be home?"

"Not too late," Kyra lied. She planned to be out as late as possible and was sure she would return sometime the following morning.

"All I know is you better be in before I am," her mother warned.

"Okay," she replied acknowledging her mother's warning as she retrieved the bottle of dark cognac from the cabinet. "You want to do this now?"

"Yeah. We might as well," her mother agreed. She stood and began to make her way to the sliding doors that led out to their picturesque backyard.

"To Daddy." Kyra's voice was tainted with sadness as she tipped the bottle back up. She poured the earth a drink in memory of her father's passing.

"To Marcus," her mother whispered in the breeze.

"We will always love you, and may you rest in peace."

Her mother solemnly repeated the sentence and closed her eyes. There was a moment of silence and a gust of air. She appeared to be almost in prayer. Then, without a bit of subtly, she opened her eyes and spoke in a normal, almost cheerful tone.

"I need to go figure out what I'm going to wear tonight." Those were the last words she uttered as she walked back into the house. The loss of her husband was too painful to dwell on, and she didn't bother to offer any soothing words of sympathy to her child.

Kyra stood outside for a moment alone. Now was the time for her to move on; she could feel it. She would not forget, but she had to let go. If she didn't she was sure she would lose her sanity. She turned to the house as a strong gust of air blew by and made her hair flutter in the wind. She looked up and smiled sadly at the sky. She emptied the liquor onto the ground and blew a kiss from her hand to her father.

It was a quarter after seven when the doorbell rang. Kyra's mother answered it in her long red and black cocktail dress to let Angel inside.

"Hello, Mrs. Jones. How are you?"

"I'm fine, thanks, honey. Kyra is in her room straight down that hall," she said while putting on an earring.

"Thank you," Angel said.

"Come in!"

Kyra stood in front of her vanity in an orange skirt set. The material was sheer and the skirt was asymmetrical, giving the whole outfit an island style. She also wore heeled sandals that tied around her ankles, and her naturally wavy hair was ironed straight.

"Angel, please tell me that's not what you're wearin'." Kyra stopped putting on her finishing touches as she looked Angel over in horror. From the small black heels accented by fake flowers to the puffed-out, almost–sixties-style black satin skirt, all the way to the matching top and the pink cashmere sweater tied around her neck, the outfit was the most unfashionable thing Kyra had ever seen, next to their school uniforms.

"This is it." Angel looked her outfit over with an innocent smile on her face. Unlike Kyra, she was pleased with her choice of clothes.

"Angel...you're my girl and all, but...no. I mean...yo, what the hell is that? It looks like you went in your grandmama's closet! Those are not party clothes, and I'm not about to roll with you lookin' like that. You won't only embarrass me but you will embarrass *yourself* like that."

"Oh...okay." Angel didn't quite know how to take the criticism, and her confusion could be heard. "What am I going to do? I don't really have anything else nice to wear to a club, and all my clothes are at home."

Kyra put her hands on her hips and thought for a minute, then looked at her closet. She had the perfect idea.

"Wear somethin' of mine."

"Oh no, Kyra. I love your clothes, but I just couldn't."

"I insist. I won't even touch your hair or makeup if you don't want. I just wanna hook up your outfit. Come on. *Please*, Angel. My clothes have practically been going to waste with us having to wear those uniforms to school. And just think of Quentin's face when he sees you." She teased and coaxed her friend into delivering an answer, which came after only seconds of deliberation.

"Okay, fine, and if we do an outfit you might as well do hair and makeup, too." She threw her hands up in defeat.

"Oh, this is goin' to be fun! Come here," Kyra exclaimed as she opened her large closet.

"You have so many clothes!" Angel's eyes were not at all prepared to take in the sight of the jam-packed closet full of designer fashions.

"I know, I know."

"Okay, don't look yet! No! Stop tryin' to peek! Okay, okay. Now you can look." Kyra touched up Angel's lip gloss in between swatting her hands away from attempting to lift the handheld mirror. Thirty minutes had gone by and her makeover was nearly complete.

Angel turned around and looked at herself in the mirror. She had on a short white skirt, a pink and tan spaghetti-strap lace top that showed off her toned stomach, and a pair of pink and white Reeboks to keep it simple. Her makeup was light, and her hair was in a simple ponytail with two strands left to dangle on the sides of her face.

"Wow, Kyra. You worked magic on me... I look completely different!"

"So I take it you like it?" Kyra smiled at her success.

"Of course I like it! It's *too* cute."

"Hey, you two, I'm about to head out. Kyra, make sure you lock up," her mother said from the doorway. "Oh, don't you look nice, Angel." She admired the new style of her daughter's friend for a moment and was gone before she could hear any reply.

"Thank you, Mrs. Jones."

"Bye, you guys!" she yelled from the front door.

"Bye!" the girls shouted back together as they listened for the click of the closing door.

"So are you ready to go now?" Angel turned to her stylist, eager to reach the party.

"Yeah, let's be out."

Xscape was packed. Bodies filled the building from the windows to the walls. The room was scorching hot. It was like walking into a human oven. The music was loud and pumping through the crowd, which swarmed the dance floor and moved with the beat.

"Oh, look. I think that's them over there," Angel said, pointing across the crowd to a group of young men sitting at a table not too far from the bar. It was so dark and so hazy with smoke they could barely see.

The girls squeezed their way across the crowded dance floor, catching the attention of other young men.

"Hey, what's up, everybody?" Kyra excitedly greeted the crew.

"Hey!" Justin stood to embrace her. He was unsure she would come, but was happy she'd made it.

"Happy birthday!"

"Thank you."

"Happy birthday, Justin," Angel added meekly.

"Angel?" He turned to the unfamiliar girl next to Kyra.

"Yup. It's me." She waved shyly.

"Q! Your girl's here." Justin nudged his brother, who was engaged in a leisurely conversation with Michael. Quentin hadn't been paying any mind to the party, but when he looked up, his jaw dropped. He jumped up and in less than a second was all over his girlfriend.

"I'm sorry, baby. I wasn't even paying attention." He gently took her hand in his.

"It's okay."

"Damn, you look so good." He stepped back and looked her body over from head to toe.

"Kyra made me over."

"*Well, thank you, Kyra.*" Quentin made sure to emphasize every word.

"You're welcome," Kyra said with a smile. She was happy they were both enjoying her work.

"Would you like to dance, baby?"

"Yes."

Quentin and Angel headed off to the dance floor and were swallowed by the crowd.

"They're so cute together," Kyra commented.

"Yeah, they are," Justin agreed.

"Damn, will they come on with the drinks?" Michael interrupted.

"We can drink here?"

"Yeah." The birthday boy informed his guest of the lenient drinking rules at the club.

"Oh, fa sho I want some." Kyra was long overdue for a night of letting loose and wilding out.

"Okay, well, I'm about to go dance. Come and join me later?" He gently held on to her hand until they parted.

"I will soon. Promise."

Kyra walked over to the bar and ordered herself a shot. One shot became two, two became three and, on her sixth shot, Justin intervened.

"Sweetheart, I think you've had enough."

"I'm straight. Just let me get one more." She motioned for the bartender to give her another round.

"I got something better." Justin watched as the bartender refilled her shot glass with 102-proof gin.

"What?" Kyra then swallowed the shot and her face became twisted.

"Come dance with me. It *is* my birthday, you know." His proposal was sincere, though it was also a means of distraction from her alcohol consumption.

"Okay." Her stumble was slight but noticeable when she stepped down from her stool.

As soon as Justin led her into the crowd, she pressed her body deep into his and began to grind her hips and move her body to the beat. His hands rested on her waist as he moved with her to the sultry tunes. As the songs changed, Kyra grinded, shook, vibrated, snaked, popped and hip-rolled Justin into desire.

As "Girls Dem Sugar" by Beenie Man, with the smooth vocals of R & B songstress Mya, emanated from the speakers,

Kyra turned around and guided Justin until his back was against a wall. She began to grind against him, and stared him dead in his eyes while she did it. He looked at her as he ran his hands over her arms, down her sides and to her butt.

"I want you," she whispered in his ear, and softly bit down on her lip. He couldn't believe what he was hearing. He didn't bother to reply. His eyes said it all.

She leaned up and kissed him, pressing her lips to his and eventually working in her tongue. He kissed her back without hesitation, and the kiss grew in intensity until Kyra stopped. She felt eyes on her. She looked over and sure enough, there was Veronica scowling at her and looking like she was fired up with anger. Kyra smirked at her and grabbed Justin's hand.

"Are you sure you're okay?" As they made the walk to her house from the ferry dock, Kyra stumbled with almost every step. The alcohol was having a noticeable effect on her speech and balance.

"Yessss, I'm fine. Damn, no, *you're* fine." She slurred her words and laughed for no apparent reason.

"Come on. Let me help you."

"I'm fine." She refused any help with a gentle shoo away.

"You're drunk."

"I'm not drunk. I only had, what? One drink?"

"More like six shots. I already know your ass is ripped." Justin placed her arm over his shoulder to help her walk to her porch. He placed her on the first stair while he stood on the ground.

"Come on. Let's go inside." She tugged on his shirt like a little girl.

"I better not." He didn't move.

"But I want it.... I want youuuu."

"But you're drunk, and that means that I'd be taking advantage of you, which I don't do. If you really want it that bad, we can get it poppin' when you're sober. I can wait."

"I'm...I'm..." With those last words, Kyra lost her balance and landed in his arms.

They stared into each other's eyes, and when she moved in for another kiss, he spoke out.

"I really need to get you inside."

Inside the pitch-dark house, Justin managed to find her bedroom and tuck her under the covers. He moved the hair from her sleeping face as she lay peaceful and admired her allure for a moment before he stood. He was readying himself to leave when he stopped and decided not to.

He took a seat in one of the wicker chairs and made himself as comfortable as possible. If she woke up and was disoriented, he wanted her to see him and know where she was. He wanted to be the first face she saw when she opened her eyes. His party was the last thing on his mind.

He double-checked to make sure everything was just right. He made sure the blankets covered her enough so that she wouldn't get chilly in the early morning when the temperature was low. He then ran his hands over her hair and gently over her face. He studied its restful look for a moment and then kissed her forehead, leaving her to sleep undisturbed.

At the crack of dawn, Kyra's eyes flickered open to the pain of a splitting headache. She slowly sat up and realized she was still in her clothes from last night.

Damn, what happened last night? she thought as she staggered out of bed and stretched her body. She then looked over at her sitting area to see Justin asleep in a chair. Her eyes bucked open and she jumped back, startled by his presence. She didn't remember anything from last night, especially not why he was in her bedroom. She patted herself down to make sure all her clothes were still on. Everything was intact, and she let out a sigh of relief. Now she could rest assured that she had no regrets.

She tiptoed over to him and gently shook his arm to see his eyes slowly open. He looked at Kyra and then jumped up to wipe his chin.

"It's okay." She let out a small giggle.

"Good morning," His voice was groggy.

"Good morning. So, um…if you don't mind me askin', how did you get in my room last night?"

"You don't remember *anything* from last night?"

"I remember a little about your birthday party, but I'm still at loss as to how you got here." She sat down on her bed and rubbed her temples.

"I brought you home last night from my party. You were drunk off ya ass, and Angel and Q had already dipped out. So I brought you here, and I was so tired I just crashed right here. Plus I wanted to make sure you were a'ight." He half lied, covering up the true reason for their current situation.

"Oh, damn. I hope I didn't ruin your birthday or anythin'."

"Not at all," he reassured her as he sat next to her on the bed. "You want me to get you some Advil or something?" He would've had to be blind not to notice the painful expression on her face.

"Please?"

"A'ight, where do you keep it?"

"In the medicine cabinet in the bathroom."

Justin came back into the room to find Kyra finishing up changing clothes. She turned to him, tying a knot in her silk robe as she carefully strutted over to where he stood captivated.

"Thanks, Dr. Hartwell," She smiled at him as she slid the bottle of capsules from his hand.

Her smile suddenly froze and her face changed to a serious expression when she noticed him staring at her silk-wrapped figure. Justin placed his hand on her chin, cupping it with his fingers, and brought her face steadily toward his lips.

"Kyra?" her mother called as she entered the house.

"Oh shit!" Kyra whispered in fear. Justin bit his lip and huffed in frustration.

They stood there with panic in their eyes.

"Shit! Here. Get in the closet!" Her voice didn't pass the volume of a whisper as she shoved him toward the door to the storage place of her clothing.

"I'm not getting in a damn closet!"

"Get in the damn closet!" she ordered, finally pushing him in and shutting the door.

She could hear her mother's footsteps making their way to her room as she darted under her covers, closed her eyes and faked being asleep.

"Kyra!" her mother yelled again, but then stopped when she saw Kyra asleep in her bed. She didn't disturb her before retiring to her own room.

Kyra waited for a moment. She barely breathed as she peeked out from under her blanket. She scrambled to the closet and freed Justin only after she heard the door to her mother's room shut.

"Shh! We have to get you out of here," she whispered.

Kyra shut the front door quietly after giving Justin a quick hug goodbye before he ran across the lawn and into the street. His sloppy plan had miraculously worked. It was only when she was in the kitchen pouring a glass of water to take her medicine that her mother startled her.

"What was that noise? I thought you were asleep. You scared me half to death," she asked her daughter, standing in the hallway decked out in her heart-print pajamas.

"Nothin'. I just came to get some water, that's all," Kyra lied, taking a sip to relax her frenzied nerves. She was sure she was caught.

"Well, just to let you know, I just got in, so I'm probably going to be out of it for the rest of the day."

"Did you have fun?"

"Yeah, it was fun. I had a really good time." Her mother yawned before leaving the room. Kyra sighed in relief when she heard her mother's bedroom door close again. She fell back against the counter with her heart pounding for more reasons than one.

CHAPTER 10

"Your mobile device is currently out of service. Please contact your service provider to reactivate your device. Thank you."

That was the automated voice Kyra heard when she dialed Natasha's number on her cell phone. She even tried to call Makai, but she got the same annoying, robotic voice. He'd had her service disconnected. After all, he paid for it. He paid for everything.

"Bitch!" She quietly voiced her anger through her clenched teeth.

This nigga done went and disconnected my phone! Damn, it's been what? Only a few weeks after I told him that I was pregnant, and he had it disconnected. I bet it was done even earlier but I just didn't know since I haven't used it in a hot minute. It's all good, though, 'cause I don't need him to do shit for me anymore. I can activate my cell later if I get a job or somethin'. Damn, listen to me, "If I get a job." Whateva. All I know is that I'm single, which suits me just fine. Fuck Makai, fuck Mercedes and, matter of fact, fuck Chicago, too.

* * *

It was Sunday night, and Kyra was fresh out the shower when the phone started ringing off the hook. Her mother didn't even budge to get it.

"I got it!" Kyra said, sarcastically rolling her eyes. She hurried to her room to answer the line, picking up on the last ring. "Hello?"

"Hi. Is Kyra there?"

"Yeah, this is her."

"Hey Kyra, it's Tasha."

"What's wrong?" Kyra was concerned as she fixed her towel around her dripping body after detecting the melancholy in her friend's voice.

"Burger King done messed with my check and I don't have enough money to make it down there this summer."

"Oh...."

"I'm so sorry. I really wanted to come down," Natasha said sincerely.

"It's okay. I really wanted you to come, too, but I understand." But Kyra was still disappointed.

"There's always winter break or something. Maybe I could make it then."

"Yeah, maybe."

"I'm sorry to call you with this bullshit."

"It's cool."

"So...how have you been?"

"I've been a'ight," Kyra lied.

"That's good. I just wanted to hit you up right quick to see how you were doing, but I gotta go. I wish I could talk longer, but I gotta hop in the shower."

"Fa sho."

"And Kyra?" she added.

"Yeah?"

"You know your cell phone is off?"

"Yeah, I know. Kai's punk ass disconnected it."

"Damn. He knows he's messed up. But ey, I'll hit you back then."

"One."

Kyra was feeling down as she slipped on her pajamas and prepared for bed. She was getting tired of things going wrong in her life. It seemed like nothing went right. She'd moved here from a comfortable life in Chicago, her relationship with Makai had gone up in flames and her relationship with her mom was shaky. To top things off, Natasha coming to see her wasn't happening, either.

It was lunchtime on Monday at school. Kyra and Angel were strolling and conversing, when Veronica purposely bumped into Angel and made the few papers in her hands go flying. Angel watched helplessly as her assignments scattered all over the rain-soaked ground.

"Ooops. My bad." Veronica snickered with her hand over her mouth.

Angel moved to pick up the papers, but Kyra stopped her.

"No, Angel, don't touch them."

"But…"

"Don't touch them! Let this bitch pick them up," she snapped.

"I wish I would pick up shit for your ass. Fuck you."

"I *said* pick them up!" Kyra snarled, shoving her adversary to the ground.

"So what happened when you took her home? You hit that?" Michael asked.

"Yeah, you didn't get in till the next day. You're lucky Dad didn't find out," Quentin stated.

"No, I didn't 'hit it.' She was all out of it, drunk and shit. I did stay the night, though."

"So you stayed the night and you didn't even hit it?" Michael was shocked and disappointed.

"Pretty much."

"Well, I don't know about you two, but I got some Friday night," Quentin proudly added.

"Yeah, Angel was looking real good."

"Hey, nigga, back off my girl," he joked with his friend while Justin turned his attention to a rowdy crowd forming not too far away from their table.

"Hey, y'all, what's going on over there?"

Veronica stood back up and pushed Kyra. Kyra then punched her in the jaw. Veronica grabbed a handful of Kyra's hair and tried to hit her, but Kyra wrestled her down to the muddy ground and began to go to work. She was clawing, slapping and punching anything she could see. Veronica reached up and got in one good hit: a punch to the mouth that caused Kyra's lip to bust open and start to bleed. Still, Kyra was an unstoppable force. The two continued to fight and the crowd cheered them on until Justin and his boys came and split them up.

Justin picked Kyra up off Veronica and held her back while his former girlfriend stood back, disheveled and bleeding.

"I told you to stay away from my man!" Veronica hollered as she held her now-dirty and ripped-open cardigan sweater. She sobbed in defeat.

"Fuck you! He's not your man!" Kyra screamed. She had streaks of mud on her face and her hair was wild, adding to her temporarily crazed persona.

"Veronica, you trippin'. Me and you have *been* over and you know it," Justin added.

"We see how hard you are when your crew ain't here to back your bitch ass up! Just be grateful I couldn't get my razors on the plane, bitch!" Kyra continued to rage as she spit blood from her mouth toward where her enemy stood.

"What is going on here? You two! Inside! Now!" shouted a short, old, bald man in a gray suit. He was Mr. McKnight, the school principal.

The girls were led to the main office and seated in front of the principal's desk. Kyra moved her seat as far as possible from Veronica's and shot a look of utter hatred in her direction. The room was thick with tension. The principal shut the door and closed the blinds before finally taking a seat at his desk.

"As I'm sure both of you know, we don't tolerate foolish quarrels here at Prince Paul Academy. Especially when they escalate to a physical confrontation. So, ladies, what prompted this confrontation in the first place?"

"I'm not sayin' nothing. Just know that she was askin' for it, and as you can see, I gave it to her ass. Ever since I got here, she's been givin' me looks, sayin' unnecessary shit, and then today she had the balls to put her fuckin' hands on me. It was curtains from there." Kyra's explanation was given with folded arms, and adrenaline prevented her from cleaning up her speech.

"But she pushed me on the ground first!" Veronica cried out.

"It doesn't give you the right to hit her, and now that I have you here, it is my responsibility to inform you that there *have* been many complaints made stating that you are being disrespectful to your peers."

"They're lying!" she squealed.

"Regardless, the situation that occurred today was completely out of hand on both accounts. You are both suspended for three days and are ordered to leave the school premises immediately. Your parents will be notified as soon as possible."

"Suspended? Do you know who my father is?"

"I am quite aware of who your father is, Ms. Pierce, but that's not going to get you out of trouble like it has so many times with your brother and the police."

"But she hit me first! It was pure reaction, Mr. McKnight!" she continued to whine while Kyra sat silently, still fuming but accepting her punishment. She almost cracked a smile when Veronica started to cry. Any sign of her suffering was a welcome sight.

"That's enough, Ms. Pierce! Now you are both dismissed!"

"Are you okay?" Justin rushed to Kyra from his seat on a bench in the hallway. He had been waiting for her while she was in the principal's office. He was at her side in seconds, examining her cut lip, his hand on her cheek.

"Yeah, I'm fine. It's nothin'." She waved her hand and moved her face away.

"Kyra! Come here!" her mother said, her voice sounding shrill. Kyra sat up in bed and took off her headphones in anticipation of the lecture she was about to endure.

"Why did your principal just call and tell me that you are suspended for the next three days? For fighting, no less?"

"Because I did and I am?"

"Who the hell were you fighting and why?"

"Nobody, just this girl Veronica. She's been disrespectin' me ever since I got here, and I never did nothin', but she went and put her hands on me today, so it was over."

"Did you win?"

"Yeah, I won. Does it look like I lost?" She held her hands out to the side.

"Okay, so now that that's established, was it worth it?"

"What do you mean?"

"Your ass is grounded for a week, so was your fighting her worth it?"

"Yeah, actually, it was." Her answer was smug.

"Don't sit over there all smug on me, girl. You were doing so well since you got here. You were bringing home good grades, you have good friends, you kept out of trouble, and now this. Shit, for this *I* should beat your ass. That's what you need."

"Well what can I say? I'm not perfect."

"I know that, Kyra. I never said you were."

"So then we can save the lectures. What's my punishment?"

"No phone, no TV and you can't leave the house for exactly seven days, one week. And don't tell me what *we* can do. I run this household girl, something you seem to have forgotten," her mother scolded as she pointed her finger in Kyra's face.

"Yeah...a'ight." She moved her head to the side.

"Now go on and get back to whatever you were doing."

Justin was at his desk doing his homework. The events of the day were replaying in his mind like a movie. After the fight, Kyra made an instant transformation. She wouldn't even let him touch her. It was like one minute she was all right and the next she had changed.

He was hard at work on his final math problem when a knock on his door disrupted his whole thought process.

"Come in." He kept his eyes on the paper as Harriet entered.

"Mr. Hartwell, your parents have sent me here to summon you. Apparently they have a few words for you," Harriet announced while adjusting her apron.

"Do you know what this is concerning?" Justin's eyebrows arched in wonder.

"They didn't tell me. I'm sorry."

"It's all right. I'll be down in five minutes."

"I was told to make it known that your father has requested your presence immediately. You have five minutes."

"Justin, have a seat," his father's voice boomed from where he stood in front of the their marble fireplace in the dome-ceilinged den. He was silent until his son did as he was told. "Did you know someone fought with Veronica today? She went home with bruises and such. Her father called me and told me that she is suspended for three days."

"So what does that have to do with me?"

"Well, you are dating the other girl, aren't you?"

"She's a friend. Nothing more, nothing less. What is this all about?" Justin asked again. He could sense the tension in the room.

"Son, your father and I have decided that you shouldn't see the girl who fought Veronica." his mother chimed in. Her tone was soft as she sipped her tea. "It is bad for the image of the family. We literally cannot afford to mess things up. Besides, what ever happened to you and Veronica dating? Last I knew, she was your girlfriend, wasn't she?"

"Mother, we broke up a long time ago."

"If you dirty the name of this family I will make sure you never inherit a penny of the business! It will all go to your brother! I will not have this family be disgraced like the Pierces!

Do you hear me? We all know what Richard has done to their name!" his father threatened.

"Dad, don't you think you're taking this too far?" Quentin interjected.

"Quentin Lamar, shut up. You speak when you are spoken to," their father ordered firmly, silencing his oldest son.

"Son, don't be stubborn about this. Your father and I only have the best intentions," his mother assured.

"That's bullshit!" Justin protested.

His parents were taken aback by his tone and use of foul language. Quentin simply sank down in his chair. Things were heading downhill, and fast.

"How dare you curse at me? I am your father! And don't you forget it! You are not a man and you still live under this roof—my roof. Therefore, you will respect me and my wishes!"

"What about me and my wishes? You two have never even met Kyra! Plus Veronica started the fight anyway!" Justin argued.

"Quentin, is this true?" their mother asked.

"Yes, as far as I know."

"I don't care about any of it! It doesn't matter! Just do as I say and leave the foreign girl be! Whether you resume dating Veronica or not is up to you, but I am serious about the American girl. You are dismissed." His father concluded their heated dialogue with a wave of his hand.

Justin stormed out of the room, and his older brother was on his heels until they reached the privacy of Justin's bedroom.

After Kyra's three-day "vacation," she returned to school to finish the remaining two weeks before summer. She spoke to Angel, but she didn't pay Justin or his boys any mind, and

Justin left her alone. They were growing apart, and while he had a powerful urge to tell her the reason behind his silent treatment, he knew he couldn't. If he did, he would surely reveal his secret, his lie. Thus, they both remained silent and exchanged glances here and there. As much as Kyra tried to push him away, something drew her, and the longing remained in their eyes.

It was Saturday and it was the first day of Kyra's summer vacation. She lay asleep in her room even after the clock passed noon. She woke to a tickling sensation on her cheek. She fidgeted for a moment and grew frustrated. She brushed her cheek, but the feeling continued to hassle her. Her eyes popped open, and she couldn't believe what she saw.

"Tasha!"

"Hey, girl!"

"I thought you weren't comin'!" Kyra shrieked in surprise as she hugged her friend to her.

"Girl, now, you know my ass was coming to see you! How could I resist coming to the Bahamas? Your house is off the chain, girl!"

"Oh my God. You had me all messed up when you told me you weren't comin'! Oh my God..." She put her hands over her mouth to hide her wide smile.

"I wanted to surprise you."

"And it worked!"

"Okay, and just to let you know, I'm staying for about a week and half and while I'm here we're gonna have fun! I wanna see some clubs, meet some niggas, go shopping and hit the beach...." Natasha listed her planned activities as she counted on her fingers.

"Well, damn, didn't you just come down with plans for the both of us?"

"Hell yeah! You know how I do! You haven't been gone from Chi-town *that* long!"

"Dang, man, I can't believe you're here! This is crazy!"

"Ain't it, though? So how have things been lately? Fill me in," Natasha demanded, flopping on the bed.

"I don't even know. I mean, you know my dad's anniversary of when he died passed. That had me messed up for a while."

"Yeah, but it always does. Not that that's not understandable. It would mess up anybody's head who saw what we saw, especially you." Natasha remembered the events that happened that tragic day.

"And of course you know how stuff went with Kai. I called him and broke it off. Then he turned off my phone. I can't believe him. I mean, he even tried to deny the shit with Cedes and sweet-talk me like wasn't no shit goin' down." Kyra shook her head, making sure to leave out the full reason for the call.

"Yeah, he's definitely the definition of trifling. I swear, you look it up in the dictionary, his picture would be right there."

"Then I was just suspended earlier this month for fightin' this bitch named Veronica. I can't stand her or her crew."

"Aww, you got haters? 'Cause if they try to boss up while I'm here, it'll definitely be on and poppin'!" She gave her best friend dap.

"Don't start no shit, won't be no shit!" The girls laughed in unison.

"Girl, yes, all 'cause of Justin."

"I heard you mention his name before. You had the li'l crush on him, but you were tryin' to front because you were with Makai. You two together yet?" she half asked and half joked.

"No, no. I am feelin' him, though, but we haven't talked in

a few weeks. We haven't ever since the fight, and we were close before that. I just never told him how I felt, you know? After that we would see each other in class and stuff, but we don't talk. It's all my fault, though. I was actin' real stank. Yesterday we did talk, even though all we said was 'Hope you have a good summer.' So I would say that's...not good, but it's not exactly bad."

"Naw girl, that's pretty bad."

"I mean, we haven't talked in so long that I don't even think I know what to say to him!"

"Dang! I can tell you like him just by the way you talk about him. You get this look."

"What look?" Kyra asked defensively.

"Man, your 'I'm in love' look. Shit is *too* obvious."

"Whateva!"

"I saw it with Makai, so I know what I'm talking about."

"Yeah...yeah..."

There was an awkward moment of silence after Kyra's trailing off, and then the phone rang. It was Angel.

"Hey!" Kyra answered the phone cheerfully.

"Hey, Kyra. Wow, you sound pretty happy today," Angel said. She was somewhat surprised at the change in her friend's disposition.

"Yeah, my friend from Chicago came down and surprised me!"

"Oh, that's great! Matter of fact, that's perfect, because I was calling you because everybody's going to meet up at Mama's. You should bring her along so she can meet everyone."

"Okay, yeah, we'll be there. What time?"

"Probably like two or two-thirty."

"Oh, okay."

"And hey!"

"What?"

"Justin's been asking about you."

"Fa real?"

"Yup. But got to go. See you when you get there. Bye." Her smile could be heard through the phone.

"Bye." Kyra hung up and faintly smiled.

"Who was that?"

"That was Angel. She's one of my friends. She invited us out to eat. I told her we would go. That way you can meet Justin and them, too."

"Oh, a'ight. Where should I put my stuff? You guys got a guest room or something up in here?"

"Naw. Just set them over by those chairs, and we can share my bed. As you can see, it's big enough for the both of us."

"You ain't neva lie. You just moved and started big ballin'."

"So I see you girls are having fun already," said Geneva Jones, who appeared in the doorway, smiling at the giggling girls.

"Yeah," Natasha answered.

"Mom, you knew about this?" Kyra suspected that her mother had been a part of the scheme. She could tell by the look on her face.

"Well..." Kyra's mother made her smile wider, revealing that she had indeed played a role.

"Aww, I see how you guys do me! Y'all are just keepin' secrets!" Kyra said, laughing some more.

"So, Tasha, are you settled? Need anything?" Mrs. Jones asked her guest in a welcoming tone.

"No. I'm fine, Geneva."

"Okay, well, I'll leave you two alone, then. Nice having you down, Tasha," she finished as she began to turn away from the room.

"Well, girl, what are you waiting for? You need to get your ass up and get dressed because, uh...all of that...ain't gonna work," Natasha said, jokingly referring to Kyra's tangled mane of hair.

Kyra dressed herself in a matter of minutes, while Natasha opted to freshen up. It wasn't long before they arrived at the café. Kyra's long legs were shown off by her denim shorts, and she immediately caught Justin's attention. Michael had his gaze fixed on Natasha, who was in a strapless red and orange sundress that she felt embodied a tropical style.

"Hey, everybody! This is my friend Natasha from Chicago," Kyra said, happily introducing her to the group. "And Natasha, this is Quentin, Angel, Justin and Michael," she said, making sure to point out each person.

"Damn, he's fine as hell!" Natasha whispered to her friend through clenched teeth.

"I told you he looked good," Kyra whispered back through a smile.

"Not him, girl! His friend...but yeah, he's cute." She had her eyes fixed directly on Michael.

"He is scandalous!"

"He don't look it to me."

"Don't fuck with him, Tash," Kyra warned.

"Why don't you two stop gossiping and sit down," Justin said, calling the two out on their activities.

"For real, girl, come have a seat." Michael patted an open spot in the booth for Natasha. She quickly accepted his offer.

"Hey, stranger," Kyra said as she took a seat right next to Justin.

"Whaddup?" Justin answered, sipping his lemonade.

"So you're from Chicago, huh?" Michael asked as he moved a little closer to Natasha.

"Born and raised, baby," she bragged.

"How long are you staying down here?" Angel asked.

"About a week and a half."

"You got a man?" Michael asked in a sly tone. He was warming up his game.

"Nope."

"Uh-uh, Mike. Leave her alone. You aren't about to play my sista like that," Kyra cut in as she caught Natasha eating up every word out of his mouth.

"Why you always hatin,' Kyra?"

She sucked her teeth at him in response.

"Well, before y'all got here we were talking about hitting up Kingston for a few days. What do you guys think?" Quentin announced.

"Uh-oh!" Natasha was quick to voice her approval of the idea. Everyone chuckled a little at her eagerness.

"Yeah, Kyra, you guys should come. We're gonna get some hotel rooms, hit the beach, go clubbin', you know, all that good shit," Justin said with a lick of his lips. His stare was intense and the table grew quiet. The thick cloud of pressure was broken only when the waitress requested orders.

"May I have your orders, please?" the waitress asked, starting with Quentin. It didn't take Kyra long to realize that she was the very same waitress Michael had picked up the last time they had come to grab a bite to eat, but she didn't offer a warning of any sort. *This is gonna be good,* she thought.

As the waitress went around the table getting everyone's orders, she stopped at Michael, rolled her eyes and skipped him to move on to Natasha. After she jotted down the selected entrées in between glares at him, she started for the kitchen.

"Umm, excuse me. You forgot my order," Michael called out with his arm in the air, waving it from side to side for attention.

"Oh no. *I* didn't forget anything, but you, see, *you* forgot to call me. Thought I wasn't just some hit it and quit it like all these other girls, huh? Whatever happened to that? And I see you up in here with another one already. We don't serve kibbles and bits here for dogs like you, so go fetch ya own food. And girl, if I were you I'd run for the hills. The dick ain't even that good anyways!" Wendy snapped, only for Michael and the rest of his company to hear. She single-handedly managed to cripple a man's ego without breaking her code of professionalism in the workplace.

"Oh, damn...." Quentin was fighting the impulse to laugh at the waitress's comment.

"Hmm, looks like someone's caught up in his own game." Kyra's sarcastic remark came as Natasha scooted a few inches away from him.

"Shut the hell up," Michael shot back. "Damn."

The rest of the meal went well. The plans for the trip were discussed, and Natasha fit in well. It seemed like she had been there from the get-go. She was cracking jokes and telling stories about her and Kyra and some of the fun times they'd had back in Chicago. Kyra was eating her food and smiling. She smiled not only because of the stories Natasha told, but also in reaction to the looks Justin was throwing her way all afternoon.

When the girls reached Kyra's house and presented the proposal of their getaway to her mother, she didn't even seem to mind. She even offered Kyra money to help pay for the trip. Her generosity caught Kyra off guard, but she was quick to shrug it off. She wasn't going to complain when her pockets were empty.

The girls were more than excited to be in each other's company, and sat up all night reminiscing and gossiping. They shared a night full of music, laughter, dancing, doing hair and trading beauty tips that was something like a seventh-grade slumber party. As Kyra sat, allowing Natasha to freely style her hair, the phone rang. She turned down the music and rushed to the phone in hopes that it was Justin, and it was.

"Hey," she greeted him with a bubbly excitement, the kind a girl feels when she answers the phone to talk to a boy she really likes after she has been waiting all day for him to call.

"Hey, sweetheart, it's not too late to call, is it?" Justin's concern was genuine.

"No, it's fine."

"Oh, a'ight. What are you up to?"

"Nothin'. Tasha was just doin' my hair."

"Oh. So are you excited about the trip?"

"Hell yeah!" She was giddy.

"Yeah, me, too. I've been wanting to spend some time with you."

"Oh." Kyra bit down on her bottom lip, trying not to smile. She was happy she was still in his good graces.

"But I'm gonna go. I don't want to keep you from your friend. See you in two."

"Okay. Bye."

"Party pooper," Kyra mumbled to herself with a slight grin as she eyed her sleeping friend. She was glad Natasha had come to visit. She had grown to appreciate her friends on the island, and Angel was a great girl. But Natasha was her roll dog. She was practically her sister except for the fact that the same blood didn't run through their veins. The fact that Natasha had come to see her made Kyra love her even more. Kyra might have lost her father, Chicago, Makai and Mercedes, but Natasha was always there. Always. Natasha rescued her from slipping back into her old ways, and this time Kyra thought it might be good.

CHAPTER 11

"Swimsuit?" Natasha mentioned one item from the small inventory the girls had assembled for their upcoming trip.

"Check," Kyra answered.

"Lots of shorts and skirts?"

"Check."

"Tanks, tees and belly shirts?"

"Check."

"Oh! Oh! And lots of shoes, sandals, flip-flops, heels...blasé, blasé."

"Check, nigga!" The girls started to laugh, and Natasha playfully pushed Kyra to the side.

"Who you talkin' to like that, girl?"

"You!"

"Yeah, yeah, whatever. All I know is...I'm so excited! This trip is gonna be so much fun!" Natasha practically squealed as she flung her body on the mattress.

"Ain't it, though?"

"I bet you want a room with Justin," she teased.

"No." Kyra giggled. "And I know you not talkin', Ms. Oh-My-God-Michael-Is-So-Fine."

"He is! But after that little scene in the restaurant yesterday, I see what you were saying about him being a dog. What a shame."

"See! I told you! That's what you get for not listenin' to me the first time," Kyra said, walking from her bedroom to the kitchen.

She turned around to see the front door open. Natasha was waiting for her on the porch.

"You know, I wish I lived here with you."

"Why?" Kyra couldn't help laughing.

"Because here it's so nice, and Chicago has changed so much since you left."

"Like how?"

"You remember how Reggie and Makai were tight? Practically like brothers? Whenever you saw one you saw the other."

"Yeah, how could I not?"

"They ain't no more. They straight beefin' now. With them both being powerful cats in the game right now, they practically run the damn hood. But you know how that goes, right? Somebody gotta be king."

"Damn, how'd that happen?"

"I don't know. I mean, everyone knows Kai's been coming up. I guess Reggie got jealous. He done branched off and started his own operation, and now they're neck and neck. Ever since they waged war, there have been so many fights and stabbings and shootings going on. It's crazy. Steve, who used to roll with them, got popped, and he was cool with both of them. Then there's the back and forth about them and Mercedes. It's too crazy."

"Girl, you act like it's any different than before."

"I know. I guess it just never really fazed me before like it does now for some reason."

"Oh."

"Oh, and you know how Cedes is with Kai now?"

"Yeah…" Kyra replied.

"She's pregnant. She even got a stomach now. I heard she's about six months already or something like that. I just look at those two and I feel disgusted."

"I bet. Nobody wants to see her walkin' around like that." Kyra was trying her best to laugh off the hurtful news, but she was having difficulty stomaching the idea that a woman she had once befriended was carrying the child of the man she had once loved.

There was a pause as Kyra sank into herself. She was deep in thought. It was painful to think about anything that involved Makai, but to know that Mercedes was having his child was devastating. The child she might have been nurturing in her womb, he rejected. Yet for Mercedes, he was willing to accept it and stand by her side.

"Tasha?"

"Yeah," Natasha replied, sounding as if she were in another place, another zone.

"I was pregnant…." Kyra confessed in a low tone. She could barely whisper her secret.

"What?"

"I said I was pregnant. Well…I turned out not to be, but I thought I was."

"What? When, by who? Justin?"

"No, no! Shh! Be quiet!" she whispered, and turned to the door to make sure her mother hadn't heard anything, "Not that long ago I found out I was…*might* be pregnant by Kai."

"And?" Natasha spoke in a hushed tone.

"I had missed my period in May, so I took a test. I actually took two. The first one was positive, and then at the doctor's they said it was negative. I only told Kai about the first test and he told me to get rid of it. He wasn't even gonna help me," she explained.

"Did you tell him about the second test?"

"No. I don't want to talk to him. It's not like he cares either way."

There was another long pause.

"Why didn't you tell me?"

"I wasn't going to tell anyone." Kyra came clean and her eyes blurred.

"It's okay. Forget about him," Natasha said, comforting her friend as she encircled her in her arms. "You're my sister. Remember that."

Villa fifteen was Justin and Kyra's, and they had no complaints about it. It was large, with shining hardwood floors and cream-colored walls. There was a small minibar and kitchen area, and the bathroom had a deep hot tub. In the bedroom area, there was an armoire, a minicouch, a chair and a small table decorated with a fresh bouquet of colorful native flowers. It opened onto a balcony that overlooked the surrounding mountains of the capitol city of Kingston and its verdant valleys. The wind blew the sheer white curtains into the room and made it that much more appealing.

"There's only one bed." Kyra stared at the king-sized bed and the sheer canopy draped over it.

"I can sleep on the couch if you want."

"No, that's okay. It's no big deal. I just wasn't expectin' it, that's all." She now found herself nervous at the thought of sharing a bed with him. She was sure she wanted him but was scared to boldly take the steps to have him.

"Oh, okay." He set down his bags and walked over to the

balcony, shutting its doors. The rain that fell gave the room an extra cozy feeling.

"So...what do we do now?"

"I don't know. It's still raining pretty hard, so we aren't going out anytime soon." He studied the approaching storm from where he sat in a chair, gazing out past the boundaries of the balcony.

"Well, I'm bored, so we need to do somethin'," Kyra said as she crawled onto the bed.

"I think they have pay-per-view. We could watch something on TV."

"That sounds cool."

Justin picked up the remote and turned on the television. He picked up the small pamphlet off the table with the list of movies that were playing and read it off.

"They have *Dreamgirls*, *Babel* and *Pirates of the Caribbean*. Pick one."

"*Pirates*," she decided, lying back on the piles of fluffy pillows.

Justin turned on the movie and turned off the lamp in order to darken the room but remained in his chair. He sat there nervous and stiff. The reality that he was going to be sharing a room with the girl he loved for the next three days was just now hitting him. It was going to be just him and her. He didn't want to make any sudden or rash moves that could ruin the opportunity in store for them.

"Justin?"

"Huh?" He swallowed hard.

"Why are you sittin' all the way over there?"

"No reason."

"Well, come over here, then, and stop actin' all scared. Come lay with me." He did as he was told. He buckled under the purr in her voice and could not find it in him to refuse her request.

Justin joined her on the bed, making himself comfortable as she leaned into him and placed her head on his chest. He slowly wrapped his arm around her side and pulled her closer as they cuddled. They watched the movie, but their minds were on each other. Neither said a word. They simply went on pretending to watch the movie while catching sideways glimpses of each other. Each was waiting for the other to make the first move.

Justin's hand slyly crept down Kyra's back, his fingers tickling the small of it. She rested her leg over his and pushed herself farther onto him. His hand then traveled lower until he rested it on her butt and gave it a firm, unshy squeeze.

She peered up at him and stared into his eyes as the changing light from the television screen was cast upon his face and around the room. She bit down on her lip, and that was all it took to have him all over her in a matter of seconds.

Through the rapid kisses, Justin maneuvered himself on top of her and held her hands over her head. He began to suck on her neck, flicking his tongue gently when he heard a moan escape from her mouth. He could feel her squeezing his hands, and he felt her legs rising and parting, leaving him to rest between them. She could feel his excitement and that only stimulated her more, quickening her breaths. Justin tore off his shirt and was working on Kyra's when there was a knock at the door that put an unwanted end to their hot and heavy session of seduction.

"Hey, Kyra! Justin! Open up!" Natasha's voice could be heard from the other side as she pounded her fist against the door.

Justin collapsed onto Kyra in disappointment and rolled off her, putting his shirt back on. She let out a long sigh, sharing his emotions, and fixed herself before she answered the knocking at the door.

"What took you so long to get the door, girl? And why is

it so dark in here?" Natasha remarked as she stepped past her friend and into the suite, turning on the lights. "Mmm, hmm. What are y'all up in here doin'?"

The light from the setting sun made everything glisten as the water reflected its golden light. The group walked down busy Ocean Boulevard, looking in shop windows and enjoying the scenery of the eighteenth-century buildings.

As they walked along, they reached Kingston's crafts market, where everyone split and went their separate ways. Justin and Kyra stuck together. They were making small talk as they walked, holding hands, when they came across a tarot card reader.

"Let's do this." He stopped in front of the small purple and red tent next to a weathered wooden sign that read MADAME DEON, TAROT CARD READER, FORTUNE-TELLER AND PSYCHIC.

"Naww, I don't like those. They're freaky."

"Will you stop being scared and come on? Let's see what's in your future according to *Madame Deon*."

"I'm not scared."

"Let's do this, then," he challenged her.

"Fine!"

The interior of the tent was dark and smoky. Kyra felt she might choke on the pungent odor of burning incense and wax candles. An old lady with white hair sat at a round table with a crystal ball in the center. Kyra wanted to laugh at how unreal it all looked. A crystal ball? This had to be a joke.

"What can I do fuh ya?" the seer said in a thick Jamaican accent.

"We want our fortunes told," Justin said.

"That'll be five dolla." She impatiently held her hand out, awaiting payment. He placed a five-dollar bill in her hand, and the old woman spoke again. *"Each."*

He looked over at Kyra as he handed over the rest of the money. She gave him a look as if to say, "This was your idea."

"You, Kyra. Come here. Sit." Madame Deon stared at the crystal ball as she dished out her instructions.

Kyra eyes shot open at how the woman knew her name. Her mouth opened to pose a question, but before she could get it out, the psychic spoke yet again.

"I said sit!"

Kyra took a seat in the small chair, and the elderly woman snatched her hand and held it tightly. She shut her eyes in deep concentration as she began to tap into her mysterious powers.

"Ya have been through so much pain and are so young. Ya don't come from here. Ya come from a place far, far away." The mystic madame paused for a minute and then went on. "Ya miss where ya come from deep down inside, but ya are unsure if ya want ta return. Ya have lost the men ya loved there. But ya are in love now with someone new...."

She paused again and a troubled look crept across her face. Her gray eyes looked dreadful and uneasy, and her furrowed brow deepened her wrinkles. She let go of Kyra's hand and let it limply fall to the table.

"What, that's it?"

"I can't tell no more. I can't tell no more. I've had a horrible vision. I can't tell no more," she whispered.

"Wait, tell me. Please...I wanna know."

The woman paused and stared her deep in the eyes. Her scowl was full of importance. When her lips came back to life, she spoke in a low, raspy voice.

"You." She turned her attention over to Justin. "You will kiss the lips of death sooner than you think. Your love will lead you to the brink of death, and I cannot guarantee nor can I see if you will live to tell of the encounter." Her eyes burned into the two of them before she stepped back behind a curtain, abruptly putting an end to the session.

"Oh my God." What the fortune-teller said scared Kyra. She knew that what she had just heard must be true—Madame Deon had known Kyra's name before she'd even met her.

"Come on, let's go." Justin pulled Kyra out of the dimly lit, smoky tent. The prediction seemed to disturb her more than it did him.

As they walked past the stands of goods, Kyra kept her face turned away from Justin and remained wordless. She was clearly shaken.

"Kyra? Are you a'ight?" he asked. He peered over at her, but she was still looking off in the distance. She didn't answer.

"Kyra…"

"Why'd you take me in there?" she snapped.

"I'm sorry, baby." He pulled her into a hug to console her.

"What if she's right?" Her muffled words couldn't quiet the sound of her worry.

"That stuff is a gimmick. Don't worry about it."

"But the stuff she was sayin' was true, J…and she knew my name…. How could she know who I am?"

"They have all kinds of tricks for that kind of stuff. Don't worry about it. Please?"

She buried her head in his chest again.

"Plus she charged us ten dollars. She's a rip-off," he said.

"Shut up." He made her laugh as she playfully pushed him back.

Early the next morning, everyone emerged rested from their rooms and met for breakfast at the hotel's outdoor deck restaurant.

"So what's up for today?" Natasha asked as she took a bite of her stack of French toast.

"How about we go swimming?" Angel suggested.

"Yeah, they got a pool here," Quentin pointed out.

"How about we go to the beach? That's better," Kyra said.

"Yeah, that sounds tight," Justin agreed.

"Beach it is, then," his brother concluded.

Justin looked over at a fidgeting Michael. He kept shifting in his chair and was failing to find comfort.

"My nigga, is you a'ight?" he asked, sipping his tart grapefruit juice.

"I had to sleep on the floor because *somebody*, I won't say any names, won't let a brotha share a damn bed," Michael growled while focusing his eyes on his roommate.

"Maybe I would let *somebody* share a bed with me if they weren't a hormonally challenged dog," Natasha retorted, looking him up and down.

"I don't even want you like that with your ugly ass," he responded.

"Aww shit…" Quentin sighed. He knew something was about to go down. Everyone did.

"Nigga, I know you ain't talking 'bout ugly with that big-ass head of yours." A few people at the table snickered at the quarrel.

"Man, whatever."

"Yeah, see, that shit right there be the reason why you sleep on the floor," Natasha teased while pointing her butter knife at her foe.

Things were better at the beach. The sun was shining, the sky was clear, and the white sand shimmered in the light as the girls lay out to sun their bodies. In the absence of the boys, who had hung back at the hotel for a minute, the talk centered on them.

"I can't stand Michael. I can't believe I have to room with him for this whole trip," Natasha grumbled as she played in the sand with her feet.

"I think you like him," Kyra teased in an innocent tone.

"No the hell I don't! And I know you ain't talkin' when you were all in the dark last night with Justin!" She twisted her neck as she spoke, and the subject made Angel sit up with interest. "Oops..." Natasha covered her mouth in sarcasm.

"Oh! You went there with it, huh?"

"What happened?" Angel asked.

"Nothin' happened," Kyra said.

"Honestly?" Tasha prodded.

"Yup."

"That's bullshit." Both girls turned to Angel, surprised by her language, and laughed.

"I know you guys didn't think I *never* cursed, did you?" she said with a devilish smile on her face.

"Um...yeah...actually, I did," Kyra answered, saying her words slowly.

"Well, anyways...I mean, spill the beans. I know *something* happened. I love Quentin with all my heart, but Justin looks good, so let's be real. It's obvious you two like each other, and now you're together for a few days away from home in a nice place. You're sharing a room, and that room has a bed. You would be dumb *not* to do him." She directly shared her viewpoint. Kyra was shocked by her sudden change in attitude, but she liked it.

"Okay. Okay, damn. Yeah, we almost did it. *But* then *someone* over here by the name of *Natasha* had to come and bust up the moment!"

"Aha! I knew it! I knew it! Kyra was gonna get her some!" Her friend fell back on her towel as she let loose with a roar of laughter.

* * *

"Where's Kyra?" Justin asked. The boys had finally made their shoreline arrival.

"She went to cool off," Natasha answered as she turned over to bronze her back. Kyra had left only moments earlier to go take a dip in the waters of the Caribbean.

"Oh."

"Baby, do you want me to rub your back down?" Quentin asked his girlfriend as he admired her tanned skin.

"Yeah," she cooed.

As Michael looked over Natasha's firm body in her lavender string bikini, he wished he could pose the same question to her but instead shifted his thoughts to the pigskin he was holding.

"J, you ready to get down with some football?"

"Yeah, that's cool. Let's go. Q, you coming?"

"Yeah, in a minute." He looked up at them for a quick second and then refocused on Angel's partly oiled back.

Justin and Michael moved a few feet away and began to toss the football back and forth. At one point Justin caught the ball but never threw it back.

Kyra had emerged from the sea in her white bikini. Water dripped down her body and its many curves, and her hair was soaked. She flicked it to the side with one smooth motion of her head. Justin was hypnotized by her. He had never seen her body so close to naked or so beautiful.

He dropped the ball, abandoning the game, and walked slowly over to her. She was just as mesmerized by his finely toned body and glistening skin as he stood before her in his swim trunks.

"Hey, when'd you get here?" she made a conscious effort to focus her eyes on his face so he wouldn't notice them roaming over his muscular build.

"Not that long ago."

"Oh."

"I, umm…like your bathing suit."

"Thanks." She smiled. "Do you wanna get in? The water feels *so* good," she said as she looked out at the rolling waves and then back at him.

"Sure."

It didn't take long for everyone else to join in. Between games of chicken and people being tossed here and there, Kyra and Justin seemed to keep finding each other's eyes. Little did they know they weren't the only ones exchanging looks.

"Mike, are you a'ight?"

"Yeah I'm fine, why?"

"Because, those fine-ass girls just passed us and you didn't say anything," Justin pointed out.

"*Nada,*" Quentin added.

"So?"

"So any other day you would've been all up on them, trying to spit game to each one *at* the same time."

"Maybe his back hurts too much to spit game." Quentin cracked a joke that only he and his brother enjoyed.

"It's not because of my back. I'm fine. But I'm going to be real for a minute. Don't laugh." He was serious.

"Okay, we promise not to laugh," Quentin said as he held back a laugh.

"I really like Natasha. No joke. And it's got me buggin' because I don't know what to do! She is not feeling me! She won't even give me the time of day. I don't know what to do to show her that I'm not playing games with her. The same reason I like her is the thing that is holding me back. She's playing hard to get," he explained.

"You know, I think this is a time for an 'I told you so.'"

"What the hell are you talking about?"

"I told you that one day you'd find a girl you would really like, and bam! Here she is," Quentin said, reminding his friend of one of their past discussions.

That night Kisses, a popular club on the island, was packed, and the line for entry stretched all the way around the corner. The bouncers were especially nice to Justin and Quentin and let them, as well as their guests, stroll in past the others in line. They were catered to like celebrities.

It was dark except for the dance lights and fog coming from a combination of people smoking and the disc jockey's smoke machine. The complex smell of cologne, coconuts and marijuana filled the air, and the bass of the music shook the walls. As soon as the group stepped through the door, they could feel the intense heat coming from the moving, grinding bodies on the dance floor. No one in their party wasted any time joining the crowded mass of people on the floor.

Kyra emerged from the bathroom in a short pink satin and lace nightgown. She sloppily pinned up her wet curls as she walked into the sitting room. Justin's back was to her as he faced the balcony. She slowly made her way over to him and placed her hand on his shoulder to offer comfort. He acknowledged her presence by taking her hand in his and kissing it softly.

"I love you." His love and passion for her was visible in the tone of his random confession. "I understand if—"

"Shh." She hushed him with a finger over his mouth, "I love you, too," she replied, shocking herself at her own sudden honesty and admittance.

"Then be my girl?"

She moved in cautiously and pressed her lips against his for a moment. "I'll be your girl," she whispered before she moved back in for another kiss.

Their kissing grew passionate, and their tongues became intertwined. Justin's hands freely roamed her body in exploration as he kissed and sucked her neck.

He picked her up and carried her to the bed, where he laid her on the cool sheets, sending shivers down her body. He climbed onto her, looking into her eyes the whole while.

Kyra brought him closer to her. She needed his body and his comfort. She needed him, period. His smile, his laugh, his voice, his touch, his protection and, most importantly, his love.

He slipped off her negligee and stimulated every part of her with his lips. Kissing down her breasts, her stomach and all the way to her belly button and south. He brushed her thighs with his mouth, teasing her, to build her desire for him. He played with her body until he could hear her whimper.

He started to massage her with his tongue, causing her moans to become louder and her hands to grip the sheets. She couldn't believe what was happening. Makai had never done a thing like this before. She had heard about it from Mercedes, and when she'd suggested it to Makai, he refused, saying it was "nasty." She'd had no idea how good it would feel. She'd had no idea what she had been missing.

Justin retraced his trail of kisses and removed his boxers. He lay ready to penetrate her when she stopped him.

"Do you have a…"

He reached down on the floor into his jeans pocket and retrieved a black condom. It was a Magnum XL. Kyra's eyes grew wide, and Justin let out a small chuckle as he tore the wrapper open and covered himself.

For a moment, Kyra thought it was all a dream. Sometimes it was hard to tell the difference, but she was more than convinced that it was a reality when she felt him inside her. As he slowly entered her wetness, she bit down on her lip and let out a moan. She wrapped her legs around him, pulling him closer to her as he gradually sped up his thrusts.

As he moved faster, submerging himself deeper inside her, her moans became louder, and so did his grunts and groans. Their breathing became heavy and their bodies dripped as they rubbed against each other.

Kyra unwrapped her legs from around Justin's waist and spread them as far as she could, allowing him to go deeper and faster than either of them thought possible. Her moans turned to pleasure-filled screams as she repeated his name and he grabbed her thighs. She clawed at his back and softly bit his shoulder as their moans became their new language.

They communicated only with moans, their eyes and their tongues. The pleasure they generated was incomparable, and it only felt better with every stroke. Sensations grew so intense neither party wanted to stop. Their bodies shook and quivered together several times throughout the night, until all energy was spent.

Finally Justin rolled over and Kyra positioned herself in the nook under his arm, resting her head on his chest. That night it was as though they became one. That night he made her feel complete. That night she knew she wanted him with her forever and he knew the same.

The next morning, Kyra's eyes slowly opened to the bright sunlight cast across the room. She looked over to see Justin lying next to her. She weakly smiled at the memories from last night that flooded her mind. She studied his features as he lay peacefully next to her in the sunlit room. She planted a gentle kiss on his lips, awaking him from his slumber.

"Hey…" Justin uttered. His voice was full of sleep.

"Good morning, baby."

"What time is it?"

"Uh…it's ten-thirty," she told him, reading the clock from her side of the bed.

"We should get up and get dressed. We have to get back home soon."

"Okay." She stood and wrapped herself in one of the bed-sheets.

"Damn, girl," he said as he watched her hips sway until she vanished into the bathroom. She let out a giggle and shut the door.

CHAPTER 12

When Natasha and Michael returned from their nighttime stroll, Kyra came at her friend with tons of questions. Natasha teased and taunted her until later that night. As the two best friends sat on the porch swing sharing Kyra's last Cuban cigar, Natasha let her friend in on her secret.

"Come on, man. Tell me! Fa real, this ain't right," Kyra was begging in frustration. She sounded only seconds away from throwing a temper tantrum.

"Okay, okay!" Natasha laughed as she blew smoke out of her mouth. "You remember when we went down to Kingston?"

"Yeah?"

"And you remember when I had got sick that night at the club?"

"Yeah?"

"Well...I wasn't *really* sick."

"I'm lost."

"I did it to go back to the hotel to be with Mike."

"Oh my God...."

"Wait, wait! Listen." She giggled.

"I'm listenin'."

"When we got back to the room, things got a little—how should I put this?—serious."

"So you guys made out?"

Natasha shook her head no.

"Oh no! You...you...you know!" Kyra exclaimed. She was practically the only person who knew that her friend was still a virgin. At least she *thought* she was still a virgin.

"Yeah, we did it," Natasha said nonchalantly.

"What made you do it? And with him? I told you about him!"

"I don't know. It just seemed like the right time. I know what you said about him, but he's really cool, and he's sweet when you get to know him. He's better than half the niggas back home, I know that."

"I been knowin' that nigga for how many months now and I haven't seen *shit* sweet about him."

"*Anyway*...me and him had our little fling while I was here and everything. That's what we were talking about on the walk. He wanted to be in a relationship, but I said no. I'm not down for no long-distance business. It was fun while it lasted, but now the fun is over. It's not like we can't keep in touch, though. I gave him my number, but that's as far as it goes."

"I feel you. You gotta do what's best for you." Kyra blew tobacco smoke through her lips.

"You know, I really had fun on this trip," Natasha concluded.

"I know! I don't want you to go!" Kyra giggled to cover her sadness.

"You should come see me up in Chi-town next summer or something."

"Yeah, maybe. I don't know. I don't know how I really feel anymore about going home."

"Man, don't let that shit keep you from home. You can't let what happened with Makai and Mercedes keep you down. You're better off without 'em."

The girls sat and relaxed, enjoying the remaining bit of the Cuban cigar and the Caribbean night breeze. After a while, Kyra began to speak. "Tash, I have one question."

"What?"

"Was it good?"

"Hell yeah!"

The girls burst into laughter, and suddenly Kyra's mother appeared in the doorway.

"What's so funny out here?"

"Nothin'…nothin'…" Kyra muttered as she cut off all signs of laughter in her voice, tossing the cigar butt over to Natasha, who slickly tossed it over the porch railing.

"Mmm, hmm." She looked the teens over suspiciously and took a sniff of the thick air. "What's that smell?"

"What smell?" Natasha innocently quizzed. She was barely able to restrain her giggles.

"You two come in soon now, you hear? We have to get up early tomorrow. Oh, and keep it down. It's late," she ordered, shutting the door and leaving the girls outside.

Early the next morning, Kyra stood on the dock with her mother and her best friend awaiting the ferry to Nassau. They all stood and watched the sun rising from beyond the horizon. It was the most beautiful morning any of them had ever seen.

"Man, I don't wanna leave," Natasha said again.

"I don't want you to go, either."

"You should really think about coming up to Chicago next summer, fa real. And if you can't, I'm gonna try my hardest to make it back down here. Please believe, I don't mind a vacation to the Bahamas every summer." Her words were half serious and half a joke.

The girls were still gazing out at the water when Kyra spotted the outline of a boat approaching the dock.

"Looks like that's your ride."

"Yeah..." Natasha said as she lifted her suitcases from the ground.

"It was nice seeing you. You're always welcome here. You be careful on your way back home and make sure you call when you get in. Tell your mother I said hello," Geneva Jones said as she gave Natasha a hug. "Kyra, I'll be in the car," she said as she walked away. She knew they would appreciate a moment alone.

"Same thing she said. Be careful, and call me when you get home. Okay?"

"Okay." Natasha pulled her friend into a tight embrace. "Love ya like a sis," she whispered.

"You, too."

Once again, they separated without a formal goodbye, and Natasha boarded the nearly empty boat. She stood on the top deck as the boat pulled off, staring back at her friend. Natasha's and Kyra's eyes locked as the ferry sailed into the distance. Neither wanted to part, but that was how things had to be. It seemed like they hadn't realized how much they missed each other until they had to go their separate ways yet again.

After Natasha left, there seemed to be something missing on the island, at least for Kyra and Michael. They both moped around for days: Michael lovesick, and Kyra feeling a touch of homesickness.

It was around midnight, and Kyra and Justin lay wrapped in her sheets. The room was completely hushed as they listened to the rain pelt the house and the strong winds of the restless storm whistle outside.

"You miss her, don't you?" Justin asked, disturbing the quiet.

"Yeah, but I'll be okay. You should be worried about Mike, if anyone, though." She let out a sigh and snuggled herself closer to his warm body.

"Have you ever thought about going back? You know, to visit some family or friends…"

"I used to."

"But…?"

"I lost my reasons."

"What about family or your dad? You don't mention him much."

"Have you ever been off the island? And I mean off any islands around here. Have you ever been to another country?" She made sure to evade his question.

"Nope," he responded. He had been everywhere from Japan to Africa, to Australia and France.

"Not even to the U.S.?"

"Nowhere. With how my father acts sometimes, I wonder if I'll ever be able to leave, even if I want to."

"Do you want to?"

"Nah. Everything I need is right here." He kissed her forehead.

"Tell me about your family. What are they like?"

"Some other time. It's late. Maybe you'll meet them someday, if you act right." He wasn't in the mood to be deceptive tonight.

"Maybe." She smirked and playfully smacked his chest.

"Speaking of family, are you sure your mom isn't going to come busting up in here at any minute?"

"Psh. She's never home anymore. She's always workin' or out with friends or whateva."

"I'm not complaining."

"I bet."

Silence fell onto the room again as Justin's fingers wound themselves through Kyra's many curls and waves. As lightning lit up the room, he voiced a question he'd never asked before.

"What was it like up in Chicago?"

"I don't know. It was loud. Real windy…" She sat up and rubbed her arms as if she were cold.

"No, I'm saying, I want to know what your *life* was like."

Kyra paused for a moment. She didn't want to be reminded of her old lifestyle. Those days were behind her, and she didn't want to bring them up. But after glancing back at the one she loved and seeing the eager look to know more about her on his face, she couldn't help letting him in.

"I was real popular, real selfish and even more stuck-up…. I got bad grades…. I would always hang out with Tasha. I knew her since I was little," she explained of her past, making sure to cut out anything involving Makai, Mercedes or her family.

"Yeah, you *were* stuck-up when you first got here," Justin joked.

"Shut up." Her laugh broke her serious thoughts. She hadn't really thought about how much she had changed until now.

"I still love you, though," he said, rubbing his hand lightly over her bare back.

"I love you, too," she cooed as she looked back into his eyes.

"Come here." Justin pulled Kyra to him and met her with a peck on the lips.

That summer went by fast as the hot sun and sudden rains of the season marked each day, and Kyra and Justin's now-exclusive relationship grew stronger in spite of their secrets.

Most days, Kyra's mother didn't find her way home from the hotel, but Kyra didn't mind the extra freedom. What with cuddling up to watch movies, cooking for her man and having daily sex, she barely had time for anything else.

Too quickly, the new school year started. Once the word got around that Kyra and Justin were officially an item, Veronica was more jealous than ever. Her vicious stares were so frequent, they didn't even faze Kyra anymore. Bottom line was that she had what she wanted.

Kyra kept in touch with Natasha sporadically throughout the year. Natasha would fill her in on all the latest gossip in Chicago and would sometimes ask about Michael. She seemed touched to hear that he had slowed things down. She had quit her job at Burger King when she had gotten back from her vacation and started working at the local mall. Working in retail was a real improvement from the fast-food business for any teenager.

"I don't get how you can work." Kyra held the phone to her ear as she turned onto her stomach in bed.

"It's not that bad. It sure as hell beats Burger King. I get discounts on my clothes and see all the new stock before it hits the shelves. I be geared out, girl! Get on it!"

"I still don't get it."

"That's because you're spoiled as hell. If you would even give it a chance, you would like it. Especially since it has to do with clothes. But who am I fooling? Putting your name and *work* in the same sentence doesn't even sound right," she said, and laughed hysterically.

"What's so funny about that? It's not like I can't do it or nothin'."

"Yeah, right. I'll believe it when I see it."

"A'ight, bet, then. I'll get a job. You're gonna be feelin' so dumb when I do, too."

"Yeah, okay. You let me know when you do."

"I'm serious!" Kyra protested.

"Mmm, hmm."

"Bitch."

"You love me, though."

"Or so you think."

"Oh! It's like that?"

"Nah, you know I love ya like my sis, girl!"

"Whatever."

"Dang, girl, it's ten-thirty already. We've been on this phone foreva."

"I need to get some sleep for tomorrow. I have a test in chemistry," Natasha sighed.

"Damn, I heard it's hard as hell."

"You ain't neva lie."

"A'ight, then, I'll talk to ya lata."

"Peace. Oh, and Kyra, tell everyone I said hi...especially Mike, okay?"

"A'ight."

Kyra went to sleep that night with one thought on her mind: getting a job. She'd never really thought about work. She'd never felt the need to. She'd been the first and only daughter of a hustler, a real boss in the midwestern streets, and when he died, she'd taken on the role of a hustler's girl. But now it was time for her to have some true responsibility. Not to mention a steady cash flow. After breaking things off with Makai, her budget had been obliterated. All her funds had dissolved.

After school let out the next afternoon, Kyra found herself walking along the shaded lane hand in hand with Justin—

Michael, Angel and Quentin by their side. When they reached the end of the lane, Justin turned toward her house, but she pulled him in the opposite direction.

"Where are you trying to go?"

"I gotta go take care of somethin' real quick."

"What is it?"

"Some stuff with a job."

"A job?" he asked in disbelief.

"Yeah, you heard me."

"Where at?"

"I dunno yet. I'm just gonna go pick up some applications from some places. Probably some boutiques or somethin'."

"Want me to come with you?"

"Naw, I wanna do it myself."

"A'ight, then, do ya thang, baby."

"Hey, we're about to be out. We have an apartment to look at, at four," Quentin said.

"Bye, Kyra, and good luck with those jobs," Angel called.

"I oughta get goin', too," Justin added.

"Okay. Call me later."

"Okay, boo."

They locked lips for a moment and Kyra started to leave, stopping when she remembered her friend's message from last night. "Oh, and Tasha said hi, especially to you, Mike."

"What?"

"Bye!"

"Wait, how are you going to do me like that? What did she say? Kyra!" Michael called out to her as she strolled down the street, smiling and chuckling to herself. The playboy of the island was head over heels for her best friend thousands of miles away.

* * *

Kyra reached Providenciales and roamed the streets to find all the opportunities available. There were a lot of restaurants and stores around, as well as hotels.

As she made her way through the streets, she spotted a store called Butterfly that she had gone to while Natasha had been visiting. She decided to stop in. It seemed to be the perfect place to begin her job search.

Kyra strolled into the boutique and approached the front counter, speaking as professionally as she could. "Hi, are you hiring right now?"

"Let me call the manager for you." The young clerk picked up a phone from behind the counter. Within minutes, the store manager arrived from the back room.

"Hello, how may I help you?" the manager greeted her with a mouth full of straight white teeth.

"Hi, I was wondering if you happened to be hiring right now?"

"Actually, yes, we do have a few positions available right now. Would you like an application?"

"Yeah...I mean, yes, please."

"Here you go. Make sure you bring this back tomorrow as early as you can. The faster the better. The positions are being filled fast." She handed over a two-page form from behind the counter.

"Thank you."

"Have a good day."

"Where have you been?" Kyra had made her way back home to find her mother in the living room eating a bowl of chicken and rice.

"I had to take care of somethin'."

"What's that?" She nodded toward the form under Kyra's arm.

"Nothin'. Just somethin' for school." Kyra did her best to lie and hide the paper, but it was too late.

"Here, let me see." Rolling her eyes and taking a deep breath, Kyra surrendered the form to her mother's outstretched hand.

"A job application?" her mother cried, keeping her eyes locked on the paper.

"Go ahead, you can laugh if you want. I know you wanna."

"No, no. This is…great. I'm just shocked. I didn't know you were thinking about getting a job!"

"Maybe that's because you're never home."

"Jobs can be very demanding you know. Especially mine. You try managing the money for one of the biggest, busiest resorts around."

"Whateva."

"But anyways, you're seventeen now and a junior in high school. I don't see why this wouldn't be as good a time as any for you to get some work."

"Yeah, I guess."

"You are going to hand it back in though, right? There's no use getting an application if you're not going to follow through with it."

"Actually, I'm taking it back as early as I can tomorrow. The lady said that the jobs are goin' really fast."

"Yeah, on the islands people are constantly coming in and out. Look at us."

"What?" Kyra demanded under her mother's stare.

"Nothing. I'm just so proud of you."

"For what? I didn't do anythin'."

"Actually, you did. Do you remember when I told you I

wanted you to come here so that you could grow? And you said you wouldn't and that you could do it in Chicago?"

"Yeah, I remember that."

"So you don't think you have? If we were still in Chicago, you wouldn't even *think* about *thinking* about a job. Plus, now you bring home decent grades and you may have a chance at college."

"I already told you—"

"I know," her mother interrupted, "but just think about it, okay? Let me know if you need any help filling out the application. I'll be in my room."

"Wait. Where'd you get that from?" Kyra noticed a ruby ring on her mother's hand that she had never seen before.

"Oh, it's nothing. I bought it the other day on Provo. Cute, isn't it?" She lit up as she looked at the ring before finally leaving for her bedroom.

The following day after school, Kyra was nervous as she walked into the Butterfly Boutique. "Hi, I'm here to return this application." She turned on her charm as she handed over the completed form to the manager.

"Oh, yeah, I remember you. Here, come with me."

"Huh?"

"I need to interview you. You do want the job, don't you?" the manager asked as she raised an eyebrow in Kyra's direction.

"Yes...but..." She was unsure as she looked down at her plain school uniform.

"Don't worry about it. You're fine. Now come on, I don't have all day to waste with you." She marched off looking over the form.

Kyra was a little taken aback by the manager's sudden change in attitude from the day before, but she followed her to a back office. As she set her bag down at the side of a chair and took a seat, she wondered just what she had gotten herself into.

"Kyra, where do you see yourself in five years?" The manager, Regina, suddenly threw the question at her as she scanned Kyra's personal information.

"In college." She was thinking on her feet, saying whatever she thought would sound best for the job. She couldn't believe what she had just said. Her mother probably would have jumped for joy if she had been there. But a stuffy little room in a dormitory with curfews and rules, stadium-style class-rooms with old professors, and too-long lectures weren't what Kyra had in mind for the rest of her life.

"What college are you considering?"

"Something in the...uh...Chicago area."

"I see here you haven't had any work experience?"

"No, I haven't."

"Not even community service?"

"No. I've never been in trouble with the law."

"You can chose to do community service, you know," Regina said, letting out a hearty laugh.

Kyra didn't understand what was so funny. The only time people did community service where she came from was when a judge ordered them to. *Who would even want to do it out of choice?* she thought.

"You make me laugh. I like that."

"Thank you," Kyra replied, more confused than before.

"From what I see here, things seem to be in order, and you seem well suited for the job, except for the fact that you haven't had any experience. Would you say that you are responsible?"

"Yes."

"I think that as long as you apply that, then you will be fine.

I won't give you the job right now, but I'll tell you what I will do. I'll try you out and see how you work for a few days. If I feel like it will work out, then I'll hire you part-time, but if I don't, then you know the deal. How is tomorrow? Saturday from two to seven?"

"That's fine. Thank you."

"Oh, and make sure you come in in something better than that next time. I'm sure a pretty girl like you has better things in her closet than a uniform."

Kyra walked out of the office with a smile on her face. *I'll show her.*

She returned home to share the news with her mother, who seemed to be happier than she was. She mentioned something about wishing they could go going to dinner as a celebration of her success, but Kyra really only caught the part where she said she wouldn't be back until tomorrow because something "came up" at the office and she needed to go there right away.

She dialed Justin's number as she watched her mother load her overnight bag into her car and drive off down the road.

"Hello?"

"Justin?"

"Hey, baby, what's up? You hand in the application?"

"Yeah, she interviewed me, too."

"Did you get it?"

"Kinda."

"Kinda?"

"I'll tell you about it when you get here."

"Another one of those nights, huh?" he asked, referring to her mother's constant absences from home lately.

"Yup. It's another one of those nights," she sighed.

"Okay. I'll be over there in a little while."

"Bye. And hurry, you know I hate bein' here alone."

Justin hung up the phone and looked over at his brother, who was sitting next to him playing a Playstation 3 basketball game.

"I need you to cover for me."

"Damn, again?"

"Yeah, her mom left again, and I don't want her there alone as much as she doesn't want to be there alone," he said, finding clothes to wear for that night. His usual overnight bag would've been ready if he hadn't put it to use only a few nights ago.

"I feel you." Justin threw on a white T-shirt and some dark indigo jeans, grabbed his bag and hurried his way down the side of the mansion from his bedroom window. He decided not to take his car but to walk to Kyra's house. It would be easier and less noticeable. It was a long walk, and it seemed he made it almost every weekend, but to him it was always worth it.

It took about an hour and a half for him to reach her home from the gated community he lived in. He walked up the dark, empty driveway to find her sitting on her porch in a peach-colored teddy, awaiting his arrival.

He didn't say a word as he walked up to her and greeted her with a kiss. He picked her up as she wrapped her legs around his waist and he carried her inside.

Justin tenderly carried Kyra to her bedroom and laid her on her crisp, cool sheets as they kissed and tugged at each other's clothing until they both were bare. Their sweating, panting, moaning and screaming went on for hours as they made love.

As Kyra stood in the shower, Justin washed her back. He watched, captivated with the way the water and soapsuds flowed over her body.

"Tell me about that job, baby."

"I gotta work tomorrow."

"So you got it, then?"

"No," she said. "She's tryin' me out to see how I work out or whateva."

"You got it." He made his statement as though it were a solid fact.

"Yeah," she plainly affirmed.

"So how long you gotta work tomorrow?"

"From two to seven."

"You want to do something when you get off? We could go to dinner or something," he asked as he massaged her back and pecked her shoulder blade.

"Nah, not really. I don't really feel like goin' out anywhere."

"You want me to come back over tomorrow and just chill here?"

"Yeah. I doubt *she* will be here."

"I understand how it is when you parents are never around. Mine are always working, too. It'll be a'ight, though."

"I really dunno why it bothers me. When she's here, all we do is argue anyways."

"She's still your mom, though. Everybody wants their parents around *sometime*."

"You know, yesterday she had on this ring. She can't afford it. I know she can't. I mean, I know what that stuff looks like and how much it costs. It was real, too. It had to have gone for at least a couple grand, and I'm just guessin'! Who knows how much it *really* cost."

"Maybe she's seeing someone. Does she have a boyfriend?"

"Like who!" she snapped, whipping around toward him.

"Whoa, chill, chill. I don't know who, I'm just saying that maybe it was a present or something?"

"She's still married to my dad, Justin. She still has his name," she insisted.

"He's all the way up in Chicago, though, right? Maybe she's lonely?"

"Yeah but still…" She trailed off for a minute and then started again. "Look, I gotta get up for work tomorrow and it's late. Let's go to sleep." She brought their conversation to a conclusion and turned off the water. She grabbed a towel from the rack and stepped out of the bathroom so rapidly, she left Justin stupefied.

CHAPTER 13

Kyra's first day of work was busier than she expected, but she handled it well. She gave out helpful fashion advice to the customers as she managed to shuffle from shelf to shelf to restock items and keep things appealing to them. More people passed through the store than she had ever imagined. Even with being on her feet for five hours as well as being under Regina's watchful eye, Kyra found working at Butterfly unexpectedly fun.

In only a few days, she became a part-time employee. Between hours at Butterfly and school, she found herself having less and less time for her friends and her boyfriend. Her paycheck helped to ease that loss, and the fact that she enjoyed what she did wasn't bad, either. As with everything in life, there were always pros and cons.

"Girl, you were right. Work ain't no joke." Kyra sat on her bed with her homework spread all around her, talking to Natasha about her new job. She stared out her window at the gleaming sun and bit her nails out of habit. She had more than enough work to do, and she was far behind schedule.

"See, I told you. And then all the shit with school…"

"I know, I'm literally surrounded with homework right now."

"But I'll give it to you. You actually went and got you a job and proved me wrong, as much as I hate to admit it."

"See! I told you so!" she boasted. She was smiling and feeling good about winning the bet.

"So where do you work at?"

"That store we went shoppin' at when you were down here. Remember?"

"Oh yeah. I remember. That store had some hot clothes, fa real."

"Yeah, they do. You should see some of the new stuff we got in on this last shipment. Woo," Kyra commented, reflecting on some of the new items that had caught her attention.

"I've been wondering why I haven't been able to reach your ass for grip now."

"Now ya know."

"Well, as much as I would love to continue this conversation, my ma just called me, so I gotta go. Who knows what she wants now."

"Okay, girl, bye-bye."

Kyra had just turned her attention to her assignments when the doorbell rang. She got up and rushed to the door to see Justin. Her face scrunched up when she noticed the dirt and sweat on him, as well as the faint odor that invaded her nostrils.

"Hey, baby." He didn't waste any time before moving in for a kiss.

"Ugh, back up. You stink and you're dirty," she whined as she pulled her face away.

"What's wrong with a little dirt? Dirt don't hurt." He mischievously moved closer.

"Stop playin'! I just got out the shower!"

"Come here!"

She dodged Justin's lunge and ran into her bedroom, where he caught her and held her down, smothering her in kisses.

"Ugh! Justin! Get off me!" she squealed.

He got up smiling and laughing as she playfully hit him.

"Go get a shower!"

"I don't have any clothes."

"I'll wash those. Please just go. Washcloths and towels are in the hall closet."

"Thanks, baby," Justin said, planting another quick kiss on his girlfriend's cheek.

"Hey, what are you up to?" said Geneva, just as Kyra finished putting Justin's clothes in the washing machine.

"Nothin', just doin' some homework"

"Then who the hell is in the shower?" She was curious after picking up the sound of running water.

Kyra's answer came without any hint of hesitation. "Justin."

"You got him up in here using my shower?"

"Trust me, he needed it."

"You don't need any boys up in here while I'm not home."

"Which is never. I need *someone* here with me."

"What do you want me to do, Kyra? Not work?"

"No, but it wouldn't kill you to make it home more than twice a week."

"Things will slow down soon."

"Whateva. And by the way, I like your bracelet. Where'd you get it?"

Geneva just ran her fingers over the new gold tennis bracelet encircling her wrist. She remained close-mouthed as Kyra walked back to her room and slammed the door.

Kyra flopped down on her bed and resumed her studies. She felt like she lived in the house alone, except when her mother made it home every now and then, each time with something new and expensive decorating her frame. Kyra washed her clothes, kept the house clean and got groceries, and her cooking was improving since she had to do it nearly every night.

"Why didn't you tell me your mom was here?" Justin whispered as he quickly shut the door behind him.

"Relax. She already knows you're here." Kyra kept her concentration on the last problem on her worksheet.

"And she doesn't care?"

"Of course *she* cares. *I* don't."

"Are my clothes ready?"

"Hold on, they should be dryin'. I'll go check on 'em," Kyra said before she went to retrieve his clothes.

She came back into the room a few moments later.

"Thank you, baby." Justin caught the clothes tossed his way.

"What were you doin' earlier?"

"Angel and Q found an apartment, so me and Mike were helping them move in. Didn't I tell you?" he said while buttoning his shorts.

"Yeah, I forgot. This job and school..."

"Maybe you should take some time off?" His suggestion came from behind his cotton T-shirt as he pulled it over his head.

"No, I'm fine."

"Are you sure?"

"Yeah."

"I barely see you anymore, and when I do, you're too tired to do anything."

"I know, I know. I think I got some time off comin' up soon," she sighed.

"Make it *real* soon."

"Where you goin'?"

"I have to get home before my parents, or yours for that matter, start trippin'." Justin said, slipping on his shoes and his fitted cap.

"Okay. I love you."

"Love you, too." Kyra savored his kiss as she watched him move past her bedroom doors. Seeing him had become a pleasure she rarely had the chance to indulge.

The next day, Kyra was busy at the store. She had worked almost every day that week, so she was more than ready to go home by the end of the day. She was finishing ringing up her last customer when an unexpected guest strolled into the shop.

"Hey," Angel greeted her with a wide smile and a happy tone.

"Hey, girl, what are you doin' here?" Kyra asked, equally happy to see her.

"Nothing. I'm about to go home and work on unpacking. I wanted to see if you wanted to come with me to see the place, and maybe if you're feeling extranice, help me?"

"Yeah, sure. I just need to check out."

Kyra was beat as the car rolled on down the street, but she missed spending time with Angel. The sacrifice of a couple of hours of sleep to see her friend's new home and make her happy was worth it.

The vehicle came to halt in front of Kyra's home. They made the pit stop for her to change out of her work clothes and into some appropriate clothes for unpacking. There was no way she would get Gucci dirty.

"Oh my God! Mom!" Kyra screamed. She had just stepped

into the house when she stopped dead in her tracks, not believing her eyes.

Her mother stumbled out of her room, frantically wrapping her robe around her.

"What the hell is *he* doin' here!" Kyra shouted as she glared at her mother and then at Matthew, her mother's boss, standing in the hall in nothing but his boxer briefs.

"Matthew..." Geneva whispered, signaling for her lover to return to her bedroom and leave her alone with her daughter.

"So that's who you're with now? Him? He's the one who been buyin' you all that jewelry?" Kyra hollered.

"Honey..."

"Don't fuckin' 'honey' me! You're never home 'cause you're out fuckin' him! He's your boss!"

"Don't get that tone with me! I'm grown, and I can do what I want and see who I want!"

"If you're grown, then act like it! You're up here sneakin' around, lyin' to me! Oh my God..." The anger was beginning to take over. "How long?"

"About three months after we moved here."

"Wow..."

"Kyra..." her mother began in a soft, soothing tone.

"Did he give that to you, too?" Kyra said, locking eyes on the twenty-four-karat-gold necklace shining around her mother's neck.

"Yes, as a matter of fact, he did!"

Kyra quickly reached forward, snatched the new gold necklace from around her mother's neck, and threw it violently to the floor. She looked up at her mother with tears flowing freely from her eyes, not caring anymore about holding them in, not ashamed that her mother saw them. At this moment, she wanted her to see them.

"You still have his name, and yet you're sleepin' with another man, in your bed...."

"It's been years since I've been with anyone, Kyra! Just because your father is gone, am I supposed to stop living, too? Is that what you want? Huh? Huh?" Her mother started to scream and push her daughter.

Kyra glared at her, taking in her tangled hair and crooked robe in disgust.

"I hate you," she mumbled. The anger was surging through her body so hard that the raw emotion escaped her without her even realizing it.

Geneva slapped Kyra so hard her head turned to the side. Kyra held her cheek in shock as she slowly let her suddenly dry eyes meet her mother's. They were on fire.

"Don't you ever say some shit like that to me! After all I have done for you!"

"Kyra..." Angel's soft voice came from where she stood rigid in the doorway. She had witnessed the scene unfolding.

"Go! Get out of my house!" her mother cried as she leaned into her daughter's red, marked face. Kyra rushed past Angel and out the door like a gust of wind.

CHAPTER 14

When she arrived home that night, Kyra could hear her mother weeping through her bedroom door. She weakly knocked and listened as the weeping on the other side died down. She could barely breathe when her mother opened the door. She was prepared to make amends.

What she wasn't prepared for was her mother pulling her into the room and beginning to pound on her. Between her mother's swinging fists, she could catch a whiff of her alcohol-saturated breath. Her mother had never been a heavy drinker.

She was screaming at her, but Kyra couldn't make out a word of what she was saying. She tried her hardest to block the shots her mother was hurling and to hold her back, to talk to her, even, but when her mother began to choke her, Kyra finally punched her as hard as she could.

Her mother flew off her, the force of Kyra's punch knocking her back, and scooted across the floor. Kyra sat herself up against the wall, gasping for air as she wiped her face of her tears and light blood.

"I want you out of here! Do you hear me? I want you out!" Her mother raged as though she were a crazy woman.

"Momma, listen...please...listen...I'm sorry. I'm sorry for everythin'. Everythin' I did. I'm sorry. I'm sorry!" she apologized while crawling over to her mother on her knees and begging for forgiveness.

"Do you really hate me that much for bringing you here?"

"No, momma. I don't hate you.... I'm sorry.... I'm sorry...." She repeated her words through gasps of air as she cried heavily.

"I just don't want you to end up like me. I want you to do better than I did. I don't want you to hurt like me. You don't want to lead the kind of life I've led," she sputtered.

Geneva Jones pulled her daughter into her arms, hugging her as tightly as she could as they cried together. It was a moment that made her flash back to the time when her husband died and Kyra came into her room one night, crying. She had taken Kyra in her arms and held her, soothing her until her sniffles and "I miss Daddy's" stopped. She looked up at the ceiling as she held her daughter and remembered the times Kyra used to come to her for comfort. She would always remember those times, but her daughter seemed to have forgotten.

Kyra splashed a handful of cold water over her face as she stood in the employee bathroom of Butterfly. She had been out of it at work today. Her advice wasn't as enthusiastic as usual, and she took longer than usual to stock the shelves and ring up customers. Last night had taken a toll on her.

"Sorry to keep you ladies waitin'." She politely excused her absence as she returned from the back of the store. She didn't look up at the customers as she got ready to ring up their items.

"Well, well, well, look who we have here?" Veronica spoke as Bridgette and Nicole snickered behind her.

Veronica laid her things over the counter as though Kyra were beneath her. To her, she was nothing but a servant.

"Enjoying the working life?"

"Yeah, it's great," Kyra replied with a fake smile.

"I bet…" Nicole mumbled.

"See, this is exactly what I'm talking about, V," Bridgette blurted out.

"What, the fact that she isn't suited for a man like Justin?"

"Exactly."

"Nicole, what do you think?"

"Hell no, she ain't."

"See, honey, the vote is in. Why don't you just give it up?" Veronica flashed a smirk.

"Over my dead body."

"Oh, I can have that arranged."

"Arrange it, then. We all know you don't have the balls to do it yourself. Don't act brand-new. You already know how I gets down."

Kyra rolled her eyes at the false threat and forced the other words that were sure to get her fired to stay in her mind and not leave her mouth.

As Kyra rang up item after item, Veronica started to laugh all a sudden.

"What the hell is so funny?"

"I'm sorry…. I just find it funny that you even have to work while dating Justin. He is of such high standards…and, well, you…we can evidently see that you are not. Whereas *I* am. Your relationship with him is such a joke. How do you two even relate?"

"Oh, we relate, all right. We relate *several* times a day, and let me be the first to tell you that he loves it."

"I guess I could be mad at the fact that you're fucking him, but it's common knowledge that if a ho is gonna let a nigga fuck, he's gon' fuck. It means nothing."

"Here!" Kyra said, slinging the bag of clothes over the counter and into Veronica's chest with force. "Your total is $895.48." She put a wide, sarcastic smile on her face as she snatched a credit card from Vernonica's hands.

"Come on, girls. My daddy is taking us on the *yacht* today." Veronica snatched back her credit card and turned from the counter, flipping her hair at her rival.

"Too bad you can't come." Nicole taunted her by making a fake sad face.

"Yeah, you gotta stay here and *work*. Have fun," Bridgette teased. Suddenly Kyra reached over the counter and grabbed her wrist. Bridgette looked terrified. She had seen Kyra fight with Veronica, and she didn't want to be her next victim.

"Here, you forgot this," Kyra said with a voice of false kindness as she handed over the receipt. She was noticeably amused by Bridgette's frightened expression as the girl scurried out of the store to join her clique in their chauffeured Rolls-Royce.

As Kyra watched the silver luxury car pull off down the street, Veronica's words lingered in her head. Veronica spoke of Justin as though he had money, when for as long as Kyra had known him, he'd told her his family wasn't well off. He even called them "sufferers," or poor people who struggled to survive. He had told her that Michael's family was the one with money and that he and Quentin would worked for their clothes and shoes to keep themselves looking nice like they did. What Veronica had said didn't make any sense whatsoever, but when Kyra took the time to examine the situation, things weren't adding up.

"Kyra! Girl, wake up! You've got things to do around here!

You are really out of it today." Regina's barking voice interrupted her daydreaming.

"Sorry, Regina," Kyra apologized as she started back to work and shrugged off Veronica's rude, snotty remarks.

At school, Kyra was late. Work and her home life wore her ragged. Her energy level was almost nil, so when she turned off her alarm clock the next morning, she took advantage of an extra hour of sleep until she woke up in a panic.

She made it to school during the day's third lesson. She stepped through the front door, her hair dripping wet from the morning mist, and into the lobby to see Richard Pierce sitting on one of the wooden benches outside of the principal's office. He was looking down, and he was obviously upset about something as his eyes met hers. She could tell something wasn't quite right just by the mood of the building.

A short man who looked as if he could be Richard's twin, only older, stepped out of the office. He wore khaki slacks and a dark blue polo shirt with matching dark blue gators. From what Kyra could see, like the gators and the Rolex she spotted on his wrist, the man was paid. The resemblance told her that he must be Richard's father.

She watched as Mr. Pierce and the principal, Mr. McKnight, talked in hushed tones, but when they spotted her, she quickly made her way to class. She reached her class and got an earful about being tardy from Mr. Cayman. He was her teacher for her junior year, and he was nothing like Ms. Kingsley. If you could find a pair of complete opposites in the world, Mr. Cayman and Ms. Kingsley would be it. They would be perfect.

Ms. Kingsley was young and witty and kept things interesting, whereas Mr. Cayman was old and dull, and you could consider yourself lucky if you made it through any of his lessons awake. Then there was always the negative factor that Kyra had a class with Veronica and Bridgette this year.

"Class, you have one more assignment due by next Monday. It will be the last major assignment of the year."

The class let out a loud sigh of disapproval as Mr. Cayman announced their fresh workload.

"Relax, relax. It will be a group assignment. All you have to do is compose a paper of three to five pages, double-spaced, twelve-point font, or neatly written in ink, about the three *E*s of Prince Paul and Providenciales: education, economy and environment."

"Do we get to pick our partners?" A young man asked from the back of the classroom.

"Sorry, Isaac, but I have already done that for you."

The class let out yet another sigh of disapproval.

"Silence!" Mr. Cayman screamed, shushing the class instantly. He was old—ancient, even—but everyone knew that he was not one to play games. "Now, here are your partners, so listen carefully...." He began to read from the list. "Bridgette Brooks and Isaac Tate, Jonathan Young and Kyle Guild, Kyra Jones and Veronica Pierce..."

Kyra's jaw dropped when she heard her partner's name. She looked back to see Veronica's expression. Kyra quickly raised her hand in protest. Her teacher tried to overlook it, but she kept it there, forcing him to call on her.

"Yes, Ms. Jones?" he finally called sounding slightly bothered by the interruption.

"Can we change our partners?"

"No. These selections are final. If I change it for you, then I will have to change it for everyone else."

He finished reading off the groups and led everyone to the newly built library, where they would work for the next week.

Every day Kyra and Veronica avoided each other as much as possible, speaking only when necessary to exchange crucial information needed for their essay. Every movement was made with an attitude, and every word was spoken with more than a hint of hostility.

"Look, get over it! Damn! I want to get a good grade on this project, okay?" Kyra exploded one day. She was fed up with the stressful situation.

"Whatever." Veronica rolled her eyes and hid behind her book.

"I'm serious. You may be able to buy yourself a good grade, but I can't. I'm workin' class, remember?"

"I don't buy my grades."

"Whateva, I just want to get this over with."

"You don't get it, do you?"

"Get *what*, Veronica?" Kyra whispered firmly.

"How much I loved Justin. Things got twisted between us and I was trying to fix them. But then here you come, Chicago attitude and all, and you snatch him right up. Right out from under me." She snapped her fingers in emphasis.

"No one *stole* him from you, if that's what you're sayin'. Y'all been over before I even got here. You need to get over it, because you have been tryin' to break us up for as long as we've been together, and the shit still hasn't worked. Cut it."

"I think anyone would try to break up a relationship that's just a front."

"How is our relationship a front? You don't know shit about what goes on between us."

"That's the thing with you. You think you know it all when

you don't know shit! You're so fucking blind while the answers are right in front of you!" she growled as she threw a book at Kyra. "Turn it to page one ninety-two and see how much you fucking know then!" She was fuming as she slammed her chair under the table and stormed out of the library.

Kyra looked around at the curious eyes that stared at her, awaiting some kind of explanation for the scene that had just unfolded. Full of embarrassment, she set the book down in front of her and turned to page 192. She scanned the page about economy on the islands and stopped when she reached the section on hotel owners. Listed were those considered to be the big-timers: the ones who owned resort after resort and were worth millions of dollars. Some families were worth billions.

She came to a section on the Pierces and was about to close the book when she caught sight of the name *Hartwell*. She read through the article about the Hartwell family. They owned fifteen resorts in the Caribbean, as well as an island: Prince Paul. The family was worth millions, and two sons were heirs to the fortune. There was additional information that Kyra skipped as soon as she spied the words *For photos turn to page 199.*

She turned to the page and looked at the pictures. She inspected them carefully, trying to understand what she was seeing, not able to accept that it was real. But it was real—as real as life, and there it was right in front of her. The truth. The truth was delivered in a form as clear as the color photo from five years ago of Quentin, Justin and their parents in front of their mansion.

There weren't too many women who would be mad at the fact that their boyfriend was rich beyond belief. Kyra certainly wasn't. What she was mad at though, was the fact that she had been lied to again. She felt foolish for not knowing, for not finding out sooner. A year had gone by, and she had been clueless.

"Looks like someone is here to see you." Kyra's new coworker, Linda, nodded in the direction of the young man waiting outside the store as they finished closing up for the night.

Kyra sighed as she grabbed her bag from behind the counter and walked out of the store, anticipating whatever Justin might have to discuss.

"Good night, Linda!" she shouted as she let the door shut.

"Kyra, can I talk to you for a minute?"

Kyra ignored him and simply kept walking down the dimly lit street.

"Baby, please." He stepped out and blocked her path, begging her to acknowledge him.

"What?" She stared off into the distance behind him.

"Look at me...." He took her chin in his hand and directed her face toward his, but she turned it away. "What's going on with you lately?"

"Nothin'."

"Don't give me that 'nothing' shit. You been avoiding me like I'm the damn plague."

"I've just been busy."

"Oh, so you're too busy for me now?" Justin assumed. His mood was taking a turn for the worse.

"I never said that.... Look, it's late, Justin, and I need to get home. I don't have time to argue with you." She sighed as she shifted her weight.

"Damn, you don't even have time to talk to me when I'm dead in your face?"

"No, it's not even like that."

"Then what's it like?"

Kyra had the strongest urge to ask him the question she had been holding in for the past week.

"Are you seeing someone else or something?" he quizzed.

"What? No, I'm not cheatin' on you, if that's what you're thinkin'!" Kyra was beginning to grow angry that he would think she was being unfaithful.

"Whatever, man, I'm tired of your little mood swings."

"I'm tired of you lyin'," she mumbled under her breath.

"What did you say?"

"Nothin'...damn."

"Look, I'm about to go. Do you want a ride home?"

"No, I'll walk." Kyra looked at the baby blue Lexus and realized that it wasn't Michael's but his. How could she have not recognized the signs that were right in front of her all this time?

"Baby, come here," he whispered as he pulled her to him and embraced her. "Whatever is going on, you know I got you, right?"

"Yeah, I know."

"And you know I love you, right?"

"Yeah."

"So why you acting like this towards me lately?"

"I told you. I've been busy."

"Do you not want to go to prom anymore or something? 'Cause if you don't, we don't have to go."

"No, I want to go."

"A'ight then, let me get you home."

Justin drove Kyra home with the radio providing the only conversation between them. As he pulled into her driveway, he noticed that the house was unoccupied and unlit.

"Your mom's working tonight?"

"Yeah, she had some stuff to take care of before prom came. She wants to make sure she's here for it. Isn't that a surprise?"

"Want me to come in?" He had high hopes that her answer would be yes.

"No, I'm okay. Thanks for the ride. Bye." She got out of the car without so mch as a kiss or an "I love you."

CHAPTER 15

Kyra fidgeted as she checked herself out in the mirror. She had to make sure everything was just right—from her hair in its upswept do with the curled tendrils hanging down, to her fresh and light makeup, all the way down to her sparkling gold dress, it all had to be flawless. Tonight was prom night, and everyone was invited.

Angel and Kyra rolled down the tree-lined lane in their rented Lincoln Navigator. The trees were decorated with white lights. Prom was being held outside the school under the starlit sky, with torches and lights that were strung through the trees to illuminate the event. There were tables all around, covered in crisp white tablecloths and set with china and silverware under a huge white tent. Dinner was to be served that night for anyone who chose to eat. Some of the finest chefs from the nearby hotels were catering the celebration.

The DJ had impressive skills and was spinning nothing but hits as Kyra scanned the crowd for any sign of Justin. The crowd of gowns and tuxedos seemed to be one mass of people all grinding against each other. The fact that everyone was dressed to impress didn't change the style of dance in any way.

She continued to search the crowd until she noticed Justin. Judging by the way his facial expression changed, he had noticed her, as well. Quentin and Angel were already all over each other on the dance floor by the time J made his way over to her.

"Hey, baby." He greeted his girlfriend with a peck on the lips and a once-over from head to toe. "You look beautiful."

"Thank you. You look handsome yourself." She looked over his tuxedo and freshly tapered hair. With how he looked, she wanted to hug him, hold him, kiss him and just let go and have a good time, but her stubborn side prevailed. "So...how's it been so far?"

"Good. But it's a lot better now."

Kyra didn't take well to the compliment but managed a weak smile in response anyway.

"Do you want to dance?"

"No, I'm actually kinda hungry. I think I'm gonna go eat." She declined his offer and clutched her handbag in front of her stomach.

"Oh. Okay. Well, when you're done come and join me on the floor? There's our table right there." He directed her toward a round table under the tent with a few jackets resting on the chairs.

After she ate, Kyra sat on the sidelines for most of the evening. She even noticed Justin dancing with a few of her classmates, but it didn't bother her. She sipped glass after glass of punch and refused every offer to dance that came her way. That was until someone made her an offer she couldn't refuse. Now was the time. This was it. This was the moment of truth.

As Justin and Kyra swayed to the slow beat of the music, she rested her head on his shoulder and closed her eyes. She was hoping he would tell the truth and terrified that he would lie.

"Why aren't you out here dancing?" he whispered in her ear as he rocked her softly from side to side.

"I got a lot on my mind."

"Like what? It's prom. You're supposed to let go of all that stuff tonight."

"Justin...we need to talk," she choked out. His heart began to race.

"Go ahead."

"Have you ever lied to me?"

"No," he lied.

"Would you ever?" She gazed into his eyes.

"No...why?" Justin lied right to her face while looking directly into her eyes. She turned away from him, knowing he was lying already.

"Because I need to ask you about somethin' and I need you to be honest with me."

"Shoot."

"Did you lie to me about your family?"

"What do you mean?"

"How they are? You know...how you live?"

"I don't get what you're getting at." He acted as though he was confused, trying to avoid the question he could now sense coming his way full speed.

"Justin, do you come from money?"

"No, I came from my mom," he joked.

"I'm not jokin'. I'm serious."

"Sorry, but no, I already told you about that. My dad is a fisherman and my mom is a housewife. I don't know about you, but I don't know too many rich fishermen," Justin said. There was a moment of silence before he spoke again. "Who told you I came from money?"

"If it's not true, then it doesn't matter," Kyra replied as the song ended and she pushed her way off the dance floor, leaving Justin alone.

That's why she's been acting so funny lately, he thought. It was no secret to the student body who was rich and who was not. It could have been anyone, but when he felt a soft hand creep up behind him and wrap itself around his stomach, he knew just who was low enough to carry out such an act.

"I just saw your girl. She looked really upset. What on earth did you do to her?" Veronica said sarcastically.

"We need to talk," he grumbled as he tugged at her hand, leading her over to the deserted pond and under a brightly lit gazebo. "What do you want from me, Veronica?"

"I don't want anything from you.... I just want...you."

"You just don't give up, do you? I don't know what I have to do to show you that I don't want you. I mean, you still blow up my phone, you mess with my girl and now you went running your mouth off about some shit you had no business in."

"She had a right to know."

"Yeah, and *I* was going to tell her."

"Well, it just happened sooner rather than later." Her remark was nonchalant and uncaring.

"You don't even know why I did this shit in the first place, do you?"

"Enlighten me, *please*."

"You! You are the reason why I did this! When we were together, you were out fucking other people. Hell, the only reason you probably fucked with me was because I had status around here. I wanted to make sure Kyra was different, and she is. I needed to know that she would hold it down for me regardless."

"You always hint at money or so-called status as the reason

for me being with you, but I have a name for myself, too. I have money. I didn't need your money then and I don't need it now. And for the last time, I wasn't out fucking no other guys!"

"So Darren, Trent, Jason and Terry were all lying, then, right?" Justin was sardonic as he listed the names of other heirs to multimillion-dollar fortunes around the island, all of whom she had been rumored to have shared a bed with. She didn't utter a word as her gaze fell to the tranquil pond. The guilt of her past infidelities was hitting her. "Yeah, that's what I thought."

"I love you, Justin, and I'm sorry for what I did. Trust me when I say I am," Veronica cooed as she rested her hand gracefully on his cheek.

"I don't know what to tell you, Veronica. I really don't," he said, swiftly pulling away.

"Do you love her?" she asked painfully.

"Yes." His answer was given without any uncertainty.

Veronica leaned in and kissed Justin in desperation. She reached his lips so fast he didn't even have time to realize what was going on before it was too late. It was too late for him to move, but not too late for Kyra to see what appeared to be him kissing Veronica in the lit gazebo.

Kyra was ablaze inside as she rushed back to the party. A part of her wished she had never moved from her seat at the table in search of some time alone. For what she saw broke her heart. But another part of her was glad. Now she had another reason to free herself from the relationship.

"Veronica!" Justin yelled as he pushed her off him.

"What does she have that I don't, Justin?" Veronica cried as she caught herself on a post of the gazebo.

"My heart." He walked out of the gazebo and into the night. He rejoined the festive party and left his ex-girlfriend.

* * *

Kyra parked the truck in her driveway as her eyes became clouded with tears. She broke down as she sat in the quiet car reflecting on what she had just witnessed. Not only was Justin lying to her about his family, but all this time he'd been with Veronica, too? The similarities between Makai and Justin were more than scary.

After a few moments of bawling her eyes out, Kyra got herself together and wiped her face. Her makeup was smudged and made her look like a raccoon. She tried to straighten out her appearance as much as she could before she entered the house. She didn't want or need to be interrogated by her mother tonight.

She stepped out of the car, her bare feet feeling the cool soil between her toes as she held her heels in her hands and trudged up the stairs to her house. When she snuck inside, she felt relieved to see her mother asleep on the couch with several papers scattered in front of her on the center table. She shook her head at her mother's strong work ethic as she slowly crept over to the couch.

"Mom…Mom…wake up." Her voice was mellow as she shook her mother awake.

"Hey, sweetie. Early night?

"Yeah. I'm really tired."

"Did you have fun?"

"It was great, can't wait until next year," she lied with a tone full of sarcasm to cover up the truth about the disastrous ball.

"I'm glad you had a good time, sweetie. Tell me all about it in the morning?" Geneva Jones said as she yawned and stretched her body.

"Sure. Good night."

"Night."

When Kyra heard the door to her mother's bedroom shut, she flopped down on the couch and let her body sink into the cushions. She undid her hair and let it fall down past her shoulders, tossing her hairpiece onto the center table. She watched the piece disappear among her mother's papers and grew curious about their contents.

She sat forward, still slightly sniffling from her crying spell in the car as she lifted a stack of them. They were too long to read individually, but the content became unmistakable when she read the big, bold font: *Name Change Kit.*

Kyra dropped the papers to the floor. She was perplexed. Her mother was going to change her name. She would no longer be Mrs. Geneva Jones but would return to her maiden name, Geneva Smith. Or maybe she would become Mrs. Geneva Daniels? With her dating her boss, who knew the outcome?

Any other night, Kyra would have been losing it—cursing, crying and breaking things, having a fit. But tonight was different. While she should have been out having a good time and partying the night away, she was at home doing the complete opposite. Kyra felt numb when she thought of her finding in the living room. She didn't feel happy, mad or sad about any of it. But when she thought of Justin, she found herself unprepared for the overwhelming wave of emotion that hit her as she stood shivering under the cold water beating down from the showerhead.

Kyra threw a bottle of shampoo as hard as she could onto the floor of the tub in frustration before she turned off the faucet. She was about to leave the bathroom, a towel wrapped around her shivering body, when she came to a standstill and found herself staring at her reflection in the large mirror.

She dropped her towel and stared at her body in this full,

unobstructed view. She looked down at her pedicured feet, up to her shapely legs, her flat stomach, nice-sized breasts, full lips and catlike eyes and finally to her dripping wet curly hair.

With a body that most girls would kill for, Kyra felt unhappy with her appearance for the first time. She had looked the same for so long. Her attitude and lifestyle had been through a whirlwind of transformations in the past few years, but her look still stayed the same, with only new outfits or hairstyles altering it now and then. There was nothing dramatic or drastic, nothing permanent.

Kyra took her hair in her hand, studied it closely, and then let it limply drop. That was when an idea came to her. She felt it was a stroke of genius. It was late at night and she wasn't in the best state of mind, but she searched the bathroom drawers for the crucial item to carry out her plan anyway. It didn't take her long to find them. They were sharp, and they shone in the makeup lights around the mirror as she took them out of their dark storage space. The two joined blades would bring her just the change she craved just the change she needed.

Kyra went into her room, making sure to lock the door behind her, and quickly threw on her purple silk robe. She snatched the scissors from where they had landed on her bed and hesitantly took a seat at her vanity. She brushed her hair roughly until no trace of a wave or curl remained, and while she held the end of one section, she slowly brought the blades to her hair.

She stopped for a second, unsure whether she really wanted to go through with her stroke of genius as she stared at her hair in the mirror and then up at her puffy eyes and the traces of eyeliner around them. It was at that moment that she did it. She cut off a lock of her hair. The scissors slicing through the strands one by one sounded good to her, and she wanted to hear more.

As she worked on her hair, she cut small bits at first and then grabbed bigger amounts. She sat there for hours, scrunching her eyes tightly shut and listening to the sound of the scissors at work. She only opened her eyes to see the new length of her hair and the pieces that littered the floor. By the time she was finished being her own personal hairstylist, it was evident that she had enjoyed the sound of her idea in action a little too much.

The next morning Kyra awoke to find herself facedown on the floor, with her headphones repeatedly blaring Beyoncé. She slowly sat up, wincing at the pain that shot up her back from her rough night on the floor, and irritably threw her headphones across the room. She was in a daze as she wiped her eyes. She was trying to grasp the concept of being awake when her vision began to clear, revealing an alarming sight.

She stared at the floor, covered in curly locks of dark brown hair. The hair looked just like hers. It *was* hers. Her hand rushed to meet her head and she felt around for her hair. She frantically sat up and stared at her reflection in utter horror, releasing a scream so loud it was a horror movie director's dream.

What had she done? Her hair looked terrible. It was uneven and too short. Her hair didn't even touch her shoulders anymore. It looked roughly cut, even butchered. Whatever it was, it was more than unsightly and she was more than discontented with it.

Suddenly the doorbell echoed throughout the house.

Shit!

Kyra tied her robe tightly and snatched a hat out of her closet as she scrambled to the door to see that Angel had stopped by to pay her a visit. As she opened the door, a worried expression crept over Angel's face.

"Hey…I, uh, came by to see how you were doing, but I…uh…see that you don't seem to be too good." She looked over Kyra's odd appearance. A silk robe and a Kangol hat weren't exactly flattering.

"Come in quick!" Kyra pulled her friend inside, looking around outside to make sure no one had caught a glimpse of her before she shut the door.

"Girl, what is wrong with you? You're acting like you're on crack or something."

"Angel, I did somethin' bad."

"How bad?" Angel asked. By her face, you could tell she was already afraid of what the answer might be.

"*Too* bad."

"What is it?"

"Promise you won't laugh, and you can't tell nobody."

"Yeah, yeah, you already know— Oh shit!" She screamed when she saw Kyra remove her hat, showing off her hair-style from hell.

She covered her mouth with her hands to try to cover up, but it was too late.

"It's not *that* bad…."

"You don't have to lie to me. I look a hot mess!" Kyra painfully admitted, throwing herself down on the couch.

"Okay, you're right," Angel admitted as Kyra threw her a glare. "Sorry!"

"What am I gonna do?"

"I don't know, but whatever it is you better do it before three."

"What's at three?"

"Quentin's graduation."

"Damn!"

"I understand if you don't want to go after last night and everything...."

"You knew, didn't you?"

"Yeah, I knew. I told him he needed to tell you..." She paused before she continued, "I'm sorry. I should've never gone along with it. That's why if you don't want to come..."

"No, no, you're cool. I'll go. It's an important day and I don't wanna miss it. Especially not over anythin' involvin' Justin's lyin', cheatin' ass."

"Are you two still together?" Angel asked with true wonder in her voice.

"Yeah, for now...why?"

"Nothing."

"Tell me." She demanded.

Angel silently looked at her friend and then down at her nails, growing nervous under Kyra's thirsty stare.

"Because last night when you left, I noticed some lipstick on him, and then for the rest of the night he danced with some girl. I think her name is Angela or something. She has a *reputation,* if you know what I mean."

"Well, yeah, we're together. Not for long, though." Kyra was heated at the new information.

"Have you talked to him?"

"No, and I don't wanna. Fuck him."

"You don't mean that."

"How are you gonna tell me what I mean?"

"Kyra, I can't justify anything he did with another girl because there is never a justification for cheating, and I know that if Quentin ever did I would lose it, too. But I can say he lied to you about everything else for a good reason."

"What kind of good reason is there to lie?"

"Ask him later. It's not my place to say."

"I already asked him and he lied about it. I can't trust what he says."

Angel took a deep sigh and looked out the window at the stretching area of green, freshly cut lawn. "Come on, let's go take care of your hair." She put an end to the subject while readjusting her purse on her shoulder.

"I'm not goin' nowhere. Not like this." Kyra folded her arms in resistance.

"What are you going to do, then?"

"I dunno."

"Well, you need to figure it out because the clock is ticking. I know a salon that can help you."

"Hell no. I don't trust a salon around here. I've seen those places and I've seen the results when people come out of them. No salons." She ruled out her friend's idea as she stood from her seat on the couch and hustled into the bathroom. She returned with a rectangular box in her hand.

"Strait Shades Colorlaxer; iridescent blond." Angel read the print on the box aloud.

"It's my mom's. She's had it for a while now and she hasn't used it. Maybe if we straighten it, it'll look longer?"

"*We?*" Angel raised an eyebrow at the statement.

"Actually, it would be more like...you."

"No. Uh-uh! If you hair falls out or if it turns orange, you're not about to blame it on me! That is what the salons are for. They got people there who know how to do this. Professionals, which I am not."

"Oh, come on. It's got instructions. All you gotta do is follow them. I don't want some stranger up in my head."

"I guess I could even it up and just follow the directions," Angel hesitantly agreed as she took in the sight of Kyra's short, uneven head of curls.

"Ah, thank you!" Kyra shrieked as she pulled her friend into a hug.

"Come on, let's go, let's go. We don't have a lot of time." She let out a chuckle as she shooed Kyra toward the bathroom.

Kyra rushed into the school building and made her way to the auditorium, one of the many renovations provided by the Pierce family after the incident with Richard. She spotted Angel in the jam-packed audience. She was calling Kyra's name and waving a scarf in the air to catch her attention. Kyra scooted her way down the long row to the seat Angel had saved, taking Justin by surprise. He was seated next to Michael on the other side of Angel. On the other side of him was an older couple Kyra assumed were his parents.

As Quentin walked across the stage and shook hands with Mr. McKnight while accepting his diploma, Kyra and Justin briefly locked eyes. That was the only kind of interaction she cared to have with him for the entire ceremony.

"Congratulations, Q! You did it, boy!" Kyra said. The ceremony had let out only minutes ago, and the crowd had dispersed onto the lawn. She was last to give Quentin her congratulations.

"I like your hair," he complimented her.

"I helped her do it," Angel interjected with pride.

"Son, who is this young lady?" Mr. Hartwell asked Quentin. He didn't recognize Kyra.

"Dad...this is my girlfriend..." Justin answered. He was unsure what his father's reaction would be, since he had been forbidden to see Kyra months ago.

"I'm his *friend* Kyra," Kyra corrected him, and shook hands with Mr. and Mrs. Hartwell.

"This is Kyra?" Mrs. Hartwell asked her son. She was in disbelief that the classy girl before her was the same person she had heard such negative things about from Mrs. Pierce and her daughter.

"Yup, that's me," she answered for Justin, who now stood quietly with his hands in his pockets.

"Won't you join us for dinner?" His mother was much more open and friendly than her husband.

"I wish I could. Really I do. But I have to go. It was nice meeting you, and congratulations again, Q." The last thing she wanted to do was sit at a table with Justin for hours over a family dinner.

Kyra began her walk back home, contemplating the fact that she was just now meeting the Hartwells when her relationship with Justin was about to be over.

Was he ashamed to bring me home to them or somethin'? she mused. She was just warming up to the wave of thoughts she felt coming on.

"Kyra! Kyra! Wait up!" Justin called to her as he jogged to catch up with her. She continued to walk, ignoring his outcries until he grabbed her by the arm, halting her where she stood.

"What do you want, Justin?"

"We really need to talk."

"We don't have anythin' to talk about, if you ask me."

"Come on, Kyra…"

"Okay, you want to talk, let's talk! Let's talk about how you lied to me! About how you kissed Veronica last night and how you were grindin' up on someone named Angela! How about we talk about that? Take your fuckin' pick, Justin!" As she exploded, Justin took her to the side of the lane. He hid her behind a tree so no one would see or hear their argument. He didn't want to cause a scene.

"Look, I know that me lying to you must seem really… bad."

"Oh, *bad* doesn't describe it!"

"Let me explain."

She went to speak again, but he hushed her.

"Let me explain…." he repeated in a gentle tone.

"I'm listenin', but make it quick. I don't have all day."

"I know I lied to you about my family, and I know that at the dance I lied to you when you asked me about it, but I swear to you I was going to tell you. I didn't know what to do at the dance…."

"How about…hmm, I dunno…tell the truth? I was bound to find out sooner or later!"

"Look, the only reason I lied to you is that coming from a family like mine, you tend to run into…gold diggers…and when I met you I wanted to make sure things were different. And they were. You were—*are*. You've been down for me and *only* me, and I love you for that."

"So you thought I was just some gold digger?"

"No, I wanted to make sure you weren't, and you aren't."

"Make sure for what?"

"I just told you!" Out of frustration, he inhaled deeply. When he went to speak again, his voice was low and relaxed. "I mean, Kyra, you made me feel different. Ever since I saw you in the market, there was something about you. I just wanted to make sure that if we had something, it was real. I didn't want it to be like my past relationships. I wanted to know that you liked me for me, not for what I could give you."

"Okay, so say you are tellin' the truth about all that, what was that bullshit with Veronica last night? I saw you kiss her, so don't try and lie about that one."

"She kissed me!"

"Oh, and you looked like you really hated it, Justin! What the hell were you two doin' by the pond alone anyways? It's no secret what goes on back there!" she yelled in reference to all the scandalous stories that circulated through school.

"I had to talk to her about something, and I swear she came on to me. I pushed her off me. Didn't you see me push her?"

"The only pushin' I saw was her pushin' her nasty tongue in your damn mouth! And then what is this shit I hear about with an Angela? I leave the party for an hour and you're dancin' on some hoochie for the rest of the night?"

"We were just dancing. It's not like she means anything to me anymore...."

"Anymore?"

"Yeah. We used to have something awhile back," Justin admitted.

"Wow. You are unbelievable." Kyra stepped back and narrowed her eyes.

"Kyra." He reached his hand out to caress her, only for her to recoil out of his reach.

"Don't *touch* me." She looked at the ground and then back up at him. "I just dunno what to believe anymore with you. I can't believe anythin' you tell me."

"We can start over...."

"I can't." She struggled to get the words out as she shook her head. This was more painful than she had anticipated.

CHAPTER 16

By the time Kyra had made her way up her street, her feet ached from her sandals. Her eyes were now dry as they took in the setting sun painting the sky as though it were its own canvas, with beautiful colors no painter on earth could create.

She stopped for a moment to take in the magnificent sight, her house only a little ways in the distance, and then she first caught sight of it. She cautiously started her trek back to her house and the cream-colored Bentley that sat in its driveway. In all her life, she'd known only one person who had money like that, or even close to it.

Despite any second-guessing, she knew deep down whose expensive car it was that sat in her driveway. Her intuition about his presence was like a sixth sense and was as powerful as ever. Now it was just a question of believability. Kyra's gut instinct was confirmed when she made her way to the stairs of her home.

There he stood on the porch in his cream-colored Armani suit with cream gators to match. His usually braided hair was tied back in a ponytail, with a custom-made cream fitted cap covering his head.

Kyra noticed the diamond in his ear, as wide as a dime, and the diamond-encrusted watch on his wrist. They shimmered in even the smallest bit of light. She was mesmerized by this new person in front of her as she watched the toothpick dance around on his soft lips, and she could not prevent her dark brown eyes from meeting his piercing hazel ones.

"Hey, baby girl," Makai greeted her with a tender tone.

"Makai?"

"Yeah, it's me, baby girl." He took a steady step toward her. "You're looking real sexy, girl. I love your hair like that," he complimented her, reaching out and caressing some of her newly short and blond hair. She jerked back as soon as his hand made contact with her body. An awkward stillness followed.

"What the hell do you want, Kai?" she bluntly asked.

"I made a promise, and I'm a man of my word. So here I am," he announced. His eighteenth birthday had just passed a week ago.

"Get the fuck out of here, Kai," she growled as she pushed her way past him and into her house, only to have him follow her inside. "What the hell do you think you are doin'?"

"So this is how you are gonna treat a brotha after he came down all the way from the Windy City just to see you?"

"No, this is how I treat a triflin'-ass nigga who did me wrong." Kyra disappeared into her bedroom.

"Where's li'l man? I wanna see him." Makai stood in the doorway and leaned against the door panel. He watched her move about the room as she cleaned up the mess she had created earlier while rushing to get ready for Quentin's graduation.

"Little man?"

"My son."

"Who said it *would* have been a boy?" she challenged.

"*Would* have been?"

"Yeah, you said for me to get rid of it, remember? Don't worry about it, though. It was a false alarm anyway. Nothin' to mess things up between you and your beloved Mercedes."

"I'm not wit' that ho no more."

"Good for you. Want a medal? You need to go get tested. That's what you need to do."

"And just to let you know now I don't have any kids wit' her, either. I know Tasha's been feeding you some chicken-head gossip. That baby turned out a spitting image of Reggie."

"Did you come all the way down here to tell me that, Kai? So what, she played you and now you come runnin' to me? What am I? Your backup plan?"

"No."

"Then get to the fuckin' point and get out."

"Before you left I promised you I would come down here and get you, or do you not remember that?"

"Are you fuckin' serious!" Kyra burst into a hysterical fit of laughter. "You can't just come back here and act like we are still...anythin'. You really think that I'm gonna go back with you just like that? That I'm just gonna run right back into your arms? After the shit you pulled, I don't think so. You must be crazy."

"You know I don't love them hoes. I been told you that. You know you're the only girl for me and you know I love you, so don't try and stunt. If I didn't really love you, then I wouldn't be here. I wouldn't be losing the money I am just to come and get you if there was even the *possibility* of you saying no."

"Oh yeah, bring business into it some way, somehow. You always have."

"Yeah, and the shit paid off," he said, looking over his high-priced outfit and jewels.

"Whateva, Kai."

"Come on, baby girl…" He lowered his tone and tried to calm her as he went for a hug.

"Get off me." She let out a grunt as she pushed him away.

"You remember what it was like when you were in Chicago? Imagine that but a hundred times better. I can give that to you. Anything you want, I can give it to you, Kyra."

"I have a life, Kai. I can't just pick up and leave because you want me to."

"I know you do, but you can come back to Chicago, too, and we can start a life there. Together: me doing my thing and you by my side, just like things always were. We can settle down and just chill. You can't tell me you ain't feeling that," Makai said with a lick of his lips.

"You wanna know what I'm *not* feelin', Kai?" She was heated as she set into him.

"I'm not feelin' how you just figured you would march your ass down here like some knight in shinin' armor to 'rescue me,' like shit between me and you is good! You just come here out of nowhere with this bullshit! Since I moved here, you haven't called me *once*. Not *one* time. Why? 'Cause you were fuckin' someone who was *supposed* to be my best friend. Then while I'm sittin' down here alone, scared to death that I'm about to have your kid, you turn your back on me and run out! And for what? For her! For that sneaky, nasty-ass bitch! You never *once* called to find out if I even had the baby or not! You never called to see how I was doin'—hell, to even see if I was still fuckin' *breathin'*, Kai! You cheated on me, you lied to me and you abandoned me when you were the only person I counted on to stand by me come hell or high water! So tell me what out of all of that I'm supposed to feel!" she screamed as tears of anger rushed down her face.

Kyra collapsed on her bed with her face in her hands as she violently sobbed. Her resurfaced emotions from the past were too much for her to bear. The wounds still seemed fresh. She looked up and stared her first love in the face.

"Baby, I know…I know I fucked up. I swear if I could take it back, I would. I'm sorry, baby girl. I would give up everything I have just to have another chance witchu. You know that when it comes down to it, you hold my heart no matter what. I can admit that I took you for granted and I did some triflin' shit. I was wrong, and I hurt you because of that. But I changed, Kyra. I swear to you on my love to you that I changed." He whispered into her ear as he took a seat next to her and took her in his arms. "I missed you so much, baby…."

"This is too much, Makai. You hurt me. You hurt me so much," Kyra sobbed, choking on her words as she hugged him back. She was weak right now, and any comfort was appealing to her.

"I know I did, and I apologize for that. Just let me make it up to you. That's the least I can do."

"No…I can't…."

"I know coming back to Chicago to stay may be too much for you right now. But just come back for the summer and see how you like it. If you don't, then you can come back here. Just give me another chance. That's all I ask of you. Give me another chance?"

"I can't, Kai. I can't," she cried as she shook her head. "I can't be hurt again."

"I won't hurt you again."

He leaned in and kissed her as she cried. She gasped between timidly returning his kisses as his hand crept up the front of her dress and tickled her thigh.

"I missed you so much, baby…."

"No, Kai."

"Just relax, baby. Just relax," he breathed, sucking her earlobe and making her melt. Her resistance was out the window.

She didn't know what had gotten into her, but seeing Makai brought her back to the lovestruck girl she was in Chicago. Even with everything he had done and put her through, as low and as wrong as it was, as much as it hurt her or caused her pain, and as much as she tried to kill the love she had for him, she discovered as soon as she saw him again that it was all still there. It was like some kind of voodoo, some kind of power he held over her that just wouldn't let her resist anything he had to offer, from Chicago to his body.

"Where are you goin'?" Kyra sat up in bed, clutching the sheet to her naked body. When he was done, he immediately started dressing, neglecting to cuddle or hold her.

"I gotta get going. I know you didn't think this trip was all pleasure."

"Business..." she sighed, already knowing the reason he was leaving her bed cold.

"As always." Even he sounded tired of the constant demands of his trade.

"Whateva."

"I know I'm busy, but when we get back to Chicago, don't worry. I'll make more time for you, okay?"

"Who said I was goin' to Chicago?" She made sure to remind him that her giving her body to him for those few hours didn't equal an answer.

"Think about it. I'll be at the Ocean View Resort. Room four seventy-eight. I'm leaving Wednesday night, so let me know if you're down." Makai fixed his silk-lined cream blazer and then made his exit.

Kyra looked down at the pink covers on her bed. She didn't know what to do, what she had done or what she was doing. Her mind and heart were all over the place, just like her sheets.

She pulled her knees to her chest and ran her hand through her tousled hair. She sometimes felt as though she was in a dreamworld, and this was certainly one those times. Makai showing up out of nowhere, looking G'd out to a level she'd never witnessed and professing his love and apologies to her, was more than surreal. She even wanted to say it was too good to be true. The day had been such a transition, from the horrific hairstyle, to the graduation, to the argument with Justin, and then to sharing her body with Makai.

She was faced with a difficult decision. She didn't want to go back to Chicago. At least, that was what she'd thought. But now she didn't know what she thought…about anything. Makai had changed that in one short visit.

The following day was a long one. Kyra and Justin were unhappy with their situation. Kyra kept to herself in the house all day with the phone off the hook.

As she lay buried under her covers, the doorbell started to ring. Kyra poked her head out from under her covers, irritated at the disturbance as she cautiously got up to make her way to the door.

"What is you doin'? Ringin' my doorbell like you are out ya damn mind."

"Girl, I been out here for damn near five minutes. Whatchu doing up in there?" Makai demanded from his position on her porch in yet another sharp outfit.

"I was sleepin'," she told him through a yawn. She had expected Justin but held in her surprise.

"It's six-thirty, shawty."

"Whateva."

"Anyways, go get dressed."

"I am dressed." She said, looking down over her cutoff sweatpants and plain white tank top.

"You're not going nowhere wit' me dressed like that."

"Who said I was goin' anywhere with you, period?" She folded her arms to purposely give him a hard time.

"I did. Now stop talking shit and go put on something nice. I wanna take you out somewhere. *That is*, if it's a'ight witchu."

"Where we goin'?"

"It's a surprise."

The shoreside restaurant was the very definition of romantic. The whole place was dimly lit with candles and chandeliers, and there was a live quartet playing music, with the ocean adding its own notes.

"This is really nice, Kai," Kyra said as she looked around the eatery from their secluded table.

"I thought you might like it." He placed his hand over hers as she looked off into the distance. "Whatchu thinking about?"

"Nothin'. It's just so nice. You really shouldn't have."

"I wanted to. Only the best for my baby girl," he stated between sips of the cold champagne he'd coaxed out of the waiter with a handful of Ben Franklins.

"Here are your orders," the waiter announced, placing the hot plates of delicious food before them on the table. "Will there be anything else for you or the lady?"

"No, we're fine," Makai replied. Then, returning his attention back to his guest, he asked, "Have you been thinking about Chicago at all?"

"Yeah."

"And? Whatchu think?"

"I dunno."

"Whatchu mean you don't know?"

"Exactly what I said. I dunno. It's not that easy."

"I don't see why it ain't. All you gotta do is ask your ma. You act like you got some nigga down here or something."

Kyra ceased chewing and picked up her napkin, daintily dabbing the corners of her mouth.

"Oh...so you really got someone? See, I was just joking. What's his name?" He was obviously jealous.

"Don't worry about it."

"Don't tell me what to worry about."

"I don't have anybody, okay, Kai? And even if I did, you should be the last one to say shit about it," she hissed. Their conversation was growing tense.

"Here we go...."

"Did you love her?"

"What? No, I didn't love her." He sounded as though her question were ridiculous.

"How come you never called me? I mean, you didn't have *one* minute that you could've called?"

"Kyra, chill ya tone. I don't want to dwell on the past. I just want to have a good time tonight. This is about the future, not the old mistakes."

"Whateva."

"To the future." He started a toast with the lifting of his champagne flute.

"To the future."

"To us."

Without repeating the last line of the toast, Kyra took another, longer sip of her champagne as she gazed out at the black ocean and the waves that crashed on the white-sand beach. The rest of the meal was quiet and calm, with a conversation comprised of pointless talk for another hour before they finished.

They exited the restaurant to retrieve the Bentley from the valet after leaving the waiter with a more-than-generous tip. Makai was showcasing his fortune as much as he could, and Kyra was as content with the evening as she could be.

The day after graduation at the Hartwell residence was full of celebration. Now that Quentin had graduated from school, he would begin working for his father.

The grill was going: there were ribs, chicken, burgers and hot dogs, with side dishes and desserts covering the tables. The display of food could bring forth anyone's appetite. The music was loud, but not nearly as loud as the laughter. Everyone but the adults filled the pool, the Jacuzzi or one of the poolside deck chairs. Everyone was more than enjoying themselves—everyone but Justin.

Justin was still down in the dumps about his breakup with Kyra, and his mother's asking him where Kyra was and whether she was coming didn't help. Nor did the busy signal he got every time he dialed Kyra's number. He was sitting on one of the poolside chairs watching the party unfold before his eyes when he was approached by Michael.

"What's up with you, man? You're over here looking all depressed when we're all out here having fun." Dripping with water from his recent dip in the pool, he took his seat in an empty chair beside his friend.

"I'm thinking."

"Oh God, it's about Kyra, isn't it?"

"Shut up. You moped for Natasha and she wasn't even your girl. Don't get me started."

"Aww, nigga, whatever. Yeah I moped. So? I got over that shit, but I never said it was easy. I really cared about that girl."

"Well, I *love* Kyra. I don't know what to do, man. This shit doesn't feel right. Like now. Right now. She should be here but she's not."

"And I doubt she will be."

"Really, you think?"

"She's the only girl I know who would trip off finding out that her man has cash."

"It's the principle of the matter, Mike. All money matters aside. This is about trust." He was serious, unaffected by any jokes.

"I know, I know."

"You know she thinks I've been messing with Veronica? Ain't that some shit?"

"Hell yeah."

"Then she found out about how I was dancing with Angela at prom. She was trippin' off that, too. It was only a few dances! I've been trying to call her but she won't answer. I always get a busy signal."

"Yeah, I saw you with Angela. Isn't she that girl who you said was a superfreak and she could do that trick with her tongue and..." Michael started. He was slowly slipping back into his old mentality.

"Yeah, that's her."

"Damn. I wish I could've got a dance with her...."

"But what I'm trippin' off is that she is trippin' off me with other females, but when we were at Q's graduation she said something like 'you're just like him.' And she wouldn't tell me who 'he' was. Who is 'him'?" Justin was growing angry at the memory.

"Damn! I know who she's talking about!" Michael exclaimed.

"Stop playing, Mike." His voice was still dull.

"Nigga, I'm dead serious! I didn't want to have to tell you

this, but nigga, last night I was at the Orchidée Violette with a *fine* young lady and guess who I saw?"

"Kyra?"

"Yup, and she wasn't alone. She was with some GQ nigga. He looked like he was stacked. Pushed a Bentley and everything. Plus, I mean, we both know that Orchidée Violette is not a cheap date. You have to come in there ready to pay that big money. That's a guaranteed. Everybody knows that."

"You think he hit it?"

"Hell yeah."

Justin sat in silence, tightening his jaw in anger and then loosening it.

Michael went on, "I don't even know who the cat is, though. I never saw him around here before."

"You sure it was her?"

"I swear to God it was! I've been seeing the girl for how long, J? I think I know what she looks like." Justin didn't say a word, but his friend continued, "See, there is no sense in sitting around here all sad and shit. She is moving on and you should, too. And by the way, Veronica is throwing little glances your way—you might as well start with her. She already thinks you two had something, so hey, what the hell?" Michael advised with a pat on the back before making his way over to the food platters.

Justin turned his attention to Veronica, who was situated across from him at the other end of the pool in a chocolate and pink string bikini that fit her figure well. He got up and made his way through the party crowd. The thought of Kyra already with another man provided him with motivation for every step.

"Veronica, can I, uh…talk to you for a minute?"

"Sure. Girls, I'll be right back." Veronica informed her

friends in a normal tone, not one of bragging, before following Justin into his abode and into the empty den. It was so calm it seemed a world apart from the energetic crowd in the backyard.

"I'm glad you came over to me, because I need to talk to you, too," she confessed.

"About what?"

"About how I'm sorry. I was really trippin' and I was acting like such a bitch. What I did to you and Kyra was really messed up. I've been doing a lot of thinking about that. I want you to be happy, and I made you the complete opposite out of my own selfishness." Veronica's words were genuine and heartfelt, but for Justin it was too little, too late. The damage had already been done.

Still, he was caught off guard by her apology. It was unlike her to apologize for anything she ever did.

"So...what did you want to talk about?" she quizzed, breaking the uncomfortable silence.

"I actually wanted to talk about me and you. I want to give us another chance."

"What? Wait. Aren't you with Kyra?"

"No. We're not together anymore. I guess we weren't meant to be. But I think me and you...I think me and you might be. You're not the only one who's been thinking, sweetheart." He was lying, trying to turn on a little game.

"I don't know what to say."

"Say yes." His lowered voice changed the whole mood of the room.

Kyra was glued next to her telephone. She was awaiting Justin's call, but it never came. She dialed his number only for all her calls to go unanswered. She waited around all day and into the evening hours, intently watching the phone and hoping for it to ring. She'd made the decision last night after dinner with Makai to stay in Prince Paul. The temptation of Chicago was strangely intense, but she felt that staying on the island, where she would be close to Justin, was a worthy forfeit. Now she just needed to make things right between them, or at least make an effort to begin. It was time to start anew, and she was ready and willing to forgive.

She was alert when the doorbell rang, and she rushed from the living room to the door. She had hopes of finding Justin on the other side but only found Angel.

"Where have you been all day?"

"Here."

"Why didn't you come to the barbeque?"

"What barbeque?"

"Quentin's family had a barbeque today. Q is going to be working for his dad now."

"Oh, I didn't even know about it. Tell him congratulations for me?"

"Justin didn't tell you about it? Because if he didn't, he was supposed to. If I had known you didn't know, I would've told you." Angel even sounded somewhat annoyed at saying Justin's name.

"It's cool. He probably tried, but I've been havin' phone problems lately, so he probably couldn't get through. I just got it fixed today," Kyra lied, covering up the reason for her lack of knowledge concerning the barbeque.

"I brought you a plate." Angel handed over the aluminum-covered plate of food.

"Good. You saved me from cookin' dinner." She laughed.

"So, what are you doing tomorrow?"

"Oh, I gotta work. I think we got a new shipment comin' in."

"That's always exciting."

"Oh yes. Mmm, this is so good," Kyra commented as she started to pick at her plate of leftovers. "How was it?" She leaned over the island in the center of the kitchen and shoved another forkful of food into her mouth.

"It was really fun. It had its weird moments, though."

"Weird moments? Like what?"

"Like Justin and Veronica disappearing into the house *alone* for about fifteen minutes."

"Are you serious?" Kyra was serious as she peered up from her plate.

"Yeah."

"How *alone* were they?"

"*Too* alone."

"What were they doin'?"

"I have no idea. All I know is they went in together and came out holding hands. After that, they were around each other for the rest of the party. It was like they were joined at the hip."

"Well! There goes my appetite!" Kyra sounded disturbed by the information as she dropped her fork and pushed the plate away.

"I didn't mean to upset you."

"Kyra, where have you been? You're an hour late!" Regina shouted at Kyra as soon as she set foot in Butterfly. Her stay at Angel's had been a little too relaxing when she woke up late for work that morning.

"I'm so sorry, Regina!" She hurried to the back room with a cup of coffee in one hand and her bag in the other.

She returned from the back room after fixing herself in the mirror and making sure she looked presentable. She had to be on point. No one would listen to a salesgirl talk about clothes if she looked a wreck.

Kyra worked hard that day, with Regina on her back more than usual—a punishment for being late, she was sure. She straightened shelves, helped customers, worked the fitting room area and even did a little inventory. She was grateful when her boss finally gave her a break and let her work the register. Or so she thought.

The door to the store opened, ringing the chime that alerted employees of a new customer, and let a gust of wind blow inside. The cool air hit Kyra, who sat at the register station reading a *Vogue* magazine to pass the downtime. She glanced up, the breeze drawing her attention from her magazine for a moment to see the new customers. She looked back down at the magazine only to do a double take: Veronica had just strolled in, and Justin was at her side.

Kyra put her head back down in her magazine, as if seeing them together didn't bother her when in reality it did. She sat at the resister, glancing at her magazine and then up at Justin and Veronica as they walked through the store selecting items with their sick lovey-dovey attitudes and public displays of affection.

She was sure she would gag when they approached the cash register, but both Justin and Veronica acted as though they didn't even know her.

"Your total is $1569.22." She announced their total with an attitude.

"I got it." Justin reached for his wallet and pulled out a wad of cash.

"Aww, baby that is so sweet." Veronica cooed as she planted a peck on his face.

"Here are your bags. Thanks for shopping at Butterfly."

Kyra handed over their things with the fakest smile she could manage on her face.

She watched as Justin and Veronica walked out of the store hand in hand, Justin whispering in her ear and Veronica girlishly giggling. She couldn't tear her eyes off them until she watched them drive off in his baby blue convertible.

"Regina, can I have a break?"

"I shouldn't give you one since you were late, but go ahead. It's slow right now anyways."

Kyra ran to the employee bathroom and locked the door behind her. She leaned her body against the door as she began to cry. Seeing Justin with Veronica made her want him back that much more.

Within seconds of arriving home from work Kyra was in her bedroom. Her luggage set was out on her bed, full of clothes and everything else she planned to take with her. It was Tuesday night. She was just in time to make Makai's deadline. Kyra was able to steer clear of an argument, since her mother saw Kyra's getaway as something she, too, could take advantage of.

"What are you doin' here?" She wiped her eyes to make it appear as though she were all right.

"I came by to talk to you for a minute. The door was unlocked...." Justin studied her luggage resting on her bed. "Going somewhere?"

"Does it look like I'm goin' somewhere?" she snapped.

"Where are you going?"

"Home for a while."

"Are you going with *him?*"

"It's none of your business *who* I'm goin' with."

"Who is he, anyway? Please do tell, because I don't recall you mentioning nobody to me during our relationship."

"You got some nerve! There was a *whole lot* of shit you never *mentioned* to me durin' our relationship!"

"Whatever, Kyra."

"And since you're so damn curious, he *used* to be my man."

"Oh, so you had me down here and him back up in Chicago?"

"No, it's not like that. Me and Makai are just...complicated. And I know you ain't talkin'. Don't even get me started on that." He sat silent in one of her wicker chairs as she continued, "It just makes me think more and more that you two had somethin' goin' the whole time."

"I told you she kissed me that night! But yeah, now things between me and her are different." His admission came without shame.

"I could see that today when you brought the bitch to my *job*. You were sittin' up there like you didn't even know me. Like I was nobody!" Her voice rose when she turned to face him.

"I didn't bring her there on purpose. She likes to shop there, and I was taking her shopping, so we went there. That's not a crime." He lied. He'd known exactly what he was doing when he took Veronica into Butterfly that day.

"Out of all the stores on that island, though, you had to come to mine? Be serious."

There was a slight pause before she started again. "You're really with her now, aren't you?" She posed the question in almost a whisper. She already knew the truth.

Justin didn't want to tell of his new relationship. It wasn't like he truly wanted to be with Veronica, but after what Michael had told him he was determined to show Kyra that two could play that game.

"Yeah, she's my girl."

"That's all I needed to know."

"We need to talk about some things, though. I mean, I know me and you aren't straight right now, but even if we aren't together anymore, we can still be friends, right?"

"Friends?" She gave him a look as though he were insane.

"Yeah, just like we were before. You know, friends?"

Kyra just stood there and stared at Justin, biting her lip and holding in the impulse to shed a tear.

"I tried calling you for the past few days...."

"I know. I was waitin' for your call yesterday, but I guess you were too busy makin' out with *Veronica* to call me, so it's okay."

"We were not 'making out.' I mean, we...but...anyways... why were you waiting for my call?"

"No reason now. The shit doesn't matter anymore. It's as done as we are." Her tone was low and angry as she closed her suitcases and locked them.

"So you're really about to go with him, huh?" He gave her luggage another look.

"I have no reason to stay," she whispered, locking her eyes with his.

"Am I interrupting something?" Makai said from where he leaned against the door, puffing on a sweet-smelling cigar. His gun was purposely on display where it hung on his waist.

"No, baby, it's nothin'," Kyra cooed with her eyes still on Justin. Justin glanced at Makai and then back at Kyra, and his eyes grew angry.

"You want me to get those bags for you, baby girl?" Makai offered his assistance as he walked over to her belongings.

"Yes, please. That would be so sweet." She mocked Veronica's tone and movements from earlier that day in the boutique.

Kyra turned her attention back to Justin once Makai had left her bedroom. She didn't know what to say and was once again faced with a goodbye.

"You're right. It looks like you don't have a reason to stay, but you got every reason in the world to go. Bye, *baby girl.*" Justin bitterly ended their conversation before walking out of the room and, as far as Kyra could tell, out of her life.

CHAPTER 17

The next day Kyra awoke to a bedroom full of bright sunshine. She rolled over expecting to feel Makai's body next to hers, but he was gone.

"Makai?" She called out his name as she glanced around the room. She rolled out of bed and tiptoed down the stairs to the bottom floor, calling out to Makai and getting nothing but silence for an answer.

"Oh great, I'm stuck here alone," she mumbled to herself, already unhappy with being stuck indoors. She'd had plans, and now they were on hold. How long they would be that way she didn't know.

Television was interesting but only for so long. The radio bored her even faster, and those seemed to be the only options. She grabbed the menu and decided to order room service, something she was more than grateful for, then made a discovery that nearly saved her sanity.

Club floor nine: the answer to her prayers. Kyra studied the map of the atrium located on the ninth floor of the plaza, which connected the east and west towers with a skylit garden. It had so much to offer: an indoor basketball court, a fitness center, a putting green, a sauna, outdoor and indoor pools, a library, a cybercafe, a business center and conference area, a garden, a running track and a sundeck.

She practically ran out the door to the club floor. It was perfect at the time, but even that eventually grew to be a bore.

Four days had gone by, and Kyra hadn't been out of the Grand Plaza or talked to anyone besides Makai. It was torture for her to watch Makai come and go as he pleased. Most of the time he only found his way home during the early-morning hours.

"Kai, I need to get out of this house."

"Not yet. Roscoe's funeral is tomorrow."

"So? Let me go with you then. I knew him, too."

"No."

"Why not?"

"I don't need to explain it to you in specifics. Just know that when it's safe I'll let you know."

"And when will it be safe?" Her voice rose and she threw her fork down on her plate in a tantrum. He didn't answer. "Exactly—never. I'm not stayin' here anymore. I can do what I want and I'm tired of this...."

Makai suddenly got up from his seat and was inches from her face. He grabbed her by her arm and yanked her from her chair.

"Kyra, I swear, if you leave this apartment...." His tone was fierce, and he spoke with such intensity it frightened her.

"Let go of my arm. You're hurtin' me," she whimpered. She was no longer as bold as she had been only minutes ago.

"I'll be back later." He let go of her arm, but his eyes still held their hard glare.

"No, wait..." She touched his arm only to have him snatch it away. "Makai! Don't go! Kai!" she cried out to him as she watched him slam the door on his way out.

She slumped down in her chair and put her head in her hands. She was alone once again, left in the apartment while he was free to do whatever he wished. She threw one of the glasses against the window in frustration, sending crystal scattering across the floor. She stared at her reflection in the window and at the skyline beyond it. Tomorrow she was going out no matter what he said.

Kyra slid on her pink sunglasses as she stepped out into the Chicago day and looked back at the Grand Plaza building. It was such a relief to finally be free of her prison.

She wandered for blocks until she found a pay phone. She punched in a number, and by the fourth ring she was ready to hang up when all of a sudden she heard a familiar voice on the other end.

"Hello?"

"Tasha?"

"Kyra?"

"Yeah, girl, it's me. Did I wake you?" She pressed the phone harder onto her ear to hear over the noisy traffic.

"Yeah."

"Too bad. Get up."

"Man, I'm about to go..." Natasha sighed. Her only wish was to get back to sleep.

"No! Tasha, wait. Come to the corner of East Chicago Ave and West Huron Street."

"Oh my God!" Natasha let out a gasp.

"See you in a few." Kyra chuckled as she put the phone on the hook.

"Hey, girl!" Natasha happily greeted her friend as she pulled her green Altima up to curb, slowing just enough that Kyra could hop in.

"Hey! What the hell took you so long?"

"I had to get ready! I wasn't about to come out looking all hit."

"You do any other day."

"Ha ha, real funny! So how long have you been here? Where're you staying? You know you can save a whole lot of money if you just crash at my crib."

"I've been here for about a week now, and as far as my mom knows, I *am* stayin' with you," she told Natasha.

"Well, she sure hasn't called….and never mind that you've been here a week and you mean to tell me you're just now getting around to seeing me?"

"Kai's been trippin'. He got me up in the house all the time talkin' 'bout, 'don't go nowhere,' blah, blah. I got tired of that shit. So here I am. Out and about."

"Makai? Don't tell me y'all…"

"Yeah, I know, I know." Kyra didn't want to hear a lecture. Her mother had given her enough to last a lifetime.

"So you're back with him now? What happened to Justin? I thought y'all were doing good?"

"No…I dunno. But I'll tell you all about it over…ice cream?"

As the girls ate their Dairy Queen ice cream, they decided to take a walk in a nearby park.

"Damn, that's messed up fa real."

"Tell me about it."

"Well, at least you're back at home for the summer. Regardless of why, I can't complain. I'm happy to see ya, girl."

"Same here."

"So, what do you wanna do now?" Natasha asked as she tossed her garbage into a nearby trash can.

"We can just chill at your house. I don't want anyone to see me out and it get back to Kai. Me bein' here is bad enough."

The girls had just begun their walk back to the car when without warning, Kyra stopped dead in her tracks. There she was, only a few feet away. She looked slightly different, but Kyra knew it was her. She could see right through all that Maybelline and Feria.

Mercedes was standing in the park in yet another ill-fitting ensemble. Her hair, which had once been a light brown color and straight, was now red and curly, the spirals hanging around her face, which held too many cosmetic products.

"Kyra, come on..." Natasha trailed off when she saw what had her friend frozen in place.

A baby girl occupied with a bouncing orange ball sat on the grass next to Mercedes. It was obvious that she was her daughter by the way she called out "mama" and stretched her hands to the sky, begging to be picked up. Kyra watched as Mercedes picked up the small girl and held her in her arms, leaning her on her hip. The child's resemblance to Reggie was striking.

Kyra's blood felt like it was on fire. She wanted to attack Mercedes right then, even though Mercedes had three other girls with her, some of whom Kyra recognized from her days at John Marshall. The way Kyra felt just now, she could take all of them, plus one.

"Don't do it, Kyra. I feel you, just not here." Natasha calmed her friend as though she could read her mind.

"Let's go," Kyra mumbled as she walked off in the other direction to avoid being seen by Mercedes or her crew. She didn't need Mercedes running her mouth to Makai and creating problems.

By the time the girls reached Natasha's house, the mood had

taken a complete one-eighty. The girls gossiped and laughed as they watched movie after movie. Kyra loved how Natasha could always change her mood. She reminded her of Angel in a way, and thinking of Angel led her to think of the island and, of course, Justin.

Kyra stared at the television. The images of *Love and Basketball* ran across the screen, but she was watching a whole other movie in her mind. She had flashbacks of the good times with Justin.

"Ay, Tasha."

"Yeah…" Natasha was engrossed in the movie.

"You got somethin'?"

"Something like what?" She shoved a handful of popcorn into her mouth. Her eyes were still watching the flick.

"You know…*somethin'*…"

"Oh! I got you! Hell yeah, I got something!" She was excited as she rummaged under her bed, coming up with a bottle of tequila and two blunts.

"That's what I'm talkin' about."

"I almost forgot I even had this under there."

"See, where would you be without me?"

Being intoxicated took Kyra's mind off things, until she discovered it was nine o'clock when she awoke from her nap.

"Oh shit." She had been gone for nine hours. Kyra rushed over to the bed and began to shake Natasha. Not a second short of three minutes later, her efforts paid off.

"What?" Her eyes were still closed as she let out a groan.

"It's nine o'clock."

"So wake me up at ten." Natasha waved her away only to realize what Kyra meant. "Oh shit!"

"Yeah. Come on. We gotta go. If Kai finds out he's gonna trip!"

* * *

"Kai?...Kai? Where are you? I'm home!" Kyra's voice echoed through the dark penthouse as she nervously felt her way into the living room. She was facing the windows for light, when Makai crept up behind her and jerked her by her hair so hard she was sure he could have torn it from her scalp had he wanted to.

"Ah! Ow..." Her voice was feeble as a result of the pain she was in.

"Shut up." He made his demand through clenched teeth as the lights of the penthouse flicked on. "Where the fuck where you?"

"Out."

"Where were you? Don't play no fucking games wit' me, Kyra." He demanded an answer as he tightened his grip on her hair.

CHAPTER 18

"Kyra!" Makai shouted from where he stood at the bottom of the stairs. It was fairly late in the evening when he finally arrived home. Kyra was surprised to hear a noise in the usually quiet apartment, and at first it startled her. She thought it was the TV show she was watching or that she was hearing things, but when his voice rang out through the apartment again—this time sounding a tad impatient—she knew it was him for sure.

"You still tired of being inside all the time?"

"Yes," she uttered from the top of the staircase. She didn't want to come any closer to the man below.

"Good." He was unemotional. "I'm taking you out. Go put something nice on."

"Okay." She watched Makai, mystified by his sudden generosity. He acted as if nothing had happened between them within the past two weeks.

"Looking sexy." He offered his compliment as he leaned against the doorframe observing her outfit. "I know you're mad at me. Don't think I forgot about all the shit that happened between us." Kyra still stood silent as she watched him in the mirror. "And I know you're mad about me being gone for a minute."

"Two weeks is a little more than a minute, don't you think?"

"You know how it goes, Kyra. Don't act new to the game."

He took his stance behind her and rubbed her arms with his hands in an effort to soothe her. Her eyes examined her arms as she remembered the bruises he had caused her days ago.

"I'm sorry."

"Mmm, hmm."

"Oh, you don't believe me?"

"No, Kai, I really don't."

"Does this make you believe me?" He pulled out a dazzling diamond necklace. A heart pendant drenched in diamonds dangled from a chain that was also studded with diamonds.

Kyra's eyes lit up. The necklace was beautiful, and no matter how angry she was at Makai she couldn't hide that. As soon as he detected her reaction, he knew he had her right where he wanted her. All was forgiven with diamonds.

"Kai..."

"I know you didn't think I would be gone all that time and come back with nothing for my princess." He clasped the necklace around her neck.

"Thank you."

"Don't thank me. You deserve that and more. I've been putting you through hell since you got here." As she admired his gift, he went on, "You see that heart? It represents my love for you. It's made of diamonds, and you know what they say."

"What?"

"Diamonds are forever, just like how I'll love you forever." His voice was lowered to a near whisper. He then turned to her and pulled her closer, gently planting his lips on hers. "I missed you."

"I missed you, too." Even with everything that had happened, he was the only company she kept, and without him around things tended to become lonesome.

Suddenly a jingle rang throughout the room. His two-way was going off. His eyes instantly tore away from hers to the rectangle that hung on his hip. He put his earpiece to his ear and began to talk, leaving Kyra to worship her new gift.

After a warm shower, Kyra put on some pajamas and listened to the Quiet Storm on a local radio station. An hour and a half after his two-way had rung, Makai left and was still nowhere to be found. She pushed back the worrisome feeling coming over her. She didn't want to worry just yet.

As she noticed the lights of the skyline become less intense and the dark night sky brighten into a light blue, it hit her that daylight had come and Makai still hadn't come home. With how things had been lately, he probably wouldn't anytime soon.

After another hour of waiting, she decided that it would be wise to head up to the bedroom. She lay there in the silk-covered bed but couldn't find a position that her body found comfortable. Sleep was not coming at all easily.

Kyra clicked on the television in hopes of finding something to watch that would make her eyes heavy. She flicked through hundreds of channels, finding only early-morning church programs and infomercials. She'd never been the religious type, and a product that would bake perfectly shaped cakes or remove unsightly hair didn't interest her. The next-best thing was the news. She figured that to be her best option.

Kyra turned to channel seven, ABC, just in time to see a breaking story. *Hmm, this may be more interestin' than I thought,* Kyra mused as she propped herself up in expectation.

"Hi, this is Judy Hsu reporting with a breaking story. In the early hours this morning, a body was found in the southwest branch of the Chicago River. The body was discovered by a family boating on the river for the upcoming Fourth of July weekend. The body has been currently identified as Robert Johnson, a notorious member of the Chi-town's Finest gang, run by suspected drug dealer Reggie Mills. Police currently have no suspects in the case." Her stare was straight ahead at the camera. It was as if she were talking directly to Kyra. *"Police believe that this was a homicide and that it is somehow tied to violence at a local club earlier last night. The incident occurred at a club run by Makai "Kai" Jackson."*

Kyra paced the living room all afternoon on virtually no sleep as she gazed out the windows at the city. She wondered where Makai was and if he was okay. The worry grew tiresome for her, and before she knew it, she was curled up asleep on one of the tan couches.

She shivered when she felt a hand touch her and wake her from her light sleep. She jumped when her vision focused on the individual before her, and she hugged him tight.

"Hey, baby girl," Makai murmured as he ran his hands over her back.

"Hey."

"You were waiting up for me, huh?"

"Yeah, what happened last night? Are you okay?"

"Yeah, I'm straight."

"I saw what happened last night on the news."

"Those mothafuckas shot up my damn club." He sounded mad as he started toward the stairs.

"What happened?" She was curious as she followed in his steps.

"A business talk just got heated."

For the next couple of days, Makai didn't leave the house, and neither did Kyra. It was nice to finally spend quality time together without business somehow being in the way, and Kyra thoroughly enjoyed having the company.

Wednesday night Makai was preparing to go out. What he did when he was gone for so long, not returning home sometimes for days, Kyra began to wonder, but never dared to ask.

She tied a robe around her body and made her way back to the bedroom, where she saw Makai coming out of the closet, looking fresh as always.

"I'm about to be out. I got something for you, though." Makai pulled a silver cell phone from his pocket. "It's my cell. You can use it to call Tasha or whatever, but *do not* answer *any* of my calls, you got me? A few of my business peeps call this line, so don't do nothing stupid."

"Okay." She agreed to the conditions while drying her dripping hair with a towel.

"Don't get nosey, Kyra," he cautioned.

"A'ight, a'ight. Damn, I said okay."

"A'ight. Now, you can go out but make sure you take Bryce and Rick witchu. You do something stupid like try that sneaking-out shit again, trust me, you will want to deal wit' me over either of them. Oh, and don't bring anyone here. I like to keep a low profile and Natasha got a big-ass mouth. I work hard to maintain it, so don't fuck that up for me."

"Okay Kai, I got it."

"Don't go crazy wit' going out, either. I'm not sure how shit is right now. Honestly, if you can help it, stay home."

"Okay baby, I got it," Kyra replied. She was annoyed by his paranoia and rambling on.

"A'ight then, I'm out. Love you."

"Love you, too."

CHAPTER 19

Over the course of the next couple of days, Kyra visited Natasha. They would go to the mall, the movies or one of a few popular restaurants in the city. Any time alone with Natasha was impossible with Kai's bodyguards following Kyra's every move.

"Kyra, I really need to tell you something..." Natasha said one day in the few moments they managed to steal in the bathroom. Her voice was low as she stepped closer to Kyra, only to be interrupted by a knock at the door and the body-guard's deep voice from outside.

Kyra sighed and ran her hands through her blond dyed hair.

"We're coming! Okay—" Natasha snapped back, trying to stall to tell the news, but she gave up after another pound on the door. "Never mind. Come on, let's just go before they really start trippin'." She sighed again and snatched her purse from the sink counter before walking out of the bathroom. Kyra hadn't paid any attention to her friend's tone.

After an afternoon movie, Kyra returned home to relax and prepare a snack for herself. Natasha had been acting funny lately, and when Kyra asked her what was wrong, she would never give her a true answer, just a "nothing." Kyra figured maybe they should spend a little time apart for a few days. She had just walked into the kitchen to make a sandwich when the cell phone Makai lent her vibrated on her hip for the twentieth time that day.

For the past few days the phone would ring and vibrate constantly, but she fought off every impulse to answer. The voice mailbox was becoming full.

She took the sleek phone and set it on the counter, focusing on the task at hand. She watched it vibrate again. She stared at the phone again for a moment, picked it up and then set it back on the counter only for it to vibrate again seconds later.

Kyra went into the living room with her plate in one hand and the phone in the other. She took a seat in the black leather chair, and set her plate on the shining surface of the center table. She leaned back in the chair, still eyeing the phone, staring as it vibrated in her hand. Her curiosity finally won and she answered the call.

"Hey, boo, I've been trying to reach you for grip. Why haven't you come by to see me?" the female voice from the other end purred in a sexual tone.

"This ain't Kai."

"What? Who is this?"

"This is his wifey! Who is this?"

Without another word, the girl hung up, and the dial tone buzzed from her end of the line.

Kyra then took things a step further and checked the messages that were piling up in the voice mail. She discovered that almost every message was from a different woman. Candi, Yolanda, Kim, Audrey, Brenda, Felicia, Sharon, Karen, Tonya, Carla, Marina and Juanita had each left their voices behind in a message. Makai apparently had more than his share of girls, and as if that weren't bad enough, it only got worse.

Her blood pressure shot through the roof at the last message.

"Hey papi, it's me, Cedes. My man ain't here right now and I'm *all alone.* I even got on your favorite set, the red one. It's been too long since I saw you last, baby. Word on the street is you brought that bitch Kyra home with you. I thought you were better than that? And if you are, you need to scoop me up and prove it to me, if you know what I mean.

"I miss, you baby. Maybe next time I'm home alone you can come keep me company. Bye."

Kyra was in the middle of packing when she heard the front door open and close. Makai was home. He wobbled up the stairs, his breath carrying the scent of alcohol and his shirt carrying the scent of perfume as he made his way into his bedroom, where he came across the surprising sight.

"Whatchu doin'?" he queried at the sight of the scattered suitcases and clothes.

"I'm leavin', that's what I'm doin'," Kyra said as she came from inside the closet with a handful of clothes to be packed away.

"And just where do you think you're going?"

"I dunno. Natasha's...home...I dunno." She was unsure of where exactly she was headed as she stuffed more clothes into an already-bulging bag.

"I leave one minute and we're good and I come home and you ready to bounce?"

"Just like I leave one minute and you ready to be up in another female, right?" Kyra huffed.

"Whatchu talkin' about?"

"You know what the fuck I'm talkin' about! Here, take this. A lot of people need you right now." She picked up the phone from where it lay on the floor and threw it at him. Even in his tipsy state he managed to catch it.

"So you answered my phone?" She kept packing as he looked over the phone.

"I heard all the messages your li'l hoes left, too!"

"I told you not to answer my phone! How hard is that? Huh? How hard is it for you just to do what I say!"

By the next morning, Kyra's things were rearranged back in the closet and her suitcases were missing. Makai had an assortment of roses delivered to the apartment with a note of apology attached, but as usual, he was nowhere to be found. Roses, fine chocolate candies, jewelry, furs and other gifts started to come like clockwork. They came as often as the abuse. Any little thing, any little mistake, any little reason seemed to be enough to set Makai off, giving him enough reason in his eyes to place his hands on her. Every time his abuse got worse, the gifts became bigger. So big, in fact, that Kyra now owned a silver Mercedes-Benz. She believed it was a cruel joke and refused to drive it.

CHAPTER 20

Kyra was in bed one night, the television off, as she sat up with her knees to her chest. Her gaze was fixed on the phone that rested on the nightstand. Makai had warned her not to use it, and she knew what would happen if she disobeyed his orders and he found out. The choices and consequences bounced around in her head: *Do it, or don't do it.*

Kyra dialed, held the phone to her ear and listened to it ring on the other end. It was already on the fourth ring and there was still no answer. She glanced at the clock on the wall and noticed that it was late and recalled that it was a weeknight. She figured her mother was asleep, with Matthew, or spending the night at the hotel, and all hopes of reaching her were crushed. As she went to place the phone on the hook, she didn't know how long it would be before the next time she could muster the courage to call.

"Hello?" Geneva greeted. Her tone was fixed to appease any caller when Kyra heard the unexpected voice of her mother. Her mouth felt as if it were wired shut, and all she could manage was silence. The only courage she needed now was the courage to speak.

"Hello...? Hello?" her mother repeated into the phone, waiting for a reply.

"Mom?" Kyra's voice cracked on her response.

"Kyra, Kyra, is that you?"

"Yeah, it's me, Mom."

"Oh, I'm so happy to hear from you! I've been trying to reach you at Natasha's forever, but you two are always out. You two aren't getting into anything you don't need to be in, are you?" Geneva, no longer Mrs. Jones, rambled on with excitement.

"You've been tryin' to reach me at Tasha's?" Kyra asked, confused. Natasha had specifically told Kyra that her mother hadn't contacted her, and Charlene, Natasha's mom, hadn't mentioned anything.

"Yeah, ever since you got there. Well, when I find the time— you know how things are down here. I figure you're almost grown, though. You don't need me checkin' up on you all the time." Geneva sounded happy as she talked.

"Oh."

"Why did you ask me that? That is where you're staying, isn't it?" Her mother was starting in on another interrogation, sounding somewhat suspicious for a moment.

"Where else would I be stayin'?" she lied. She didn't want to risk hearing the reaction she was sure to hear when her mother discovered where she had really been all this time. "So how are things down there?"

"Things are good. Business is really thriving, and Matthew and I are engaged now! Can you believe it?"

"Fa real?" Kyra tried her best to sound enthusiastic, but her voice rang false.

"Yup. I tried reaching you. I left a few messages to call me with Charlene, but I didn't get in touch with you to tell you until now. You and Natasha seem to be having a ball up there."

"When's the wedding?" Kyra inquired.

"We didn't set a date yet. Truthfully, I wanted you to help me plan it when you come home in August." Kyra didn't like the idea, but she couldn't manage words to protest it. "Kyra, are you there?" Her mother's question brought the dead line back to life.

"Yeah, yeah, sorry. Congratulations with everythin'." She kept up her attempt to sound upbeat.

"Thanks, sweetie. *So*, how are things up there?"

With that question, Kyra broke down. The reason why she didn't know, but she couldn't stop the tears from coming.

"Kyra?" Geneva sounded worried when she picked up the sniffles from the other end of the phone line.

"Mom, things are so bad. I want to come home. Things are so bad...." She softly cried into the phone.

"Baby doll, what's wrong?"

Kyra became as alert as a cat when she heard the front door open and shut, signaling that Makai was back from running the streets.

"Mom, I gotta go."

"Kyra, wait...."

"What are you doing?" Makai asked as he entered the room. Kyra had returned the phone to the cradle only seconds before he made an entrance.

"Nothin', just about to go to bed." She clicked the light on her side of the bed off and turned her back to him so that he couldn't see her moist eyes as he prepared to join her.

She lay there all night with her head spinning. Her mother's words regarding her undelivered messages didn't make any sense, and she wanted answers. She needed them, and little did she know she would get them soon enough. The only question was, was she ready to hear them? Could she handle the truth?

It was a humid day. Clouds blotted out the sun, but the heat was just as powerful as if it were visible and shining. Makai woke Kyra up that afternoon, demanding more than asking that she accompany him to the pool. Even with only three and a half hours of sleep, she didn't dare refuse his plan and made sure to quickly change into one of her many swimsuits and get ready to go.

At the pool, Makai glided in the water while Kyra sat poolside in a lounge chair, pretending to read. She kept her eye on him over the top of her *Glamour* magazine. She had an inexplicable suspicion that he was somehow responsible for Natasha's deception.

Too hot to sit out any longer and realizing that Kai didn't seem to be coming out of the pool anytime soon, Kyra waded in. She swam over to him as he soaked in a small whirlpool tucked behind a waterfall.

"It's hot as hell out here."

"Yeah, it is," she agreed as she took her seat next to him.

They sat quietly behind the waterfall, looking at the distorted images through the water. Her eyes kept darting to his face and then away, looking straight ahead. She wanted the answer without having to ask, but her distress went unnoticed, or so she thought.

"Speak your mind, baby girl."

"Kai...baby...what did you tell my mom about me comin' to Chicago?" she cooed, trying to sound innocent while probing at what she wanted to find out. She was dancing around the information she truly wanted to uncover.

"Why you ask that?"

"See, I talked to her yesterday and…" Her mumbled words made her sound ashamed of what she had done.

"You called her from the house?"

"No."

"Where, then?"

"A pay phone down some blocks."

"Did Bryce or Rick go witchu?"

"No. They went to get some food or somethin', I think." She lied again, surprised at how well her mind was adapting to the art of trickery and how quickly her mind managed to spit out a lie.

"Mmm, hmm. Don't sneak off without them. I told you about that shit before." He looked at her from the corner of his eye. He undoubtedly knew she was lying, but he gave her a break. After all, it was her mother.

"I'm sorry, baby."

She had to bite her lip and look away to keep from screaming out for him to give her an answer that very second.

"I didn't tell her anything. Think about it—when have I talked to her?"

"True…true…"

"Tasha is the only person I know of who's been talking to your mom."

"What? I don't get it."

"You wouldn't."

"Tell me?" she begged as she grabbed ahold of his arm.

"It's simple. I paid Natasha and her momma to play along and say that you were staying wit' 'em. Charlene called your mom up one day at her office, chitchatted wit her, and next thing you know you were on your way here wit' me. You handled the rest of the work from there, really. I knew you weren't really dumb enough to stay on that island."

"You paid them?" Kyra wasn't able to grasp the news right away. She couldn't believe what she was hearing. When she first saw Natasha and Charlene, they'd acted as though her being in town came as a surprise to them.

"It was business, fair and square. But the answer is yes, I paid them."

"How much?"

"What?" A passing girl in a string biking had snatched his attention from the topic at hand.

"How much did you pay them?" Her voice was firm.

"Five grand each."

"Five grand each...five grand each..."

"That's how it goes, baby girl." Makai pecked her cheek with his lips and then swam out from under the waterfall.

After a long shower back at the suite, Kyra returned to the bedroom, where Makai was up, eating a bowl of sweet cereal and watching an old episode of *The Sopranos*. She disappeared into the closet only to come out in an all-black outfit. Her hair, which had grown out, was pulled back into a ponytail and she appeared ready to go out, not to go to bed.

"Where you trying to go?"

"I need to go see Tasha real quick," she said. She was going regardless of what he said.

"For what?"

"I just need to talk to her, that's all."

Kyra's Benz screeched to a halt in front of Natasha's home that night. The pounding music system that was loud enough to wake the neighborhood was silenced when she took the key from the ignition.

Kyra jumped out of the car, slamming the door, and marched her way to the front door of her traitor. The house looked dark inside, but she didn't care if anyone was asleep. She was on a mission.

She planted herself on the porch for about two minutes, ringing the doorbell and pounding on the door as if she were the police. A few neighbors were stirring in reaction to the commotion outside, but she wasn't worried. In that type of neighborhood, nobody was quick to call the Chicago PD.

Natasha swung the door open, and her face looked disgruntled by the obnoxious disturbance. "You better get the fuck on...Kyra? What are you doing here? And why the hell are you knocking on my door like you the police?"

She opened the door as a signal for Kyra to step inside, but Kyra simply stood on the last step, glaring at her friend. They both stood in the night on the porch in silence, neither one knowing what to say.

Just as Natasha was getting around to posing a question, Kyra lunged at her without warning and pulled her down onto the lawn. She stumbled and fell to the ground, taking Kyra with her.

On the ground, Kyra was like a wild animal, clawing and slapping while keeping a tight grip on her betrayer's hair. Natasha fought back the best she could without injuring her. She just wanted Kyra to get off her, not hurt her. The girls rolled in the grass, grunting and yelling, drawing attention to their squabble.

It was an even fight.

Natasha straddled Kyra's body and lifted her fist in the air as though she was going to strike again when she stopped herself. "What the fuck is your problem!" she shouted through the heaving of her chest.

"You sold me out...." Kyra was exhausted from the exchange of blows and only muttered a reply.

"What?" Natasha softened her eyes from their hard glare to a look of bewilderment.

Her body flinched when the sprinkler system switched on, soaking the lawn and the girls.

"You sold me out for Kai. You and your mom lied for him," Kyra muttered again, choking on the water that was splashing in her face.

Natasha regained her footing and let Kyra go. She looked down at her friend, who was rubbing her jaw, and looked down the block, becoming aware of the small crowds that had formed. Her neighbors were motionless in the privacy of their porches as they gazed at the girls for their own personal source of entertainment after dark.

"Come on." Natasha reached down to help Kyra up so they could head indoors, but Kyra refused her helping hand and got up on her own. Natasha knew they couldn't discuss anything involving someone as made as Makai out in the open like that. Anyone could be listening.

Once they were inside, Natasha slammed the door shut and stormed through the living room. Kyra followed her closely while keeping enough distance between them.

"You're lucky my ma is working third shift tonight," she warned as she picked up one of her mother's cigarette cartons from a side table next to couch. She put the Newport cigarette to her lip and lit it, puffing on the tobacco and blowing the smoke up to the ceiling. Kyra just stood there silently, scowling at her friend as her body dripped.

"You're fucking crazy."

"Bitch, fuck you."

"Oh, so I'm a bitch now?" Natasha asked with a surprised expression.

"Apparently you've been one."

She climbed the stairs to her room and Kyra followed.

"Not everyone has it easy like you do," Natasha stated as she took a seat on the edge of her bed. Her back was to Kyra as she bent over and snatched a used towel from the floor.

"Who the hell said I had it easy?"

"Please, Kyra, you've always been better off. Your mom has a good job and Makai spoils the hell out of you. Even when Marcus was here you always had more."

"Don't you dare bring my dad into this," Kyra warned. Her voice was harsh.

"And what do I have? A mom who works as an underpaid nurse and a dad who's locked up."

"So you did this shit out of jealousy? I thought you were better than that. And damn, I really thought I was worth more than five grand to you."

"You act like I did something horrible! I mean, he came to me and asked me for a favor one night and I said I would help him out. It was just to get you up here, and since he asked I assumed that must've been what you wanted. What the fuck is so bad about that?"

"What's bad about it is you been keepin' secrets from me! Especially on some shit like that! Then you tried to play it off like you didn't know I was here in the first place! Like me bein' with Kai was a surprise to you!"

"What did you want me to tell you? I mean, it's not even that big of a deal...."

"Tell me one thing."

"What?"

"Did you know how things would be once I got here?" she asked.

"Yeah, of course I did—shopping sprees galore."

"Did you know things would be like this?" She wiped the

remaining bit of makeup from her face. Natasha didn't move a muscle. "Look at me! See how it is. See how good I'm livin'. Look!" she screamed as she grabbed her friend by the shoulder, forcing her to see the bruises from a bad night at home.

Natasha's eyes welled up at the sight of Kyra's face. It was bare of makeup, and all scars and bruises were revealed. Kyra stood there, for the first time not ashamed for someone to see what Makai had done to her.

"Oh my God…" Natasha quietly gasped, reaching her hand out to touch her face, but Kyra smacked it away.

CHAPTER 21

It was storming heavily outside, the rainy season reminding island inhabitants of their vulnerability. Justin packed his things away in suitcases. He had to make his move and the time was now. With his parents out of town on a business trip in Mexico, it was all too perfect. Being the only person left in the house, he sent the household staff home, leaving him free of watchful eyes.

Being alone in the mansion was eerie. He was paranoid listening to the creaks and other odd noises he heard that he never used to when the mansion was full and bustling with workers or family. He shook off any strange feeling and continued to cram clothes into his bag, as a sudden flash of lightning and clap of thunder occurred.

"Going somewhere?" Veronica startled him from where she stood in the doorway of his bedroom.

"How did you get in here?"

"The door was open. I just came by to talk and see what you were up to," she said. Justin had been unhappy lately, and Veronica thought she knew why.

"Oh..." Justin awkwardly replied. He gripped the bag

tighter, remembering that it was there and that he had somewhere he needed to be. His eyes told his story.

He noticed her eyes filling with tears and tried to explain or offer some kind of apology or comfort.

"Veronica…"

"It's okay, Justin. You love her, so go to her. *Go* to her." Her words were soft as she caressed his cheek. Her legs shook with anxiety and she bit her lip.

He placed his hand on hers, moving it from where it rested on his face. A tear dropped from her eye as she managed to squeeze out the words "I understand."

Their tender moment was cut short when it was interrupted by the ringing of his phone.

"I'm here," Michael said.

"I'll be out in a minute."

"One."

Justin turned around to say goodbye to Veronica, but by then she was gone. She was out of his life without a goodbye, and he felt that things were best that way for her as well as for him.

Michael drove through the ferocious storm to a private hangar on the far side of Prince Paul. They made their way to the only open hangar to meet the pilot Michael had somehow rustled up. Justin took notice of the bags in Michael's hand but didn't get a chance to say anything before the pilot appeared from inside the plane.

"Taye, mi man," Michael greeted him, switching on his accent. It was clear that he and the pilot were on friendly terms.

"Good ta si ya, mi bredda. Dis is ya frind, ey?" Taye returned the greeting in a thick accent, his attention eventually focusing on the new face.

"Yah, dis him." Michael nodded toward his friend, who was quiet in anticipation.

"Wi betta git going if ya wan go tonight. Di storm is ongle gon' ta git worse, truss mi." Taye peered out at the pounding rain and strong winds with his hand on his white hat to keep it on his head.

Taye took his seat in the cockpit and started clicking the necessary switches to control the aircraft, while Michael and Justin took their seats in the cabin of the small private airplane. As the engines roared to life, Justin began to speak. "So I take it you're coming with me?" he asked, looking over at his friend as he fastened his seat belt.

"You didn't think I was about to let you go alone, did you? And miss an opportunity to see Tasha again? I don't think so."

Justin chuckled at his friend and shook his head. Michael had been slipping back into his old player lifestyle, but it was clear that even after a year, he had still it bad for Natasha.

Justin felt the plane creep forward and head toward the runway for takeoff. His senses were going wild. This was it. He was on his way. Nothing was going to stop him from getting to Kyra. Nothing would keep them apart anymore—nothing and no one.

Justin dialed Natasha's number and anxiously held the phone as it rang. He could hardly breathe as he hunched over the hotel desk. Someone answered on the other end, but he failed to recognize the voice.

"Hello, may I speak to Natasha, please?"

"Who?"

"Natasha?"

"Boy, don't cop no attitude with me! You little thugs these days think..." The woman started going off on a tangent. It didn't take long to figure out that it must be her mother.

"Ma...who is it? Give me the phone." Natasha's voice could be heard in the background as she retrieved the phone. "Who's this?"

"Tasha it's Justin."

"Oh hi.... Look, if you want me to tell Kyra anything else, then—"

"Actually, I'm in town, and I wanted to know where I could reach her. Do you know where she is?"

"No. I don't know," she lied, not wanting to help because of her own bitterness.

"Oh..." he sadly responded, with a moment of silence following.

Natasha was guilt ridden as she leaned her body against the kitchen counter. She tried to be stubborn to the best of her abilities, but she was unsuccessful in her efforts.

"Look, there's a party tonight at Club Pandemonium. It's down on South Michigan Ave. They hold it every year and it's real hype, so she should be there. That's the best I can do." She avoided giving Kyra's real address. Leading Justin to the Grand Plaza would be leading him into a death trap.

"Thanks," he said, jotting down the helpful information on a handy notepad.

"Listen, J, you gotta be careful if you find her. The nigga she's running with these days is no good. Trust me, I know what I'm talking about," she warned.

"A'ight I will. Here, I got somebody who wants to talk to you." Justin threw the phone in his friend's lap as he went to dress for the party.

"Hello?"

"Mike!" Natasha shrieked in delight at the sound of the voice on the other end.

* * *

Kyra sighed as she sat alone on one of the couches in the VIP section of the popular club. She sipped a glass of Raspberry Bacardi with Sprite as she nodded to the music. She was there physically, but mentally, she wasn't part of the scene. Not even the famous faces she spotted floating around the area could bring her back to life.

On the other hand, Makai seemed to be thoroughly enjoying himself. He was sitting on a couch across from her, seated next to the girl she had spotted the last time they went out clubbing.

Kyra was in the middle of sipping her cocktail when suddenly and without warning Makai tried to pull her into the party atmosphere.

"Come on, baby girl, dance for me," he tipsily requested.

"I don't feel like it."

"Come on…come on…"

She downed the rest of her drink in one swallow and looked him the eye with a hard look that told him she was getting tired of him bossing her around.

"Yeah…get up there." He was unsure how to interpret her look as he motioned her toward a wide platform that stretched across and above the dance floor.

Kyra looked at the other girls who were on the platform and how provocatively dressed they were. One girl even had on a see-through dress that between the length and sheerness, might as well have left her naked. By the way they moved and danced, combined with the way they looked, Kyra took them to be exotic dancers.

That was when she first discovered that her value had decreased in Makai's eyes. She glanced at the breathtaking girl whose name she didn't know and saw how she had a hawk's eye on her and Makai. She tried to put a name to the face out of the list she'd heard back when she'd listened to Makai's cell messages.

Makai held out his hand to help Kyra onto the platform, diverting her attention from the nameless girl. She gave him an ice-cold stare and took his hand, stepping onto the platform with the rest of the dancers. She wanted to prove that she wasn't scared of him and that his tricky actions wouldn't embarrass her the way she assumed he wanted. She was going to flip the script and put it down.

Kyra started to dance. She danced harder and with more sexuality than any other girl up there. Any male around had to take notice of her movements, and many of them did, but slyly, so as to not offend their boss. Kyra moved her hips and shook her butt so fast and with such a passion that even she was shocked. Makai appeared pleased and watched her rhythm from his seat on the couch next to one of his many mistresses with a look of lust. All eyes were on her.

She stayed on the platform and let her body sway slowly to the music. She didn't want to look out of place while she was trying to solve the mystery of who this person was. Then she saw his face. She was sure her heart stopped when they made eye contact. She could have sworn she had died and gone to heaven. There beneath her on the club's dance floor stood the person she had ached for, for so long. Chills ran through her body. It had been too long since she had been in his presence.

Justin and Kyra locked eyes for mere seconds as she mouthed his name and stopped moving. Everything felt like it was moving in slow motion. She was fixated on his face when she felt another pair of eyes on her. She forced herself to tear her eyes from his and look at Makai. His eyes were on her with a look of curiosity as she hustled off the dance platform to offer him an explanation before he had the opportunity to question her abnormal actions.

"Baby, I don't feel so good," she lied. Her talent for deception was improving.

"What's wrong? You look like you just saw a ghost."

"I dunno. I'm about to go to the bathroom, okay?" she said, fixing up her voice so that she would sound ill.

Kyra made her way down the curved flight of stairs and past the specially decorated white and black velvet ropes onto the crowded dance floor. As she nudged her way through the crowd, she spotted Justin near the DJ booth and quickly nodded for him to follow her. She couldn't risk anyone seeing them talking.

She pushed and shoved through ocean of sweating bodies on the dance floor and made her way down a short corridor to the women's bathroom. Justin kept his distance while tracking her movements and eventually caught up to her. Kyra pulled him into the bathroom and occupied a stall just in time, before anyone had a chance to catch a glimpse of them.

As soon as the lock on the door clicked, assuring their privacy, her lips instantly found his with a renewed passion. As they stood in the cramped stall, their lips reacquainting themselves with each other, Kyra even felt a warm tear drop from her eye and glide down her cheek. She was overwhelmed with happiness.

Justin broke their kiss to admire her bright smile he had missed so much. Whenever Kyra smiled, her entire face lit up with happiness and her eyes sparkled. However, a small bruise under her eye also caught his attention, and he was automatically concerned.

"I missed you so much," she breathed.

"I missed you, too.... What happened right there?"

"Nothin'.... I, uh, fell...." Kyra lied, realizing that her

fading black eye must have been showing. The hot show she'd put on had caused some of her makeup to sweat off.

"Who did that to you?"

She wasn't as good at telling lies as she thought.

Kyra put her hand on the spot Justin had caressed feeling his touch again for the first time in what seemed like forever. She shut her eyes to savor the moment and then let them slowly reopen. She knew that as worried as he was for her, he was powerless against Makai and his people.

"Listen to me. You have to lay low. I can't tell you why right now, but I'll get in touch with you, okay? Just watch what you do in public. If you see me, act like you don't know me…" she whispered. He opened his mouth to speak but her protest interrupted him. "Trust me. Whatever you do, be careful."

"I'm staying at the Sutton Place Hotel, suite seven."

"I wish I could stay here with you, but I know Bryce and Rick are probably gonna come lookin' for me at any moment…."

"Who are—"

"My bodyguards."

"Bodyguards? If you got *bodyguards*, how do you expect to come see me?"

"Shh, don't worry. I'll find a way to get to you. I promise you. I'll find a way." She gently pressed her forehead against his and he held her in his arms as she weakly sobbed. She was in over her head and she knew it.

A few days later Kyra managed to carry out the plan she conjured up to see Justin at his hotel. Her bodyguards were around less and less so she figured the task would be an easy one. They were more than likely Asiah's watchmen now, and for that she was appreciative. She didn't like having eyes on her day in and day out. They were nothing but a nuisance that she was sick and tired of dealing with on a daily basis.

Kyra's first glimpse of him had a smile wider than the Grand Canyon spreading across her face. He immediately pulled her to him and greeted her with a kiss, picking up where they had left off.

"Hello to you, too," She let out a giggle as she slipped off her sunglasses and dropped them on the table in the living area of the suite. She wrapped her arms around his neck and reintroduced her lips and tongue to his, the kiss quickly getting emotionally deeper. "I missed you so much, you just dunno."

She pulled back from the kiss and embraced him, resting her head on his chest.

He ran his hands over her hair as he held her in that blissful moment. The silence of the room was perfect. He had come all the way from Prince Paul for a moment like this.

"Hey, J, we're about to go...." Michael interrupted the cherished moment and invaded the living area with no other than Natasha by his side.

"Uh-uh! What is *she* doin' here?"

Justin and Michael exchanged looks of confusion at Kyra's odd reaction, but Natasha was well aware of what was going on.

"Mike, let's go." She pulled on his arm, trying to make her way out the door.

"Goin' to spend your new-found fortune?"

"Shut that shit up, Kyra!"

"Fuck you!"

"Whoa, whoa, hold up." Michael didn't understand.

"Naw, tell this bitch to hold up," Kyra argued.

"Look, just because we aren't friends anymore doesn't mean you're about to be disrespecting me."

"Whateva. I'll do as I damn well please. What are you gonna do? Beat my ass?"

"Look, I said sorry. That's all I can do. Why can't you understand that I made a mistake?"

The girls' eyes made contact, but Kyra was close-mouthed. Natasha had a certain longing in her eyes that said she wanted to speak to her old friend, but Kyra was too stubborn to participate.

"Mike, I need to use the bathroom real quick and then we can leave."

"Okay."

Natasha excused herself to go to the bathroom. Her eyes were glossy with tears as Kyra maintained her cold attitude in the living room.

"You should go talk to her."

"There ain't shit to talk about, Justin."

"You two were tight. What happened that could be that bad?" He was clueless to the secret cash deal Natasha had made with Makai to get Kyra away from the island.

"Fuck her, she ain't shit. J, I'm tellin' you, she's just a greedy, selfish, sneaky—"

"Kyra..."

"What?"

"Please go talk to her baby? Do it for me?"

Kyra shot him a mean look, but his puppy-dog eyes made her weak. How could she say no to something he asked of her that was so simple? After he'd made a trip all the way to the U.S. just to find her, she couldn't refuse.

"Fine. I'll do it."

"Thank you." He showed his appreciation with a kiss on her cheek.

"What was that all about?" Michael whispered his puzzlement as he watched Kyra walk off in the direction of the bathroom.

"I don't even know," Justin whispered back.

Kyra rapped on the door a few times and then walked in to find Natasha sitting on the swirled blue and green marble sink top.

"It's you," Natasha said, trying to build up an attitude.

"Yeah, it's me," she sighed as she shut the door behind her.

A thick feeling of awkward tension fell on the room.

Another awkward moment halted their conversation. In all their twelve years of friendship, neither one of them could remember getting so mad at the other that they'd stopped speaking.

"Kyra…" Natasha was starting in on another round of apologies.

"Don't. What's done is done. I'm here now."

"Yeah, but it was still messed up."

"I'm not gonna sugarcoat it, 'cause we both know it was, but I can't be mad at you forever. We've been friends too long to let Kai fuck that up. I ain't sayin' we cool or anythin', but I ain't got no beef with you."

"How are things at home?"

"Better."

"Does he still…" Natasha cautiously hinted at her question concerning Makai's physical abuse.

"Sometimes. It's been a while."

"You shouldn't have to put up with that."

"I know, but it's like right now I don't got a choice but to deal with his bullshit. I hope he'll get tired of me and let me go. He got other girls anyway. He even has another girlfriend. I don't know why he's still draggin' me along."

"Who?"

"Some model chick...I forgot her name.... Who cares...?"

The girls just sat there quiet again, each miniconversation coming to an abrupt end. Kyra played with a small hand towel on a nearby rack while Natasha studied the floor.

"I gave the money back," she blurted out. Her eyes never left her focus spot on the floor.

"What?"

"I gave Makai the money back. All five grand."

"Why? You might as well have spent it."

"Don't be like that. I just didn't realize what I did until you showed up at my house that night. After that, having the money just didn't seem right. And then to go out and spend it? Uh-uh. Plus, you know I hate that nigga," Natasha declared with a hint of laughter in her voice.

"Me, too."

"Never thought I would see the day." She giggled.

CHAPTER 22

Once Michael and Natasha left, Kyra and Justin had the suite all to themselves with time to waste. A day of relaxing, talking and lovemaking was a pleasant one, as was every other visit Kyra made following that day. Their casual hook-ups at random hotels around Chicago were considered precious.

By the end of the month, the undercover couple had seen the inside of almost every hotel in the Chicago area. Kyra had to ensure that if Makai caught her, he wouldn't be able to track Justin down at the Sutton. To ensure Justin's safety while he was in Chicago, Kyra was more than ready to sacrifice her body to abuse at the hands of Makai. She was determined not to let anything happen to Justin.

On an unusual night, Makai stayed at home. He once again occupied himself on Kyra's side of the bed. Any other night she would have wanted to get it done and over with, but tonight it was different. Tonight she was into it, moaning and screaming, her body wet with sweat as he plunged deep into her. Tonight she fantasized that Makai was Justin.

It was late the next afternoon when Kyra awoke. She tried to raise her head from where she lay but winced with soreness.

Her head was throbbing. *What happened last night?* She asked herself as she carefully sat up in bed.

The emotional toll of living under Makai's rule was affecting her in more ways then one, and if it didn't stop, she was fearful of where it might lead. That single thought was scary in its own right and was all the more reason to take action. She needed counsel. She needed another opinion. The morbid thoughts of pushing Makai down the stairs to his demise, as well as committing an assortment of other violent acts, were ones she would attempt to pursue if she didn't receive help, and quickly. She needed Justin.

Kyra caught two cabs just to make her meeting with Justin at their new destination for the day, the Econo Lodge. It wasn't one of the nicest places they'd had the luxury of staying in, but it certainly wasn't one of the worst. Being fussy wasn't an option. Anything would do.

Once Kyra stepped in the room, Justin shut all the blinds to hide them from the outside world. She hadn't even sat down before she started to remove her boots and make herself more comfortable. Justin watched as she unzipped the knee-high boots, and his eyes traveled up her legs to her tan tank dress. He couldn't resist the urge to run his tongue across his lips. Their location was perfect for the things running through his mind.

He flicked on the light switch out of his desire to see her body in all its glory. Kyra was just removing the green camouflage hat that shaded her bruised face. Justin's hormones were meaningless when he caught sight of her assaulted face.

"He hit you again?" His jaw tightened in anger.

"Last night..." Her voice was a mere whisper.

"Why? What happened?"

"Because...I said your name by accident.... Anymore questions?" She didn't want to dwell on the incident and didn't want to reveal the details as to when she'd let his name slip out of her mouth.

He didn't answer but took a seat on the edge of one of the two queen-sized beds.

"I swear, if I see him..." His temper was increasing as thoughts of violent payback raced through his mind.

"No, no. Don't do nothin' crazy, *please*, baby." The image of what would happen to him or anyone else who hurt Makai greatly disturbed her. Whoever the perpetrator turned out to be, they would surely suffer a slow and painful death at the hands of Makai's henchmen, after hours of excruciating torture.

"Why are you so worried about this cat? I can handle him. Any nigga who puts his hands on a female ain't shit."

"You don't know what you're talkin' about. He's not like you...."

"So you're really trying to stick up for him? After how he beats on you? You're gonna take his side?"

"No, no. You just don't understand."

"Then *make* me understand! Make me understand how I have to sneak off just to see you, and how I have to sit by and let another man beat on you and God only knows what else! It's bullshit!"

Kyra flopped down on the edge of bed with a sigh. Things were difficult. She hadn't told Justin much about Makai, especially not what he did for a living. She'd never had the need to discuss him in Prince Paul and never found the time to now. She could never seem to find the right time to mention the subject, but this seemed like it was the best opportunity she'd got. She couldn't let it slip by. There was a time for everything, and the time for the truth was now.

"Makai...well...he's a...he's a hustler. He's not like you dad or your brother….. He's…in the drug business. And he's been in it for years, long enough that now he has power, and a lot of it. This is his city. We just live in it." Kyra fumbled over her words.

"You mean to tell me you been up here all this time when you got an easy way out?" he exclaimed. The whole situation was beginning to frustrate him.

"An easy way out? What the hell do you mean an easy way out? If there was one, don't you think I would've took it by now? How dumb do you sound right now?" she yelled, offended by his comment.

"All you gotta do is call the cops and have them arrest his ass. Tell them what he does and then boom! He's in jail and you're free. That's pretty easy if you ask me."

"Are you fuckin' stupid? Kai has connects with the cops! And God knows who else. They would probably come to the door, see that it's his place and bounce. And if he *did* get locked up, hypothetically speaking, and it was *my* fault, his people would track me down. They wouldn't stop until they found me, and if they find me, they find you, they find my mom, they wipe all of us out. Do you have any idea what they would do to us? To me? You must be tryin' to get me killed!" Kyra exploded at his insensitive statement as she got up and began to pace the room. "Look, I'll figure somethin' out, okay? I'll figure somethin' out!"

"I'm sorry, baby. I shouldn't have brought it up." Justin apologized as he took her in his arms, feeling guilty for the tears that were now streaming down the slopes of her cheeks.

He pulled back and took her face by her chin to kiss her lips. She winced and pulled back for second, the presence of her cut reaffirmed. Her body then melted into his, their kissing becoming more intense as they gently fell back onto the bed.

He held himself over her, his lips making a trail down from

her face to her neck, and with the removal of her dress, her chest and stomach. Things were getting hotter by the second with the removal of each article of clothing.

With Kyra's whimpers and moans coming quicker, Justin reached down into his pants pocket to retrieve protection. He could feel his time to perform approaching.

Kyra soaked in the deep bathtub, surrounded by bubble bath and warm water. She lit all the unused candles for the first time, and their light vanilla scent calmed her as she soaked and reflected on her still-fresh encounter with her lover. She had returned to the empty and tranquil apartment just as predicted, pulling off yet another visit to see Justin undetected.

She shut her eyes and was letting the atmosphere relax her when suddenly her eyes popped wide open. A loud crash emanating from the first floor startled her out of her peaceful state. Kyra sat stiff. She heard another thunderous crash. Her heart was racing. Someone had come for her.

Absolutely petrified at the thought of who was in the apartment, Kyra cautiously climbed out of the tub, her body dripping wet as she grabbed a white cotton robe to cover herself. Her curiosity overpowered her fear and enabled her to tiptoe down the hall to the top of the stairs. The sound of breaking glass sliced through the silence.

"Who's there?" Her throat was tight as she shouted down into the darkness. There was no answer. "I said who's there?"

A glass object struck the stairs in front of her and she jumped back, clambering to the hall light and switching it on. The glow only managed to light the hall and the upper half of the staircase. The face of the prowler still could not be seen below.

Makai stepped out from the darkness into the light. He was

out of breath and his eyes were red. Something was gravely amiss.

"Come down here." He then disappeared into the darkness.

Kyra hesitated. She'd never seen Makai look like this before. He looked upset. Had he found out about her affair? He was obviously angry, yet sadness could be seen in his eyes. Sadness was an emotion she couldn't place with him, even after all the years she'd known him.

She carefully descended the stairs, avoiding the shards of glass from the form that used to be one of the crystal glasses that decorated the dining room table.

She was uneasy after evaluating the condition of the bottom floor of the duplex. The once-stunning dining room was a shell of its former self, with the exquisite china in pieces across the floor. Down the hall, the mirror in the foyer was cracked, and the statuette that used to rest on the center table of the living room had been split in two. It was the reason for the mirror's destruction.

Kyra didn't know what to make of the situation as she entered the living room. Plants were lying on their sides, a couch was overturned, as was the center table, and the glass ashtray that used to rest on it was in pieces on the rug. The dark wood chair also lay overturned in front of one of the large windows after Makai's futile attempt to send it flying into the Chicago sky.

Makai sat on the only upright couch with a bottle of whiskey in his hand. He took a swig and wiped his mouth. Kyra could have sworn she saw his eyes beginning to glisten and began to question her sanity.

"Kai...what's wrong?"

"Deshawn..." He hung his head low and let his hands cover his eyes.

Kyra stood amazed at the scene before her. The monster she

had been living with for the past two months was sitting before her crying like a baby.

"Kai..."

"They killed him. Those mothafuckas...they killed Deshawn.... They killed my little brother...." His voice was calm but his eyes poured tears as she rushed to his side. She took a seat next to him on the couch and placed her hand on his shoulder in support.

"What happened?" She shared his sadness. Deshawn had always been a nice boy, ever since she'd first met him when he was only ten years old.

"Reggie and them...they raided a house of ours, and it was the one that De was working.... They killed everyone and took all the product we had in there. Cleaned the place out. There was nothing left. No white, no survivors, nothing."

"Who else was there?"

"Just De and some other people. No one else from my crew, though. Just some workers...." Makai waved off the other deaths as though they meant nothing. "You know they took ten kilos of my shit? Ten fucking keys. With all that money in their hands, they're waging all-out war...." The attack Reggie had pulled had caught Makai off guard and weakened him in more ways than one. Not only had Reggie and his crew hurt Makai financially, but now they would have equal firepower. The throne was up for grabs.

Kyra sat still. She searched the depths of her soul to find the right words to say, but she found none. Not that anything she said would have made a difference. Deshawn was dead, and no one and no sweet words or gestures could bring him back. That was something she had learned the hard way, but it was also something that Makai recognized. "And the thing about the shit is that I can get that shit back.... No matter what I can't get De back. I would give all the shit we got in every last one of my spots to bring him back, and I can't. I was responsible for him...and my ma, oh my God...." He tossed between fury and grief.

"You can't blame yourself, Kai," Kyra murmured as she let her hand massage his shoulder.

"That was my little brother. Ever since we were little, I had his back. Every day and every night. Every night *except* tonight. I should've been there.... I would've been there any other night.... There's no one else to blame *but* me...."

Being an only child, Kyra never quite understood the connection between siblings, and she couldn't quite relate to what he was feeling. She kept quiet, not wanting to say the wrong thing at such a pivotal time.

"I need to get the crew together...." He thought aloud. "Kyra, do me a favor?"

"Yeah?"

"Grab me a suit from the closet upstairs. Any one; it doesn't matter." He requested the favor as he took another swig of his whiskey and planted the earpiece of his two-way in his ear.

"Okay."

"Thank you, baby girl" He gave thanks with a look of appreciation in his eyes. It was as though for that split second the old Makai, the man she used to know and love, had resurfaced.

Kyra was lying in bed asleep when a powerful early-morning storm woke her. She sat up in bed with her clothes from the previous night still on. Her tired eyes fell to Makai's side of the bed to see that he wasn't there. He had been gone all night.

She turned her attention to the window as the pounding rain smacked against the glass, and listened to the distant rumble of thunder. She wasn't happy that the storm had woken her up, considering she had only fallen asleep four hours ago.

She rolled over, fetched the remote from Makai's nightstand, and clicked on the television. Its bright light illuminated the dark room. It was only six in the morning.

Kyra was irritable as she clicked though channel after channel of infomercials and workout programs. The news was once again the only thing that held her interest.

After about half an hour of traffic reports, stock exchange updates, a weather forecast and sports recaps, Kyra was just about to push the Off button when she paused. A breaking news story was just hitting the air.

She leaned forward and turned up the volume in fascination as the reporter began to relay the juicy information.

"I'm Karen Lee, and I'm here live on the north side of Chicago in a quiet suburban community where last night a horrific crime took place. Shots rang out from what witnesses say was a black SUV. The victims: a young mother and her daughter," the woman reported in a yellow slicker. She was standing in front of a house blocked off with yellow crime scene tape as the rain poured. "The mother, eighteen-year-old Mercedes Alvarez, is currently in the hospital and in critical condition after being struck twice. Tragically her infant daughter, Lauren Mills, was fatally wounded and pronounced dead on arrival at Children's Memorial Hospital. She was only one year old." She paused to give a more dramatic effect to the story before she went on, "The two were believed to have been enjoying a quiet evening at home when suddenly the lights went out and bullets went flying. You can see here that the telephone line, as well as the power lines, have been severed. This is believed to have been a planned homicide."
The reporter pointed out the cut wires dangling from a metal

box on the side of the house. "Police say they have no leads or suspects in the case, but it is believed to be another crime in connection with a shooting that occurred months back in a local nightclub. Reggie Mills, who is reported to have lived in the home and has been identified as the father of the young girl, was not home at the time of the shooting. His whereabouts are currently unknown, but he is believed to have been somehow involved with the shooting at the nightclub Bahama Breeze back in mid-July. Mills has been linked to drug activity within the city and is wanted on several warrants. If you have any information on who may have committed this gruesome crime, please give us a call at 312-555-8019. Back to you, John."

A picture of a smiling Lauren was put up on the screen with the phone number. Kyra felt sad for the little girl. She was so young, and she was adorable. Kyra felt a wave of guilt wash over her even through her bitterness for Mercedes's past actions. She knew the information they asked for. She knew who did it, and yet she had no choice but to sit by and do nothing. There was no way she would snitch. Her lips were sealed.

Kyra jumped at the company of Makai, who without a noise had entered the bedroom. She hadn't even heard him come into the room.

"Hey," he whispered as he held his position by the door.

"Hey."

"Whatchu doin' up?"

"The storm..." She looked over to the window to avoid his stare.

"Oh." He then paused for a minute. "I'll be in soon. You should go back to sleep," Makai softly advised as he walked off down the hall to the bathroom.

Kyra lay in bed thinking as she listened to the rushing water coming from the shower down the hall. The incident last night reminded Kyra of something: if it weren't for her father jumping in front of her all those years ago at the picnic, she would have died just like Lauren. He had made the ultimate sacrifice and willingly given his own life for hers.

For the next few days, Makai kept himself holed up in the house. He spent his days drinking bottle after bottle of beer and liquor and doing an assortment of drugs. Kyra was worried that the mix of narcotics and alcohol would leave him on edge. She expected the beatings to get worse and to be dished out more frequently, but instead they stopped completely. Between his mourning and being wasted, Makai was quiet and mellow. Even though he was there, Kyra felt as though she were there alone.

The mix of illegal substances and booze often left him passed out for hours at a time, giving Kyra many opportunities to sneak out. The risk was as high as ever, but she took it time after time, and most importantly, she got away with it. She was slick. The chances of getting caught seemed to be slim to none.

Nothing is ever as it seems.

"Mom?" Justin pressed his ear to the pay phone on the loud Chicago avenue. For the first time in weeks, he was contacting home. His funds were running low and he was in desperate need of assistance. An uninterrupted hour of deliberation had gone into making this call.

"What on earth? Where are you? What have you been? I have been so worried…. What is all that noise…? Henry no…" The loving voice of his mother shakily rattled off question after question before her husband wrenched the phone from her hands.

"Justin? This is your father speaking." His voice was still at its usual Barry White-like volume, but his son could feel the heat of his temper thousands of miles away.

"Dad, listen…I…I need your help with something…." Justin checked each side of him on the sidewalk. He wanted to make sure no one on the street could hear his conversation.

"Help? You want my help? With what? Money? I knew you would call once you ran out of money."

"So it was you who froze my accounts?" His question came after a trip to an ATM machine and his inability to withdraw any cash.

"That's right, and your credit cards, too."

"Dad! What the…" He bit down on his lip in anger. He ran his free hand over the waves in his hair out of disappointment as he took another look around the street. He knew Kyra was growing antsy back at the hotel room they'd rented for the day.

"Don't think you're going to go running off with that little foreign girl and think I'm bankrolling you! You wanted to act like you're such a man, now be one!"

"Look, I'm coming home, I just need more time…."

"You are not setting foot in this house! Do you hear me? No son of mine—"

Justin was furious as he slammed the phone down, silencing his father's fit. It hung from its metallic wire, and a busy signal could be heard. Justin pushed on with determination as a chilling wind of an abnormally cool summer day infiltrated his baggy T-shirt. He needed to make a move, and soon. He needed a plan and he needed assistance. He was surely cut out of the inheritance and disowned, and he would soon be homeless if he didn't figure out new living arrangements. He had to leave Chicago, but he had to have Kyra by his side. He would not lose her again for anyone. Not even his family.

* * *

Justin returned to the three-star hotel to see Kyra sprawled across one of queen-sized beds in nothing but her underwear, watching basic cable TV. She tore into a grape Laffy Taffy as she greeted him from a bed covered with candy wrappers.

"Hey, babe, did you get in touch with your parents?"

"Yeah..."

"And? What'd they say? Are they gonna send you some money?"

"No."

"So how are we gonna leave Chicago by Sunday?" She was dumbfounded by his reaction. She perched herself on her knees in the middle of the bed as she racked her brain for solution. They had spent hours that afternoon planning the details of their escape. They were going to start a new life in California and lie low until things died down and they were sure Makai wasn't looking for them anymore.

"I have no idea—"

It was a Friday night when Kyra came through the door of the apartment with several plastic bags of groceries. Shopping was one of the excuses, from her list of them. She always managed to scheme up something to cover up her whereabouts, and as long as she came back with something to smoke or drink Makai didn't seem to care.

"Hey, baby." She greeted Makai with a fake giddy voice as she noticed him awake and sitting in the dimly lit living room. She set the bags on the kitchen counter before returning.

"Baby, why you sittin' here in the dark?" she asked as she flicked on the other black floor lamp.

He didn't give any kind of response as he sat on the couch. His eyes freakishly seemed to be the only things that moved.

"What's all this?" She picked up one of the overturned photos and papers that swamped the center table. She hadn't noticed them in the dark.

Her body froze as she studied the Polaroid in her hands. A lump formed in her throat as she gazed at the photo of her and Justin leaving the Econo Lodge. She was caught in the act, and this time there was no excuse she could make to cover it up.

She set the picture down and looked at another photo, and another. Each colorless picture was of her and Justin going in and coming out of the hotels they visited for their trysts.

She was dismayed. She never thought Makai would go so far as to have a private detective follow her. She assumed that her bodyguards had been her only obstacles.

Kyra couldn't help feeling foolish as she stood there remembering how she thought she had pulled it all off. She should have known it couldn't be that easy.

"I have everywhere, baby girl. The Sutton is a nice place. Never stayed there, though." His remark was casual, but he subtly revealed that he knew where Justin was.

Kyra tossed the last photograph to the side and stood firmly as he rose to his feet. She knew what she had coming, but she wasn't scared. She wanted to make sure that he saw that and that he recognized it.

"Seems like you've been quite busy these days…. I got about…what, forty pictures here?" he estimated as he tossed the pile into the air, sending photographs raining down around them.

"Kai, don't start this…" she sighed. She could feel an argument coming on.

"I'm not starting anything. I'm finishing it."

There was a moment of silence.

"So, how long have you known?"

"I just got 'em today. So where'd you go? And don't try and lie 'cause I know you went somewhere else besides the damn store. Did you go see him?"

"Yeah…I went to see him." She boldly told the truth as she folded of her arms.

"Oh, look at this. Kyra's bossin' up. How cute is that," Makai laughed sarcastically.

"Whateva, Kai, I don't have time for your bullshit. You don't see me up here trippin' off Asiah."

"You don't need to worry about what I do."

"See, that's your problem. You wanna play that double-standard shit."

"What double-standard shit?"

"You got your hoes and can see whoever you want, while you got me at home. I'm expected to be exclusively for you to do whatever you want with and treat however you fuckin' please. Well, fuck that, Kai! I'm through!"

"Okay. Listen to what you're saying. They're my *hoes* and you're my *woman. And as my woman* I expect you to be by my side after the death of my brother. But naw, you're out there fucking some other nigga on some straight scandalous shit," Makai said.

"Let's get one thing straight right here and now," Kyra started with an attitude. "I am *not* your woman, nor will I ever be again." She spoke coldly. She never flinched as she stared into the eyes of her old love.

"You're whatever I fucking say you are." He grabbed her face. "If I find out you go to see him again, I'll kill him, and then when I'm done wit' him…I'll come for you." His threat was grim and lingered with Kyra long after he walked off.

She flopped down onto the couch and looked through the

pictures with tears in her eyes. She'd always known it was risky, but she hadn't realized that it was truly a life-and-death situation until that moment. Her seeing Justin was putting them both in danger.

"What are you doin'?" She posed her question after entering the bedroom to see Makai packing a duffel bag.

"What the fuck does it look like I'm doing?"

"Looks to me like you're packin'. *Where are you goin'?*"

"Out of town for a few days. Probably up to tha D. Me and Brandon need to make a run. We fell behind after Reggie and them mothafuckas pulled that li'l stunt."

"When are you leaving?"

"Later tonight."

"When will you be back?"

"Probably Sunday night. Deshawn's funeral is on Tuesday."

"Oh."

"I'm keeping Bryce and Rick here again, just to let you know. So if you need anything, let them know. I need to be out, though. Fucking witchu done made me late."

He picked up the half-full duffel bag as he approached the doorway where Kyra stood. He leaned in for a kiss, but she turned away with a look of disgust. Makai looked her over with a cross stare before he stormed out of the house.

It was Sunday, the day of Makai's return home, and Kyra was bursting with energy. Tonight was it. Part two of the plan: the end, the getaway.

Burning candles were the only light in the living room as she awaited his return. She had wanted to be gone before he was even back within the city limits, but her babysitters were staples outside the front door. She wasn't going anywhere until they were gone, and they would only abandon their posts once Makai gave them the okay.

She sipped the white Zinfandel from her flute. Makai would be home any minute now. She tapped her fingers against the glass out of her wearing patience.

She peered out over the city. The beauty of the lights and the water beyond reminded her of why she loved Chicago. No matter where she went, her roots were here, and she could never deny that even if she tried. No matter where she ended up, she wouldn't forget it. This was the place that had made her who she was. This was the place that had shaped her. This was the place that had offered her lesson after lesson in life.

Kyra rested her hand on the wall-sized window and shut her eyes, sharing a private moment with the city. She slowly opened her eyes and turned to see Makai coming through the door. He dropped his duffel bag as soon as the door shut behind him. He slipped off his shoes and set his pistol on the foyer table.

"How was your trip?"

"Business as usual. We'll be all right. How have you been? You haven't missed me too much, have you?" he said sarcastically.

"Oh, I'm good."

"That's good, but hold that thought." Makai lifted his heavy bag and began to climb the stairs. Kyra hadn't anticipated him bringing a collection from one of his stash houses in the city as soon as he got home. He was headed right for the safe, and Kyra didn't hesitate for a minute to slip out of the penthouse, adding his gun to her bounty.

"Kyra!"

She heard him yell her name from where she waited for the elevator in the hallway. Without thinking, she bolted down the stairwell until she reached the parking level.

Meanwhile, Makai looked at his bare stash and was furious. He had had enough of Kyra's games. Now she had crossed his line. No one robbed Makai Jackson and lived to tell the story.

"Come scoop me from my crib now. She's running," Makai said to his partner in crime, Avon, on the phone. He was ready to go in seconds, re-dressed in all black, with a backup gun from his large collection hung on his hip, fully loaded. He was headed for the kitchen.

CHAPTER 23

Justin was in his bedroom of the hotel suite repacking his belongings. He moved with lightning speed as the thought of being with the woman he loved kept him on his toes. He wasn't sure how much time he had left before she reached him.

"What are you doing?" Michael said from the doorway. Natasha was right behind him with a light jacket wrapped around her waist. It was clear they were heading out.

"I'm leaving."

"We don't leave for another week."

"I know, and I'll explain everything later. Kyra is going to be here any minute...."

"Where are you two going?" his friend asked. He was somewhat aware of Kyra's situation, but the specifics were still cloudy.

"I don't know," Justin answered as he finished stuffing the rest of his clothes into his bag.

"Well, what do you want me to do?"

"Honestly, I would get home as soon as you can."

"Man, what the hell..." Michael spoke with frustration. He wasn't prepared for the plan, but neither was Justin.

"Look, Mike, I don't have time to argue. Just know that I have to do this." He looked his best friend in the eyes with a serious expression.

"Ey, do what you got to do," Michael replied without understanding.

Why his friend seemed in such a rush to leave the city at this hour of the night, he couldn't grasp. He was aware of Justin's motivation on their trip up to Chicago, but why Justin and Kyra now wanted to flee he had no idea.

"Look, I'll be at Tasha's. Call me if you need anything."

"Fa sho."

"Good luck, man. See you back home."

"A'ight, man." Justin gave his friend dap and a hug before the two parted ways, unaware that it was the last time they would see each other.

Makai flicked the butt of his cigar onto the lawn and straightened his jacket as he strolled up the pathway to the porch steps. Avon tapped on the door; neither replied to Natasha's question of "Who is it?" from inside.

Natasha opened the door to see her visitors and her body grew tense.

"Kai." Her greeting was plain and she barely made eye contact.

"Tasha."

"Baby, who is it?" Michael asked, coming from behind her.

"Nobody." She spoke to Michael before turning her attention back to Makai. It was obvious that she was bothered by his presence. "What do you want?"

"I need to talk to you right quick."

"I'm busy," she replied. She didn't want to be mixed up in anything else that involved him.

"Well, get your ass unbusy, ho." Avon flashed his gun in her face.

Both Natasha and Michael froze in fear at the sight of the gun. Makai led Natasha out onto the lawn by the arm while Avon stayed behind with Michael.

"What do you want?" Natasha's voice was shaking as her eyes stayed glued on Michael and Avon, as well as the gun between them.

"Where's Kyra?" Makai demanded. His grip on her arm was getting tighter.

"I don't know…. Get off me." She tried to jerk away but couldn't free herself.

"Don't fucking lie to me, Tasha. I know you know," he grunted as he jerked her by her arm.

"Look, I don't know shit."

"You don't know shit, huh?"

"No!"

"Avon, she said she don't know shit!" Makai yelled with a laugh to his partner.

Avon then punched Michael in the stomach with all his might, knocking the wind out of him. Michael groaned as he grabbed his stomach.

"Tasha, I know she told you where she was going."

"No, she didn't! Thanks to you, me and her aren't even friends anymore!" she partly lied.

"Bullshit."

"It's true!"

"Avon, have fun."

With the signal from Makai, Avon started beating on a defenseless Michael while Natasha winced at every blow.

Several neighbors emerged from their homes due to the racket but scampered back indoors at the sight of Makai.

Natasha became vexed as she looked around at person after person shutting and locking their doors. No one even tried to help. They wouldn't dare.

Michael had enough of being hit and decided to strike back. His blow sent Avon staggering. Avon was quick to draw his gun and shove it in Michael's face after recovering his balance.

"No!" Natasha screamed as Makai grabbed her flailing body around her waist, holding her back as she stretched her hand toward Michael.

"Tell me!"

"I told you I don't fucking know!"

Avon cocked his gun. In the blink of an eye, he would more than willingly end the life of the man before him.

"Okay…okay…I know where she is."

"Tasha, don't tell them," Michael groaned.

"Nigga, shut up," Avon grumbled as his pistol made contact with Michael's head, silencing him.

"She's at the Sutton Hotel…. I'm not sure if she's still there, though…. That's where I last saw her…. I swear I don't know anything else."

A flash of lightning and the sound of thunder filled the sky as Makai threw Natasha to the ground. She crawled over to Michael, who lay injured on her front lawn. She cradled him while her misty eyes watched the sleek car disappear down the road. As Michael rest in her lap, she sobbed for what she had done. She could feel the small drops fall then, not from her eyes but from the sky. A storm was coming.

CHAPTER 24

"God, I can't believe it. This is really it." Kyra smiled in exhilaration and pecked his lips.

The elevator ride was an awkward and silent one as the jittery occupants stood and faced the sliding doors. They held hands for support until they reached the ground floor. By this time the following day, they were sure to be fast asleep in another state and worry free.

Justin stepped out into the lobby with determination, and Kyra hustled to keep up with him. Her bags, filled with money, outweighed his by a great deal.

The couple made small talk as they stood on the curb. The warm rain was something like a tropical mist as they stood in the elements to hail a cab to the airport.

Kyra had just stepped into the street to better their chances of being picked up when she lost all concept of the world around her. There Makai stood, casually leaning against the hood of his Rover.

"Shit!" She turned around to see Avon already behind her with a gun to Justin's head. The surrounding onlookers looked mortified, and several shrieks could be heard as people scrambled for safety. The hoodlums were completely undaunted by the law. They were untouchable.

"Going somewhere?"

Her legs told her to run but her heart wouldn't allow her to leave Justin behind.

"Well, well, well, Ms. Kyra Jones. You have been a very bad girl," Makai taunted her from where he now stood in front of her. "Is this your little lover boy here?" He waved his gun in the air.

"Kai, please...." She pleaded for their lives.

"Shut up!"

"Just let us go."

"Shut up! Ain't nobody goin' nowhere until I have my goddamn money!" He now aimed his gun at her. She held her hands up in surrender.

"Don't shoot. It's all there in my bag, under the clothes."

"You should've known better than to steal from me, Kyra."

She didn't say anything as she saw him reclaim his profits. She stood powerlessly as he loaded the bags into the trunk of his car. She wasn't going anywhere tonight.

Makai stepped closer to Kyra and moved his lips as if he was about to say something when without warning, he struck Kyra across the face with the butt of the pistol, sending her crashing to the wet pavement.

"Leave her alone!" Justin boldly hollered in Kyra's defense from his vantage point at the other end of Avon's gun. He was on fire as he watched her shift on the ground in pain. The street was empty and they were alone. Makai and Avon's wild antics had sent everyone running. No sirens were heard. An entire city street was Makai's playground.

"And you! If anyone should be mad here it should be me! Not only have you been fucking my girl, but you mean to tell me you had the balls to rob me?" Makai was in Justin's face in seconds.

"He didn't have anything to do with it," Kyra confessed.

"You, shut up!" Makai frowned at her as he watched Kyra hug the ground.

"Yo, fuck you!"

Makai turned and without a word punched Justin in the mouth. Avon and Makai started to pound on Justin's body. They used anything they could to do damage—the butts of their guns, their hands and their feet. Justin did his best to fight off his attackers, but he was on the losing end of the beating.

Kyra came to Justin's aid and began to pound on Avon's back, but he shrugged her off, sending her flying into a brick wall. Kyra couldn't take Justin's being hurt, let alone just sitting by and letting it happen. That was when she remembered the gun. She had to get to it, but it was in her car. It was their only hope of survival. If Makai won, both she and Justin would be dead. She was going to make a run for it.

Kyra dashed from the sidewalk and a sprinted toward the parking lot across the street.

"Get her!"

Avon ran to Kyra, his Air Forces proving to be better suited for the situation than her heels. He snatched her up by her waist and lifted her from the ground. She tried to wriggle her way out of his grip and attempted to fight him off but was unsuccessful.

She screamed for the heavens to hear her as he carried her closer to where Makai stood and farther from the gun. Tears of frustration fell from her eyes, mixing with the rain as Avon set her on the ground. He grabbed her arm and his gun touched her temple. Their fate had been sealed.

"Look at your man now, baby girl. Isn't he handsome?"

Makai whispered his taunts in her ear as she painfully surveyed the damage to Justin, who looked away from her in shame. Makai then went to kiss her lips, purposely for her lover to witness. Her teeth bit through the flesh of his bottom lip as soon as she felt it on her own.

"Bitch!" he raged as he slapped her, causing her head to turn and her cheek to sting.

He laughed as he grabbed his bleeding lip and examined his fingers.

"I'm gonna have some fun witchu. I thought you knew I liked that feisty shit." He laughed again as he rubbed his bloodstained fingers together.

"I hate you," she grumbled as she glared at her old flame.

"I know, I know. But the thing is…I don't give a fuck." Makai accepted her hatred with a chuckle.

Kyra stood in the rain, her body shaking and shivering from the falling temperatures as she locked eyes with Justin, who was still on his knees on the ground. He was slowly recovering from the previous scuffle.

"It's sad it has to end like this. I really did love you, nah mean? The shit just got complicated," Makai said as he glanced at Justin and then back at Kyra, taking notice of the gaze she fixed on the one who held her heart. "Ey, Avon, should I let her see him die?" Makai coldly asked his main man.

"Hell yeah." Avon pushed his weapon closer to Kyra's face.

Makai turned from Kyra and rushed up to Justin, kneeing him in his chest.

"Come on, get up. Fight me, bitch," he provoked Justin as he listened to Kyra's screaming in the background.

Justin's eyes grew dark as he looked at Makai towering above him. His anger was immeasurable, and using that energy, he caught his adversary off guard with a concentrated push that sent him to the ground.

"Oh shit. This nigga got heart," Makai chuckled as he lay on the wet ground.

Avon's body flinched at Makai's landing. He was ready to jump in.

"It's cool. I got this. Here, hold this for me." Makai handed his gun over to his accomplice. He wanted Justin for himself.

He stood up and faced Justin, who now was in a firm fighting stance. He was ready. Makai threw several jabs to his body, and Justin wasted no time in throwing fists back. Their fists were flying so rapidly it was difficult to tell where each punch came from before it hit its target. Kyra almost forgot to breathe as she watched the scene unfold. It was Justin and Makai, one on one.

Justin moved with ferocity in the rain. His fists slammed swiftly into Makai's body, one blow after the other. He moved so quickly that by the time Makai could register that he'd been hit once, he was struck again.

Makai lost his balance and Justin pounced on him, tackling him to the ground and pinning him beneath his weight. He wrapped his hands around Makai's neck and began to squeeze. Kyra felt her heart in her chest as she watched Makai squirm under Justin's body, gasping for air and beating at his attacker's hands. He had no effect on Justin's grip.

"Get up!" Avon hollered as he cocked his gun and aimed it at Justin.

The noise of the gun caught Justin's attention for a second, causing him to look away from Makai and be caught off guard by Makai's backup knife, which he kept in his back pocket, as it was thrust deep into his abdomen.

He fell back. His death grip around Makai's neck was now gone and his hand held his wound.

"Hand me my shit!" Makai raged as he held his hand out to catch his firearm. "I'm finna kill this nigga," he growled as he put his gun to the side of Justin's head and cocked the weapon. He was prepared to fire, his embarrassment fuel for his anger.

"No, Kai! Stop! Stop! Makai, please!" Kyra wailed as she once again tried to fight her way out of Avon's grip.

A sudden roar of laughter and applause emanated from the darkness.

"Reggie?" Makai queried through squinted eyes. He couldn't believe what he was seeing. He had assumed his rival was dead.

"Makai, Makai, Ma-fucking-kai," Reggie shot back as he stopped where he stood, Curtis standing to his left. "Damn, partna, I see you ready to take another life tonight, huh? You're good at that. I should know. After all, you killed my daughter," Reggie continued. As he spoke, he ran his fingers over the barrel of his gun, toying with it.

"Nigga, fuck you and your mothafuckin' daughter! You killed De!" Makai hollered. He was enraged to see his enemy in the flesh, alive and well. He quickly turned his gun on Reggie and fired several shots in his direction. Avon threw Kyra to the ground as he joined the fight. She lay on the ground covering her head as she heard the four enemies open fire on each other. The barrage of bullets discharged from their chambers was deafening.

Kyra lifted her head just enough to see what was going on around her. Everything seemed to be moving in slow motion. She saw Curtis hiding behind an old car parked on the side of the road. Every so often he would peek around the side and shoot at Avon, but he was eventually silenced by Avon's aim with a bullet between the eyes.

Reggie used Makai's own Range Rover against him by opening a door and using it as a shield while he emptied his clip. Avon and Makai stood out in the open and fired without fear, both aiming to kill Reggie, and doing so faster than anticipated. His body slumped to the ground behind the bullet-riddled door, and they knew that this time for sure their job had been done.

"Shit! I'm hit!" Avon cried out in pain as the burning sensation become intense. He grabbed his torso and fell back onto a building wall in an attempt to catch his breath while coughing up his own blood. He hadn't realized he was hit until the shoot-out ceased and the smoke cleared.

Makai didn't bother to acknowledge his pain as he checked the site. He stood motionless as he held the smoking gun in his hand. His eyes were fixed on the body of his old friend turned enemy.

Meanwhile, Justin struggled to become vertical again. His stab wound had a negative effect on his posture as he stood and pulled the knife from deep within his flesh. He let out an agonizing grunt as he dropped the bloodied knife to the ground. Kyra cautiously started to rise in order to help, her eyes not leaving Makai's back. He was unpredictable and dangerous.

He stood quietly as he listened to rocks crunch beneath Justin's feet. It served as a reminder that he was not alone and that he had a job that needed to be done. One down, two to go.

Makai casually gripped his gun tightly in his hand and slid his finger over the trigger. Kyra was crouched in a running stance when her eyes caught his movement. Her eyes darted to Justin, who stood unaware, still trying to regain his balance.

Kyra's eyes darted back to Makai as he quickly turned and

raised his gun to Justin. His eyes were cold and hard. She knew his intention. There was no time for words or warnings before Makai carelessly fired two shots into Justin's frame.

Justin's body hit the ground with a thud, and to Kyra, time stood still. She felt her heart explode in her chest and her breathing was suspended.

"Why did you do that, huh? Why did you do that?" As Kyra pounded her fists against Makai's chest, the sound of approaching sirens could finally be heard. Makai was stiff as he watched Kyra break down. He could see the blood running out from under Justin and knew deep down in his heart the wounds were fatal.

"Come on, man, that's five-oh! We gotta get out of here! Let's go! Kai!" Avon panicked through his short breaths as he clutched his stomach and started to limp toward his ride.

Makai looked over at his injured friend and back at Kyra, who was in hysterics, as he heard the sirens come closer and closer. His shock didn't take long to wear off; it was dominated by the fear of being sent to prison. He knew there was no way he could get out of this one, regardless of how many police connections he had. His time was up. In one fluid motion he pulled the trigger and sent a bullet through his head. He had retired from the game. Avon dropped to his knees after witnessing Makai's suicide.

Blood spattered on Kyra's dress. She was frozen in the middle of the street, shaking and rocking over Justin's irresponsive body until paramedics arrived.

Several police units accompanied by ambulances arrived at the scene. Their sirens were blaring and their lights flashed through the darkness of the night as the police officers and paramedics spilled from their vehicles to rush the area.

The police were baffled as they took in the situation. Two

of their most-wanted drug dealers, Reggie Mills and Makai Jackson, were dead.

The paramedics quickly made their way to Avon, who through a fit of cursing was taken into an ambulance and rushed off to the local hospital's emergency room with a punctured lung. He wouldn't make it through the night.

Several paramedics hurriedly lifted Justin's body onto a stretcher, rolling him past Kyra toward one of the medical vans.

"Justin? Justin? Please say somethin'. Please." Kyra tried to pull at him as the paramedics went to work on him. Between their bursts of EMT lingo, she was able to make out that he was still alive, and to her that was all that mattered.

"Sorry, but you can't come in here." A paramedic pushed her back as he went to close the door.

"I need to be with him. You don't understand." She pleaded to accompany him to the hospital as she held the door open.

"Sorry," the paramedic apologized before yanking the doors shut.

"Dammit! Fuck you!" Kyra yelled at the vehicle.

"Ma'am, please come with me…. Ma'am…" A police officer tried to escort her to another on-scene ambulance to receive medical attention.

"You don't understand. I can't lose him. He's all I got left…. He's all I got left…."

Kyra calmed herself as she watched the ambulance roar down the road and listened as its sirens echoed through the night. She was on the verge of losing what little control she had left. Her plan had gone horribly awry, and now she faced the possibility of losing yet another man she loved to the Chicago streets. She was unstable and was unsure she could stomach another loss.

CHAPTER 25

After Kyra endured a lengthy interrogation by the police in one of the hospital staff rooms, a woman's voice on an officer's radio interrupted their conversation. The officers were needed somewhere else immediately, and that meant Kyra was free to go. What with her fidgeting, trembling and incoherent mumbling for hours, Kyra seemed to be losing her mind and was unable to give them any valuable information.

Once the police left, Kyra didn't waste any time. She had to find Justin. She had to know if he was all right. The uncertainty was killing her inside.

As Kyra sat in an uncomfortable chair in the waiting room, she entertained herself by flipping through month-old magazines left on the end tables and watching the syndicated television program.

She watched the clock. She had been there for only three hours, but it felt like an eternity. She remained a fixture in the waiting room as other families came and went. Some left with grave news, screaming and crying. Others left with good news. Kyra prayed to God she would be one of the lucky ones.

After buying a snack from the vending machine, Kyra

couldn't sit any longer. She began to quietly pace the hall, her hands shaking and her face sullen. In the middle of her pacing, the opening of the hospital doors grabbed her attention. She watched as a middle-aged doctor strode toward her. His scrubs were bloodied, and under his full beard his face seemed heavy.

"Excuse me…? Excuse me?" she called out to get the attention of the passing doctor.

"Yes? May I help you?"

Kyra fainted before she could get the words out of her mouth.

"Nurse! Nurse!" The doctor, who had just finished surgery, held her limp body in his arms until a nurse came to his aid.

Birds chirped outside the hospital window as Kyra came to her senses. It was morning and the sun shone between the clouds scattered throughout the sky.

She sat up to yawn when an unexpected voice spoke to her.

"Good morning, baby."

Kyra flew from her chair to where Justin was sitting up in bed. He was hooked up to several machines, and a regular beep disturbed the silence. His voice was hoarse and an IV was inserted into his arm. Her eyes welled up when she saw his condition.

"What are you crying for? I'm okay."

"That's why I'm cryin'." She gave a weak smile and gently kissed his forehead.

"Girl, you better give me a kiss."

She let out a short laugh and gave in to his demand, kissing him on the lips.

"Okay, I'm better now."

"Stop playin'."

He grew serious before speaking again.

"Are you okay?"

"I just had a few cuts and bruises, no big deal. What did the doctors tell you?"

"I have two broken ribs and I've fractured my hand in three places. They said I got lucky, though—the bullets went right through."

"Did they hit anything?"

"My spleen. They had to remove it." He began to cough.

"Here, have some water."

"Thank you."

"You really got lucky, then. At least you can live without that."

"Yeah, I know."

Kyra sensitively laid her head on him from where she sat beside his bed.

"God, I was so scared. You have no idea. I thought I'd lost you."

"But I pulled through, so no more crying, a'ight?" He twirled a strand of her hair in his fingers.

"So now what? What are we gonna do?" Kyra asked.

"I don't know. Where's the money?"

"Forget the money. We don't need it. All it does is cause problems, and the last thing we need right now is more problems. You just need to focus on gettin' better for me, okay?"

"So you're content with it being just us two, huh? What are we going to do? Live off our love?"

"It's a start."

"Just me and you, huh? You sure you know what you're getting yourself into?"

"Just me and you. That's all I need." She chuckled and flashed Justin a smile.

"Just me and you."

Justin repeated those words and then closed his eyes as he inhaled her sweet perfume. His medication was taking effect and he was becoming drowsy. As he drifted off, Kyra tenderly held and caressed his hand. As she felt his chest heave up and down, she stared out the window. The wind rustled through the trees. She watched as a leaf soared through the air, carefully descending toward the ground. Fall was approaching. The season was changing and Kyra was hopeful that everything was behind them. She closed her eyes, and her body relaxed. She was just where she wanted to be, and for once life seemed to slow down enough for her to truly rest. Living the fast life had left her exhausted. Now as she drifted off to sleep, she was ready for a new and peaceful life.